James Butler Bonham

James Butler Bonham
Messenger of Defeat

by William N. Bonham

LANGMARC PUBLISHING

AUSTIN, TEXAS

James Butler Bonham
Messenger of Defeat
by
William N. Bonham

Cover design: William N. Bonham
Sketches: William N. Bonham
Editor: Sandra Bonham

Copyright © 2003 William N. Bonham
Printed in the United States of America
First Edition, First printing: 2003

Published by
LANGMARC PUBLISHING
P.O. 90488
AUSTIN, TEXAS 78709-0488

Library of Congress Control Number
2003108418

ISBN: 1-88029287-4   U.S.A. $18.95

FOR

Sandra and Cody

never flinch

ACKNOWLEDGEMENTS

In writing this book I learned many things. One of the most pleasant and surprising revelations was the number of people, many of them strangers to me, who offered their help and encouragement. To all, I am grateful, and some I must mention: Mrs. Patience Chappel (Bonnie), granddaughter of Milledge Luke Bonham, who generously shared family history with me; Elizabeth Cassidy West of the University of South Carolina Archives; Roberta Copp and staff of the Caroliniana Library at the University of South Carolina; Bela Herlong and staff of the Saluda County Historical Society; the Daughters of The Republic of Texas and staff at the Alamo library; Jan Lund for her helpful critique; and Sandra Bonham for her help, her patience and extraordinary editing skills. Any failures of insight, or mistaken conclusions are mine alone.

CHAPTER ONE

The bleak plain rolled relentlessly as it descended league after wearisome league toward the Rio Grande. The gnarled cedar trees and oak scrub, which had dotted the landscape as they left Bexar, had now become more sparse with mesquite and tumbleweed ever more dominant on the rocky ground. Occasionally they were blessed by crossing a small stream, first the Rio Medina, then the Frio, and now looming into view, the welcome green growth that marked the course of the Nueces, the cool, refreshing Rio Nueces. Miguel was grateful that they were crossing the northern desert in March before the heat came and turned it into a burning hell, but that small blessing paled beside his great good fortune at being away from Santa Anna's army and the battles that surely waited beyond the Alamo.

As a lieutenant and junior member of Santa Anna's personal staff, Miguel had been entrusted with the mission of carrying back to the capital the dispatches announcing the great victory over the rebel ragtag who had tried to defy the Generalissimo by defending the old mission of San Antonio de Valero, the Alamo. The humiliation General Cos had suffered last December at the hands of the rebellious *Tejanos* had been avenged, and those who had sought to prolong the disgrace had been taught a lesson they would not soon forget. It only remained now for Santa Anna to continue the campaign and drive the adventurers and criminals beyond the Sabine, and restore order to the state of *Tejas y Coahuila*.

If Miguel had opened and read the description of the battle in the dispatches he was carrying, he would have had trouble reconciling it with what he had witnessed, as would his companions, an escort of four lancers and a sergeant. They, like Miguel, could not believe their luck at receiving this assignment and had not yet ceased, in the silence of their souls, thanking God for it. They had seen too many of their comrades bravely die, and they had been totally dismayed at the devil-like ferocity of the *norteamericanos* even as they faced certain defeat.

It was their second night out, and as they reined in to make camp on the banks of the Nueces, Miguel marveled at the manners and temperament of his mount. She was a handsome dove-colored mare that he had first spotted standing in a grove of cottonwoods just to the east of the fortress shortly after the battle. It had happened when the Generalissimo had sent him with a squad of men to search the perimeter for stragglers immediately after the battle. Miguel had found no men, but he had taken the horse, which had only a bridle. Seeing she was fine-bred and spirited, he hoped fervently that somehow he would be allowed to keep her for himself. The wish became reality when, upon reporting back, fortune smiled as Santa Anna remarked, "Oh, I see you have found yourself another horse. Good! The one you are riding is needed by the lancers."

It was important to Santa Anna that his troops be all spit and polish, with matching horses to the extent possible. And since they had ridden many of their horses to death in the rush to get to Bexar, the general wanted all of the black mounts that could be had to reconstitute the appearance of his troops. Miguel never knew for certain whether it was because of this concern, but a moment later Santa Anna continued, "You may take your new horse and deliver my dispatches to his excellency, the foreign minister, in the capital. Tell General Almonte to arrange for a small escort to accompany you and be prepared to leave this afternoon."

Fighting to conceal his joy at receiving this assignment, Miguel replied with a crisp and military, "*Sí, mi General!*"

And so here he was—accompanied by five soldiers whose horses, bays, or at any rate, not blacks, did not conform with Santa Anna's vision of the proper appearance for his elite lancers. Men and horses can be exchanged, of course, and Miguel wondered if he and these soldiers had been selected at random, if indeed it was the color of the horses they rode, or if there was some other reason. In his own case, he suspected that, at least in part, he had been selected for this mission for the same reason that landed him on the Generalissimo's staff in the first place, the prominence of his father.

If that was the case, he now happily accepted it, and sitting there watching the ripples from the pebbles he threw into the river, he was surprised to think that just a few days before he had felt uneasy being a general's aide and would have much preferred to be in the direct line of combat. But all that was before he had seen those grim images: the frozen faces of death all around him on the battlefield, the young lads from Toluca, the brave men of Guerrero, wizened veterans from Guanajuato — all now gone—died bravely, for what? Could they not have starved those people out of the Alamo? *Was all this death necessary?*

But even viewing the carnage up close in all its stark reality had not touched him so much as a single death he witnessed from a distance. As he sat astride his horse among Santa Anna's staff watching the melee grow in intensity with the dim light of dawn, he became aware of the rebel flag flying from the ramparts of the old chapel. And then he recognized a familiar figure, his old friend José, now a brother lieutenant, begin to lower the flag and replace it with the flag of Mexico! *Bravo!* It was an inspiring sight as he watched the halyard slowly moving up the staff.

In the next moment, an immeasurable bit of time, he was shocked to see José slump behind the parapet, apparently shot, and the flag he was attempting to raise, the flag of his beloved country, begin to slowly settle down over him. Then, he realized that though much noise and shouting continued, the firing had stopped. And moments later, as if in obedience to a signal from heaven, all was silent. The battle was over. *But José was dead!* Killed as the battle ended! Miguel was dismayed to think that he had envied his friend the chance to be in the thick of the fighting. His first impulse was to run to José, but he realized that even if he could leave his post beside the Generalissimo, it would be unseemly in his resplendent uniform to be moving about among those who had suffered so much, now covered with grime and blood, and all of them a little crazed. As these thoughts flashed through his mind in an instant, he suddenly became aware of the Generalissimo's voice ordering him to begin the scouting action around the perimeter, "You will probably find that some of those cowardly dogs have tried to escape," he said.

Miguel did not think so.

But now, with the carnage well behind him, he looked once more at the horse he had found. He called her *Guapa* and realized even more what a fine and worthy animal she was. He wondered to which of the rebels she belonged. He would never know, of course, but the thought reminded him of their corpses piled high outside the old chapel and that gruesome pyre, which marked the only grave they would ever have. The grim truth of war! Often necessary, he knew, but "glorious" as he had been led to believe? Never! That was only a word used to motivate young people to fight the battles. Now, he wanted no part of it.

But he was troubled. If duty called again, would he be able to go into battle and fight bravely for his country? He knew his reasons for doing so could never be the same as those he had brought with him as he crossed the Rio Grande into Texas just a few short weeks before, but *yes*, he thought, *I would*. Of course he would never know for sure. He was out of it, and his mind began to be at ease. Just then his thoughts were interrupted by the sergeant, whose demeanor was noticeably more relaxed than had been the case when they departed Bexar. He was reminding Miguel that the time had come to eat.

As they quietly ate their simple meal, Miguel could see—was it *gratitude*—in the face of each man? He was sure that it was not for the food. He was right to assume that the men felt as he did, although they feared speaking of their good fortune, even to each other. They went about their tasks in a military manner, brisk and businesslike, but there was underlying joy and relief among those who slept in that camp that night. The feeling continued through each day of the long trek down into the valley of Mexico—six men riding light-colored horses.

CHAPTER TWO

Only days before, the horse had borne a different rider bringing news of quite another sort. A lieutenant of cavalry in the revolutionary army of Texas had ridden his horse Sal into the Alamo, not away from it. He had been returning at the end of a sortie of more than two weeks, and in his absence the fortress had been besieged by a Mexican army, which had not been expected for at least another month. The horse had carried him on a mad dash through the Mexican lines to rejoin his comrades within the walls.

* * *

The chain of events, which had led up to this desperate ride, had begun with the defeat of General Cos and the expulsion of Mexican military forces from Texas. This had raised the hopes of the American colonists that victory in their long struggle to shed the yoke of Mexican rule was at hand. Although none believed the matter to be finally settled, there was a sense of quietus in the conflict, and most of the settlers who had been fighting with the army had returned to their farms for

Christmas and to begin preparations for spring planting. They knew that eventually they must fight, but
many, particularly those from the more populous settlements to the east, still persisted in the hope that the
inevitable conflict would not occur until late spring. But
those in the western settlements, constituting a frontier
of sorts and being less insulated by distance, knew that
time was short. The exodus back to the farms had
seriously depleted the army units in the field, leaving
the frontier posts weakly defended, their principal safe-
guard being the great desert that separated them from
the heartland of Mexico.

The most important place on the frontier was San
Antonio de Bexar, or simply *Bexar* as many called it.
There, taking over the Alamo lately occupied by General Cos, the garrison had set about making preparations for the battle that surely lay ahead. For weeks they
had been doing what they could: building up the battlements, husbanding grain, drying beef, scrounging for
powder and shot . . . and seeking help.

With each passing day, information continued to
trickle in that Santa Anna would soon be coming. And
no one disputed it. There could be little doubt of his
purpose—to expel once and for all, by annihilation if
necessary, the rebellious colonists—who called themselves Texians—from the state of *Tejas y Coahuila*. Their
revolutionary activities had gone unchecked for too
long, and the ignominious defeat that his cousin, General Cos, had suffered at their hands in this very place
had been the final straw. Now, they must go!

As the threat became more imminent, the Texians,
with their supplies low and their ranks thin, knew that
if the Alamo was to be held, they would need to be
reinforced, and quickly. So it was decided that the
lieutenant would go forth—first to the *presidio* of La
Bahía in Goliad where Colonel Fannin commanded

nearly five hundred men, and then perhaps to other places: Refugio, Brazoria, Gonzales, and use his presence, his ability as an advocate and as a leader to underscore the urgent appeals–which the new commandant of Bexar, Colonel Travis, would be sending throughout the region.

The lieutenant was James Butler Bonham. Called "Colonel" by some, "Jim" by most everyone, he was one of the officers of the regular army posted in the Alamo. He had no uniform but wore a military style greatcoat and a buckskin jacket, breeches and boots of a type that might be favored by a planter. Tall and lean, straight as an arrow, with black hair and intense dark eyes, he had the look and manner of a gentleman—benign, but toughened by countless days living away from what might be expected to be his normal surroundings. Warm houses, fresh linens, well-tended clothing, regular habits and good food were things he had experienced only intermittently over the past few months. He was not dismayed by long hours on the back of his horse and making do with whatever shelter was available at night — usually the welcome confines of a settler's house or a makeshift inn. But sometimes his broad-brimmed hat was the only thing between him and the sky above.

On these occasions whatever kind of lean-to or shelter he could fashion from what he found around him would do. On the Texas frontier this often meant taking care not to build a fire, or if so, concealing it in such a way as not to attract hostile Indians. Despite the discomforts, he found pleasure and excitement, a kind of fulfillment in such tasks, particularly so in this case, as he regarded it to be an undertaking of the highest moment. There was no boredom here, no ennui; his blood seemed to rush faster, his senses were keener, and his awareness of life was honed to a sharp edge. Jim was well served by his horsemanship, for which he had been renowned throughout his life, and he was acutely aware that time was short—the most should be made of every minute. His own endurance was not in question . . . only the limits imposed by nature: the endurance of his horse, *thank God,* a powerful and noble animal; the weather, unpredictable, but now improving; and the terrain, including the many streams and rivers, often difficult to ford at this time of year.

Although he could have passed for either, Jim was neither frontiersman nor professional soldier, but a lawyer, late of South Carolina and Alabama. He had come to Texas to make his place in the world. But first he had to fight for it, and his mission now was part of that struggle.

The first day out had been almost pleasant. Leaving the Alamo and proceeding down the familiar road to Goliad, he had made good time. He had to be on constant watch for Mexican patrols and also be wary of the Comanches. He had been warned to take care to avoid ambush by them, and he knew he could never outrun them on a tired horse. He had soon learned how to deal with this threat as part of the elementary education of settlers and soldiers alike who had any hope of survival. Massacres were almost all reported eventually, but lone riders often disappeared without a trace.

Attacks on travelers were often made late in the afternoon. Many had been lost because, anxious to reach their destination, they pushed their animals too much during the day, leaving no reserve of energy for what was sometimes a mad dash for safety. The Comanches were familiar with the settlements and way stations, and would often position themselves within an hour's ride of these points, poised to swoop down on the victims when they and their animals were the most vulnerable.

Knowing this, Jim always paced his horse carefully.

Sal was a powerful animal. Jim marveled at her strength and had never seen the limit of her endurance, but he rested her frequently and chose the places carefully.

He had found a good place to spend his first night out and on the second day, knowing that La Bahía was within easy reach, he prepared to pause once more before descending into the countryside leading to Goliad. He was watching for a place he knew, marked by a crooked tree and east of the tree line which traced the course of the San Antonio River as it wended its way down to the Gulf. He had been watching for some time, and just as he had almost given up finding it, sure enough, there it was! Just over a ridge at the top of a long gently sloping plain that led down to a bend in the winding river. A couple of smaller trees were nearby and just enough scrub growth around them to provide the cover he and Sal would need to rest unobserved. Best of all, there were the ruins of a little stone hut . . . a *jacal* . . . which would afford some shelter should the towering clouds become capricious.

The suitability of the place was made complete by a small brook trickling out of the rocks and providing all the water he and Sal would need. He dismounted, and satisfying himself that no rattlesnakes or scorpions had taken over the place, he settled down to relax for a few minutes. Not really tired himself, he sat with his back against a tree and watched Sal munching the little sprigs of green, which were the first signs of spring.

Had he the good fortune to be in this place a few weeks hence, he would have been treated to the sight of the vast meadow which stretched out before him covered in a stunning blanket of blue; thousands of tiny blue flowers joined together as if a piece of crisp blue sky had fallen. Although it was a sight he was never to see, the vast openness of the landscape itself fascinated him. He sensed the incipient vitality of something about to happen. The serenity of the place gradually took over and he was inevitably distracted from the anxiety and urgency that lay both behind and ahead of him.

Although it had been cold and rainy in recent weeks, a warming trend had begun. The coming spring was indeed in the air—breaks in the overcast combining with the unmistakable balminess in the soft breezes blowing up from the Gulf—a fresh day full of life; it could not be ignored. It had become a day that brought joy in simply being alive, the kind of day that charged any undertaking with energy and optimism, no matter the circumstances.

Captured by the sight before him, his thoughts had been inescapably drawn back to his youth, evoking memories of times long forgotten. He was transported back to Red Bank creek and the Saluda river valley. He could not but compare this vista with that of the long gentle slope leading down the hill to his home—the creek lined with trees on one side and the vast cotton fields on the other.

He was overcome by images of carefree days which would live forever in his heart—he and Simeon with little Luke always tagging along, swinging out over the creek on a rope and the exhilarating shock of the cool water as he dropped in, catching those black bass, lying in the tall grass with his brothers and feeling the warm earth beneath them as they watched the clouds go by in endless succession, the sudden thunderstorms that sent them all scampering, talking and dreaming of the future and the heroic deeds they would perform.

Chapter Three

Jim's reverie took him to a time when he was eleven. As with the western world in general, 1818 was a year of profound change in South Carolina. The prosperity brought about by Mr. Whitney's cotton gin was wearing thin as the impact of another momentous event—the Louisiana Purchase—made vast lands available for the planting of even more cotton to satisfy what seemed an insatiable worldwide demand. As a result, the enormous new plantations to the west in what was being called the Deep South, were becoming the principal force in the cotton economy. Though plantations in the Carolina uplands such as those of the Bonhams and their extended family—places called Flat Grove, Wine Hall, Mount Willing, and Red Bank—were withstanding the pressure, an uncertain future loomed.

Although born at Flat Grove, it was at Red Bank that Jim Bonham had spent most of his young life growing up. Stretched out along the creek from which it had taken its name, the plantation was near the center of Edgefield District, an area that dominated the western part of the state. Home to many soldiers and politicians who were already legendary, it extended north and east from the Savannah River to the smaller Saluda River and breached a geologic line that generally separated the Carolina uplands from the more developed low-lands that included Charleston and the tidewater. Save for the village of Edgefield itself, it was mostly a collection of plantations, and the changing times were manifested primarily by the westward migration of people drawn from every strata of the population. The result was an almost palpable restlessness that neatly complemented the volatile temperament, which from the earliest days had been associated with Edgefieldians.

As a product of this environment, Jim was not only restive, but idealistic, fiercely independent, and head-strong. He came by these traits naturally. His father, James, for whom he had been named, had gone off from his home in Maryland to fight in the War for Independence at the tender age of fifteen and, together with *his* father, Absalom, had been present when Cornwallis finally surrendered at Yorktown on that memorable day in October of 1781. After the war, his mother having died and father remarried, young James set out to make his way in life—a way that eventually led to his arriving in Edgefield in 1796, by then a widower with two young children. It was there that he met Sophia Butler Smith who awaited him as if predestined to take the stage in a drama that had already been carefully plotted. They were married within a year after his arrival, and before long, young John and Ann began to welcome new brothers and sisters.

But now, as Jim remembered the old times, his thoughts returned to a morning in late fall. The first snow of the season was descending on Red Bank. A light snow, but a sure reminder that winter was coming. Dawn had just broken, the rolling pasture and the fields beyond were becoming uniformly white, and Jim was already with the horses. Toby, the black gelding his mother sometimes used as a riding horse, and the matched pair of bay mares that pulled the family buggies, were stimulated by the brisk air of the new day and were clearly restless, even a little fractious. Nevertheless, they remained patient as they waited for Jim to measure out their oats and eventually open the door leading to the small paddock just outside.

These animals, pampered and carefully segregated from the other farm animals, were a source of endless delight to Jim. He admired their graceful movements, their shining coats, and their intelligence, which had become more evident as his understanding of them grew. When he wasn't peeling their lips back to look at their teeth or searching for burrs in their tails or manes, he would simply sit and watch them, losing track of time. He would often gaze into their eyes, almost expecting them to speak at any moment. He even imagined that they spoke with each other in a language he just might learn, if he could. Whatever it was seemed only barely out of reach. Nevertheless, he felt that he was able to communicate with them. The horses, normally made uncomfortable by eye contact with humans, would often return his gaze as if they, too, were trying to make a connection. Certainly they understood some of his words, or was it his tone of voice—his manner?

His boyish notions notwithstanding, Jim remembered what his father had taught him: there was a practical side to dealing with these animals he admired so much. He must always be in control and never show fear. Fear never entered his mind, but he had noticed in the beginning that the horses always seemed to be watching, waiting for any sign of—what? Weakness? But by now, even though he was just a boy, his position as master had been established. It had become natural and instinctive, and he and the horses got along just fine.

Feeding the horses was one of Jim's chores and, with the benign approval of his mother, he had also taken to currying Toby. He was anxious to put into practice what he was learning from Zeb, the blacksmith, and from the other hands who trained and tended the other horses and mules. He spent hours watching them at work and had become so engrossed with the animals that even on days when he really didn't want to get out of bed, like this morning, a few minutes with the horses was all it took to shake the shrouds of sleep and launch him on a new day of discovery and adventure.

Of course, like most boys and men, he had to *know* horses. They were an integral, even essential, part of life. But there were also other things. Fishing and hunting satisfied instincts of another kind and brought different kinds of fulfillment. Not just catching a bass or bringing down a turkey, but honing the skills it took to do these things was a source of pride to Jim as well as to his friends.

Although the present intensity of these shared interests and experiences might eventually fade, or at least be overshadowed as adult concerns overtook them, the lore would remain buried deep inside and would link them, and boys like them, together throughout their lives. These things, so close to the natural world, also formed the basis for kinship with an older generation of men who, perhaps out of nostalgia, enthusiastically led the boys down the same roads they had traveled and, in so doing, formed another kind of bond that created continuity as it transcended generational differences.

Underlying all these interests was the fantasy world of boyhood, a world in which every activity, no matter how mundane, was translated into a noble exploit. Leading a horse to water became preparing it for battle; the split rail fences that zigzagged along the roads, often and magically, became ramparts, and any trip was likely to be a perilous journey. Inspired not only by fictional heroes, but by the real heroes of the age in which he lived, the notion of great deeds was always with him. It had not been even forty years since his father and grandfather were at Yorktown, and the French revolution was more recent still. Even now, as Jim sat looking at the horses, Napoleon brooded on St. Helena. The Louisiana Purchase and the exploits of Lewis and Clark, still fresh events, were influencing the lives of people right here in Edgefield.

Although Jim was unaware of the full significance of these events, the principal players were popular figures, and many of them still lived. Jim even remembered, or thought he remembered, the news of Andrew Jackson's great victory at the battle of New Orleans. In his world of hero worship, the line between the likes of a Francis Marion and Rob Roy tended to disappear; the Lady of the Lake resided somewhere upstream on the Saluda River. And of course, what would heroes be without heroines? Girls, too—other than his sisters—were looming on Jim's horizon, and they fit neatly into the dream.

But now as the snow fell, the pangs of hunger were competing for Jim's attention, and he became increasingly aware of smoke pouring from the chimneys of the house, signaling warmth and good things to eat. Sure enough, within the house his mother and Louisa were already busily engaged in the morning routine. His mother with the children, and Louisa getting breakfast ready, a task that only she could perform to the satisfaction of her mistress. Sophia Bonham believed that each day must begin with a hearty breakfast and, if appetites were sluggish, a few chores—like tending horses—would sharpen them soon enough. She was right! All of her children, sluggish appetites or not, had regular chores to perform, and heaven help them if they should ever fail to meet their responsibilities.

Within the kitchen, the warm glow of oil lamps was

gradually giving way to the purer white light reflected from the snow as daylight came. Along the back wall was a fireplace with the usual pot brackets on either side of the opening and a brick hearth along the floor providing a base for a cook stove on one side and a porcelain oven on the other. The wood to fuel all these fires was in a neatly stacked pile just outside the back door, but a few pieces for immediate use were always kept in a big brass pot beside the oven.

Along the opposite wall were several wooden cabinets in which were stored the ordinary cutlery and dishes. Other cabinets with fabric-covered enclosures were provided for the protection of finished foods such as pies, bread and roasted meats. On the wall beside them were long rows of open shelving upon which were placed the large ceramic jars in which cured meats and most other foods were stored. Drying herbs and a few hams hung from pegs which projected from the wall at the end of the shelving. Two large oak work tables extended along the middle of the room and at the far end, near the door to the outside, was the wet area, a long shelf containing a sink and space for the several casks of water.

Louisa's son, Hertha, had been up for hours kindling the fires, hauling water, carrying in the milk, and doing everything he could to prolong the time he could spend in the presence of Mercy, the young girl who helped his mother with the cooking. But Louisa had a keen eye for just how long she could allow Hertha to stay before helping became loitering, and she had finally fed him his breakfast and shooed him out to start his other daily chores.

Louisa, with her husband and their children, had moved with Sophia and her family from Flat Grove when they had built this house at Red Bank creek nine years before. It was the same year Jim's sister Elizabeth was born and before the birth of Julia and his younger brother, Luke. Sophia and her husband, James, had made their home in her father's old house at Flat Grove since their wedding day.

But eventually, as the family grew, a new house had become a necessity. Equally important, James was not the kind of man who could settle for simply managing the lands of his wife's family. His instincts were strong to build something of his own. So he bought the land at Red Bank creek and built their home. Little more than five miles from Flat Grove, it was considerably more distant in terms of size and comfort, and became the center of a new plantation which grew steadily as James added to the lands in the years before his death in 1815.

Now, Sophia was embarked on a new life, unexpected and challenging. Surrounded by her kin and sustained by strong religious conviction, she had been able to endure the loss of her husband as she had that of her young son, Jacob, who died the same year Jim had been born. But she was thankful that she had borne James seven other children. Now, with oldest daughter Sarah having been married the past June, and Simeon and Malachia away at school, she found herself with her four youngest, two boys and two girls, still at home. In this environment, reflecting the infectious exuberance of youth, Sophia felt rejuvenated. She began seeing things though their eyes, looking to the future rather than to the pain of the past, and she was pleased to see her own naturally optimistic and happy outlook return. With many disappointments behind her, she counted her blessings as she savored her daily life.

Thirty-eight, slight of build, with dark brown, almost black hair contrasting with a flawless complexion, Sophia remained a handsome woman—not because the years and the child-bearing had not exacted a toll from her body, but because her inherent vitality was expressed in the impact of her presence. Her hazel eyes were always intent on whatever or whomever she beheld. She was naturally poised and cheerful, full of energy, and she communicated a sense of serenity and self-confidence that captivated those around her. Within her family, not just with her own children, but with nephews, nieces, cousins—all of them—she was a favorite, and they would remember throughout their lives the joyful times spent in her home. Although they were a restive and striving lot, there was much happiness and laughter in the Bonham household during those years.

Sophia herself had the great good fortune to have wise and loving parents who also possessed the means to provide her with the education and material goods, which enabled her to realize the potential of her intelligence, energy and interests. Within this privileged environment, her parents, Jacob Smith and Sally Butler, instilled in their children a healthy respect for the Almighty and worked hard to develop their children's better instincts, as well as the virtues of honesty and hard work.

In raising her own children, Sophia conscientiously sought to pass along these same values. But she added something special of her own. She was endowed with exceptional insight, more than mere intuition, and this enabled her to establish a strong rapport with each of her children. Her children were all, in varying degrees, of independent nature, disdainful of regimentation of any kind, and definitely knew their own minds. There was difficulty in teaching strong-willed people, but Sophia worked hard at it, was equal to the task, and the entire family benefited.

By some inner force, and certainly following their mother's example, the children were all motivated to excel at whatever they might undertake. This impulse was particularly strong in the younger boys, James and Milledge Luke. Moreover, each of them seemed to have been born with a sort of natural perspicacity and a disdain for pettiness, traits that did not preclude acts of foolishness and rashness, but might, as Sophia would one day speculate, even encourage them.

All the while, Sophia was much aware that she could never fully take their father's place. Fortunately, there were male relatives close at hand, uncles and cousins, whose willing help—although a collective effort—together provided a sort of surrogate fatherhood. The children learned much from these men, not the least of which was a sense of responsibility, which fit in well with the virtues taught to them by Sophia. But she struggled with the memory of the children's father. Inculcating the family with his values was easy, because she shared them. It was, in fact, an exciting and rewarding task, the evident success of which both surprised and delighted her.

But drawing an accurate picture of him, especially for the younger children, escaped her. She wanted them to know about him, and know him as a man if they could, but each passing year made it more difficult. In a way, however, the family continued to live in their father's presence at Red Bank. In a material sense, the place represented a good part of his life's work, and the environment he had created contributed to the shaping of his children's lives.

The house stood between Red Bank creek and the road which, generally paralleling the creek, ran through the plantation. It was close to the trees that lined the creek but faced the road, which rose gently in both directions. On the other side of the road opposite the house were the family stables and paddock, separated by a stand of trees from the barns and other working buildings of the plantation, vegetable gardens, and slave quarters beyond. Cotton fields extended in both directions alongside the road as it moved away from the enclave. Followed far enough, the road eventually led to the Red Bank Baptist Church, which to those living thereabouts was the real center of community life, even more than Edgefield village. In this happy place Jim and his brothers and sisters grew up.

At the church, in this house, along the creek, and in the fields beyond, the brothers heard the gospels, devoured books, fished, played in the fields, learned about the land, and about horses and life. While their sisters shared some of these experiences with their brothers, they also learned different things—how to play the piano, to cook and to sew and how to deport themselves as proper young ladies.

The insular nature of their lives notwithstanding, the changing times were becoming more evident with each passing day. They were already familiar with the term *Alabama Fever*, used to describe the wave of westward migration, which was beginning to touch all of their lives. To Sophia, *Alabama Fever* was but a symptom of more fundamental change, and it served to heighten her awareness of the temporal nature of all things.

Cotton prices were going down, and it was becoming ever more obvious that the larger plantations to the west were taking over. As those giant enterprises grew and the planters in Edgefield and throughout the Carolinas were forced to diversify into other crops, Sophia was horrified to realize that to many in the Old South, the most profitable crop was becoming the slaves themselves.

Import of slaves had been banned since 1807, but because of the huge demand for them generated by the western plantations, a new internal trade had developed. It made unavoidable the ugly realities of the institution, realities that to many people had long been obscured by the routine and patterns of a settled and established way of life. No matter the truth of these sobering thoughts, Sophia was caught up in the system, a system in which cotton was the financial engine, an engine that drove the factories and shipping interests of the north and the spinning mills of England, as well as the plantations of Edgefield. She regarded the slaves as part of her extended family, a family entrusted to her and for whom she was responsible to the Almighty. Red Bank, Flat Grove, and the rest were home to them all, mistress and slave alike, and Sophia intended to keep it that way. Although it was a flawed institution that underlay their lives, it was the way things were, and concerns with the moral dilemma took second place to the immediacy of daily life.

Indeed, such thoughts were far from Sophia's mind as she dealt with the hubbub of her awakening family on this chilly and bleak morning. She was in high spirits that could not be dampened by the winter winds. The very chill of the day served to underscore the warmth and vitality within the shelter of her home. This crisp morning life seemed serene, even with the chaos four children can generate as they start a new day. Elizabeth and Julia would be taken off by Louisa to their tutor a little later in the morning. The boys, of whom Jim at eleven was the oldest, would soon be setting out for the field school that they attended some two miles distant. But now, the two girls and their brother Milledge Luke, snickering all the while, were speculating over what Jim might be tracking in from the stable as they buzzed in and out of the kitchen.

Louisa stood at a cupboard beside the main table serving up oatmeal into large clay bowls, all the while admonishing the children, "You chil'n get y'selves over here and eat these oats," and nodding towards the table upon which had been placed a large platter of ham and two larger bowls, one filled with biscuits and another with pears, "and eat plenty of that ham, and lots of butter and preserves on d' biscuits. It's cold out there! … an y'all needs to put some meat on them bones anyway!"

Jim, having carefully cleaned his shoes this time, came in through the back door and quickly demonstrated what it really meant to have a good appetite.

Eventually, breakfast was finished, and as the boys bundled up for their departure, Sophia called to her daughter.

"Elizabeth, please check to see that Milledge has his muffler on!"

"Yes, Mama!"

As the two boys stood there smiling, bathed in the attention of their sisters and the watchful, yet proprietary glances of Louisa, Jim opened the door, once more feeling the icy wind. He called out, "Let's go Luke, the world's waiting for us!"

Sophia, hands on her hips, palms out, head cocked to one side as she imperceptibly shook it in mock apprehension, which was belied by the smile in her eyes that bespoke both love and pride, finally broke into full laughter as she called out, "Get on now you scalawags, and stay out of trouble!" And with the loving smile of their mother following them, they set out for school. For Sophia, this was a moment of purest contentment and pleasure.

As they left, Elizabeth, who by then had bundled up herself, called out, "Mama, can I go with them just to the top of the hill?"

It was a daily ritual between Elizabeth and her brothers; indeed Jim and Milledge had already stopped and turned, waiting for Elizabeth to join them on the first part of their journey.

"Just to the top of the hill!" Sophia called out as the trio departed.

With little Julia waving from the window, the three trudged away, up the long, gently rising hill. But before they were far from the house, and knowing the result it was likely to bring, Milledge squeaked out, "My feet are cold!"

"Well, get up on my back little brother! Help him Elizabeth."

And after he was securely in place, Jim continued, "How's that Luke?"

"Why do you always call me Luke?"

" 'Cause it's your name."

"But it's my middle name; mama calls me Milledge."

"Well, she calls me James Butler—isn't that a mouthful! I think she just likes the sound of it. Anyway, to mama you're Milledge, but to me you're Luke! What do you think, Elizabeth?"

Elizabeth, always teasing and looking for fun replied, "I don't know. To me, he seems like a little varmint!"

Luke half turned and shot back, "I may be a varmint, but I'm riding!"

Luke's remark triggered the same thought with each of them, but it was Elizabeth who spoke first.

"Jim, didn't mama say she was gonna let you get a horse?"

"She sure did, but not 'til I'm twelve," Jim said.

"Well, you're almost twelve. Don't you think we... you . . . could talk her into it now?"

"You know mama, twelve means twelve!"

Just then, as they reached the top of the hill, Luke interrupted, "Jim, my feet are still cold!"

"Well hand me your shoes, little brother, and put your feet in my pockets!" This seemed to satisfy Luke, and as he wiggled his feet into the warmth of Jim's pockets, Elizabeth helped him to complete the operation, gave him a peck on the cheek, and turned to make her way back down the hill.

"You two stay out of trouble now!"

As Jim and Luke moved along the road, they eventually came to the point where Will, Jim's friend, would usually join them for the rest of the walk to school. But last summer the Travis family had moved to Alabama, and ever since, when they passed the spot, they thought of Will and sometimes spoke of him.

"You still missin' Will, Jim?" Luke asked.

"In a way I do, but you know, it's gettin' to where I have a hard time even picturing him now."

His brother did not answer, but he knew what Jim meant. The two trudged on in silence for a while longer, when finally Luke, more quietly now, spoke up again.

"Jim, tell me about daddy."

"Do you remember daddy at all?" Jim asked.

Luke stammered, "I don't know. I don't think so."

"Well, most of what I know is what mama has told me. I'm not even sure whether I really remember him, or if it's just a picture she has painted for me."

"She's hardly told me anything."

"She's probably been waiting for you to ask, or maybe it grieves her too much. You should ask her to tell you all about daddy."

"But Jim, what do you remember?"

"I remember him talkin' about all the things happenin' in the world . . . the explorers . . . the battle of New Orleans . . . the war he was in for independence . . . and him carrying me on his back just like I'm doin' you now. I remember his laugh. I can still hear it." Jim paused for a moment, and then continued, "And there's other things, but I'm not sure . . ."

"Like what?"

"Oh, like him sitting at the head of the table telling us about horses, and that we could never flinch."

"What does that mean?"

"It means you have to be strong no matter how scared you are." Seeing the puzzled look on his little brother's face, Jim continued. "You remember when Simeon was home a couple of weeks ago he told us about daddy's story of the sea captain?"

Puzzled, Luke said, "Yes, I think so, but what's a sea captain got to do with horses?"

"Well, it's sorta' like a parable."

"A parable?"

"You know—like in the Bible. A story to teach a lesson." Seeing that Luke still had not made the connection, Jim continued. "When there's a storm, a really bad storm, and everybody in a ship is scared, really scared — daddy said they would all look at the captain to see if he was scared, too. But if he didn't show it, didn't flinch or seem scared, then they would figure everything was all right and not be so scared themselves."

"That's not the same as with horses."

"But the lesson's the same—don't flinch!"

All at once, it was clear to Luke. Jim was speaking of instincts with which he was already familiar but had unconsciously accepted as a natural part of his make-up . . . resist fear . . . never give in. The crisp sound of his brother's feet crunching through the crusted snow seemed to demand that he give voice to his understanding. "That's right! Never flinch!"

Jim looked over his shoulder at Luke, and as their eyes met, they laughed aloud and then, as if following some unspoken command, shouted in unison, "We don't flinch!"

The boys grew silent as each put together his own picture of their father in his mind's eye, and Jim was finally moved to sum it up.

"So try to always think of our dad, sittin' at the end of the table tellin' us that story, teachin' us how to behave."

Luke said nothing, but he had made a little connection with the father he longed to know and would always cherish that little piece of advice received straight from him.

CHAPTER FOUR

The road from Bexar to Copano Bay was one of the oldest in Texas. It generally followed the San Antonio River as it meandered down to the Gulf and marked a line, which was sort of an unofficial frontier between the Anglo settlements in eastern Texas and the vast lands to the west and south extending down into Mexico proper. Less than fifty miles inland from the bay, the *presidio* of La Bahía was a key point on that road. It was situated on a slight hill above the right bank of the river and was only a short distance from the town of Goliad, which lay within a wide sweeping bend on the opposite side.

Within the *presidio* was the largest single force in the revolutionary army of Texas, nearly five hundred men, commanded by Colonel James Fannin. They were mostly volunteers, mostly American, a combination of men who had been part of the garrison and those who had come up from Copano with Fannin earlier in the month when his plans to embark on an expedition further down the coast had gone awry. A fortnight had passed since Fannin had come into La Bahía and now, entering the last half of February, the men were becoming increasingly restless. They were anxious for news of the other expeditions, friends of theirs who had gone with Colonel Johnson and Dr. Grant intending the conquest of Matamoros at the mouth of the Rio Grande. But they were also reacting to mounting rumors that Santa Anna would soon be coming north with a powerful army.

Uncertain as to what would happen next, they had a growing sense that a decisive chain of events had begun—some giant wheel had been set in motion, leading to an inevitable confrontation. They worked hard to be ready, but ultimately could only wait and wonder what lay ahead. Each new arrival, whether an express rider, a returning patrol, or simply a traveler, was greeted with a voracious appetite for news. Sentry duty, normally shunned, was welcomed. Posted on the battlements around the perimeter of the fortress, the sentries were first to see each new cloud of dust or wisp of smoke on the horizon, or the approach of a rider. No lookouts on a ship were ever more vigilant.

So Jim had been in view for some time as he approached. Since he and his horse were familiar figures to many of the men in the *presidio*, his identity had long since been established. As he came closer, Jacob Coleman, one of the men who knew him well, called down to his comrades below.

"Colonel Bonham is approaching. Open the gates!"

At about the same time, Jim urged Sal into a gallop, unconsciously wanting to convey a sense of urgency to his arrival. He circled around to the south gate, which by then had been opened. As he entered, he looked around at the familiar surroundings with new eyes and could not help wishing that the Alamo were so sound a fortress as this place. Here, the walls were all intact and well-buttressed, the area they enclosed was larger, and the place was positioned to have good command of the approaches of any enemy. By comparison, the Alamo, with its crumbling walls and irregular perimeter, seemed an outpost.

Having heard the ruckus in the quadrangle, Fannin stepped out from the room in the west wall where he made his headquarters. He immediately recognized Jim who, as their eyes met, dismounted and began to walk over, his magnificent mare moving easily beside him as if she had just come from a canter in a park. Fannin welcomed him with mixed feelings; he was vaguely uncomfortable with Jim's presence, but curious to know why he had come. *Perhaps he has brought news, or more than likely, wants something of me,* he thought.

If anything was welcome about Jim's arrival, it was that Jim was Sam Houston's man. Fannin was beginning to feel the need to explain his recent actions to Houston or, in his absence, then to anyone who might eventually have his ear. Nattily dressed in full uniform, Fannin, his usual sallow and inscrutable countenance showing signs of fatigue and anxiety, self-consciously straightened up, and assumed an air of authority as he waited for Jim to come to him. He affected a cordial demeanor and an openness he did not feel as he spoke.

"Good afternoon, Mr. Bonham. What brings you to La Bahía?"

Jim was not of a mind to suffer fools and scoundrels, and although he was not sure that Fannin answered to either category, his recent actions had raised doubts. True, Fannin had been a steadfast participant in the movement for liberty well before Jim had even set foot in Texas. Indeed, he had befriended Jim almost from the day he arrived. But there was no doubt that he had since fallen in league with two individuals who most assuredly were scoundrels: the overbearing Colonel Johnson, erstwhile commandant of the forces in Bexar who, by commandeering weapons and provisions, and persuad-

ing a goodly number of volunteers to follow him to
Matamoros, had sacked the Alamo just as surely as
could be expected of any Mexican army; and the schem-
ing Dr. Grant, who had engaged in the political intrigue
that had made it all possible. These three: Fannin,
Johnson, and Grant had allied themselves with a rump
political group that sought to break away from the duly
formed revolutionary government, impeach the governor, and challenge the authority of Sam Houston.

So it was with a great deal of reserve that Jim approached Fannin, whom nevertheless he recognized as
probably the best, if not the *only*, hope for reinforcing
Bexar. Whatever the reasons for Fannin's recent actions,
Jim was intent on putting all misgivings aside, giving
Fannin the benefit of any doubts, and focusing on the
urgent business that had brought him here. He could
not fail.

"Colonel." Jim nodded as he replied to Fannin's
greeting with all the pleasantness he could muster.

Sensing Jim's mood, Fannin realized that they should
get straight to business, whatever it may be. He motioned for his orderly to tend to the horse. Turning once
again to Jim, he said, "Let's go inside."

Fannin watched as Jim warmed himself at the fire,
gratefully accepting the hot tea and biscuits which he
had been offered. Then Fannin sat in the big oak chair
behind his desk and quietly waited for Jim to speak.
Jim's words were no surprise.

"I suppose, as with us in the Alamo, you must have
been hearing that a large Mexican force has been assembled, and even now may be marching towards Bexar
with the likelihood of arriving there sooner than we had
expected."

Fannin nodded. "And here as well, I fear."

"As you might imagine, improving the fortifications at the Alamo goes on apace, and we have made just

about as good a fortress of the place as ever we are likely to. But to hold it will require a much larger—and better equipped—force. Not only are we short of men and every kind of supplies from cornmeal to powder, but many of the men are ill."

Jim squelched the impulse to remind Fannin that these conditions were primarily owing to the actions of Colonel Johnson. He knew such a remark would serve no purpose except perhaps to anger or alienate Fannin, and that was something he was most assiduously striving to avoid. *Like walking on eggs,* he thought.

"Travis is in sole command now, and he's laid it all out in this dispatch."

Fannin set aside the dispatch as Jim handed it to him.

"And he wants me to reinforce the Alamo?"

"Join forces with us, is the way I would put it. But yes, as far as we know, you command the only force capable of doing it quickly. We don't believe there is much time and from what we hear, the people back in the settlements haven't fully come to realize the urgency of the situation."

"And what of Goliad . . . the link with Copano? Would Travis have us abandon it?"

"Of course not, but this place is more readily defended with fewer men, and it is certain that Bexar is the more immediate prize for the enemy, while at the same time having the weaker defenses."

"Mr. Bonham. Jim, let me make it clear to you. I understand and sympathize with the plight of the forces in Bexar. While we have men, we are ourselves short of supplies, uncertain of the enemy's intentions, or even his whereabouts. We have to wait and size up the situation. After all, Goliad is also a key point on the frontier."

"I understand your concerns, Colonel, and as important as this place may be, we know that Bexar is the main objective and that Santa Anna may be there in a matter of weeks. There is very little time!"

"Weeks?" Fannin rejoined, "How can you be sure that he will arrive so soon?"

"By the increasing number and consistency of the reports we are receiving from places along the Rio Grande!"

Fannin nodded, as if accepting the validity of the evidence.

"Again, I must tell you, if my only concern were this command, I could act, but as the senior officer on the frontier I am compelled to be prudent! I must see what develops . . . and await orders!"

It was the word *orders*, which caught Jim's ear. Throughout their conversation he had thought that Fannin's views, while reasonable, reflected vacillation more than deliberation. But when Fannin had alluded to a command structure, something that by now everyone knew to be in shambles, he was sure of it. Fannin lacked confidence. He was confused and did not know what to do! It was worse than Jim had thought. So he took a deep breath.

"Orders? From whom?"

"Governor Robinson; the Council. They have appointed me ranking officer—their agent."

So now it was out on the table! *Good,* Jim thought; but still he had to chose his words carefully,

"With all due respect sir, you know that the Council lacks legitimacy, and Robinson is not governor. He is the lieutenant governor, and Henry Smith remains the duly appointed governor of Texas! Likewise, General Houston is the commander in chief of the army."

Fannin's face flushed; he could hardly contain his anger as he almost shouted.

"But Houston's not here. He's gone! If he is commander in chief, why isn't he here to command?"

I've done it now Jim thought. But trying to remain calm, he kept his answer simple.

"He'll return soon." Then doing his best to adopt the tone one would use with a brother officer inveighing against misguided directives from above, "But don't you agree that we cannot afford to let the wrangling in San Felipe and Washington carry over to our situation here? The fate of Texas depends on our solidarity. We're here—*now*. The duty has fallen to us, and what we do may well be decisive. If the frontier doesn't hold, Santa Anna will move directly to the east and do God-knows-what to the settlers there!"

Smarting from the patronizing nature of Jim's remarks and with his guts churning, Fannin did not answer immediately, but soon regained his composure.

"I understand all those things. I don't need to be lectured on the situation. But how can you—how can Travis—expect me to leave this place weakened? Don't you see the dilemma posed by your request?"

"Just so! I do appreciate your position, and I apologize for the tone of my remarks. The weight of your responsibility here—indeed along the entire frontier—is clear. But that is the point. Can Texas afford to have her army split? Wasn't it Ben Franklin who said something about taking the risk of hanging together to avoid the certainty of hanging separately? With our forces combined, we may even be able to take some offensive action while there is still time. The Mexican army will be strung out across the desert all the way from the Rio Grande."

"But what if they come by sea up from Copano?" Fannin interjected.

"Do you really believe they have enough ships for that? As I told you, we've heard that they are marching directly up from Mexico. But either way they will be strung out; this place will remain defensible, and their ability to sustain a prolonged siege will be severely limited, particularly if we are able to harass them with cavalry. Bowie even thinks there's a slight chance that the Comanches might get after them as well. Apparently there's no love lost there!"

"Nonsense!" Fannin grumbled, "We can't count on the savages as allies."

Jim swallowed hard and hoped his passion would not lead him to irritate Fannin again. So he said calmly, "Colonel, I agree; you must act prudently. But really, we can't wait for things to be crystal clear. If we don't act now, almost certainly it will be too late!"

Fannin, obviously torn and faced with what seemed to him the worst of dilemmas, began to weaken.

"You know, even if I agree, it may not be possible. As I've told you, our provisions are low. I'm waiting daily for resupply from Victoria. It's all very well to speak of bold action, but going off half-cocked, it can— it *often* leads to disaster."

Taking the polemic to what he hoped would be a less personal level, Jim replied, "Yes, but sometimes it is the only road to success. Think of where our revolution would have been had our army not made the bold move of crossing the Delaware through a storm at the onset of winter."

Fannin responded with inscrutable silence. But Jim sensed that Fannin might be pleased with the idea of comparing himself with George Washington. So, shamelessly, he continued.

"They realized that they had to take advantage of whatever opportunity was available and get across that river and surprise the Hessians. It was small step, but it turned the tide."

"But they had the ability to sustain many losses before that. Circumstances were different—there were the French."

"True, of course, but at the bottom of it all, there was the will. Think of the misery of that winter in Valley Forge; it must have far exceeded what we are going through. Men have faced impossible odds many times in history, but they never prevail if they don't try. Victory in the revolution was won in spite of overwhelming odds."

Fannin seemed receptive to these arguments, and Jim was beginning to feel that he had gained a little bit, although he dare push the pedantry no further. As the afternoon wore into evening, the conversation continued but became increasingly repetitive, and finally both men grew silent. Fannin stood facing the fire, his back to Jim.

Despite his rank and his military experience, he had for some time realized that he was most comfortable as a unit commander carrying out a strategy formulated by others. He could never be comfortable as commander in chief, a position to which he had aspired and even schemed to achieve. Now, as he was being forced by circumstances to make a command decision, he had no stomach for the role. Finally, he turned, looked hard at Jim.

"I'll think on this overnight. I'm disposed to help if I can, but as I've told you, I can't go running off half-cocked. As you've observed, this is the only viable military command in Texas. I can't put it at risk without weighing all the possibilities."

Jim allowed himself a little rush of exhilaration and thought that maybe, just maybe, he had won his case. And by way of sealing the unconfirmed bargain, he responded vigorously.

"With your permission, I'll go to Victoria tomorrow, find the quartermaster, and make sure that whatever supplies he has found are sent here post haste!"

Fannin smiled wryly at Jim's remark. "I've got some

men over there now doing just that, but I'm sure they'd welcome your lending them a hand, and making use of your special powers of persuasion." Fannin laughed aloud.

It was clear that the discussion was over, and his growing consciousness of the yellow glare from the lamps told Jim that, outside, night had fallen. Despite a perfunctory offer of supper, he knew that Fannin had seen enough of him that day, so he bade him good night and went out into the cool evening to find some of his friends, some food, and a bed.

* * *

Jim was up at first light and quickly made ready for his departure to Victoria. He shared breakfast with men who had come to Texas with him: Burke and Mac-Manomy and other volunteers from Alabama. As they ate, he could not but notice their frayed clothing and ragged looks. *Not exactly ready for a parade ground,* he thought, *but still enough spunk to do what they have to do.* But there was something else about them, something almost melancholy, a sort of disillusionment. Was this a product of floundering leadership? He did not know, could not even be sure his impression was correct, so he buried it with all of the other unanswered questions, and soon the time came to say good-bye.

It was not without trepidation that he made his way to headquarters. He hoped that by now Fannin would have reflected on their conversation, would have read the letter from Travis and decided to join forces with them. But he also half expected and was prepared for some sort of ambiguous answer, in which case he felt that the effort would have at least opened the door for Fannin's conscience to do the rest over the next several days.

However, Fannin's decision proved to be both surprising and shocking: an unequivocal refusal. Jim listened quietly as Fannin repeated the same familiar arguments. But as Fannin went on and on, Jim began not to hear the words. All he could do was wonder why. Surely Fannin understood the situation. Why didn't he seize the moment and act?

At first, anger welled up inside Jim as he fought to understand. Then doubt; perhaps Fannin was right; but no, the situation was clear, and Jim had little time to speculate. Perhaps Fannin's intentions were good. Maybe he was not being driven by the same devils that infected Johnson and Grant. But it didn't matter. Whatever lay behind Fannin's decision, time was being wasted. There was nothing more to be gained here, save frustration and anger. He felt he had to move on to other places where his efforts might prove more fruitful. It was a struggle to keep his composure as he mouthed the words.

"I accept your position, Colonel . . ." and then with a bit more feeling added, "but surely you must know how ardently I hope, we all hope, you will reconsider! Meanwhile I'll go on to Victoria, as we discussed, and see if I can be of any help."

Fannin said only, "That would be most welcome."

Within the hour Jim was ready to leave and Fannin had come over to shake hands and bid him farewell. He muttered, "Godspeed" as Jim swung into the saddle, wheeled about and slowly rode away. As he headed for the gate, Jim found himself surrounded by many familiar faces, some of whom had come with him to Texas. Momentarily, they lifted him from his gloom. Now, soldiers of La Bahía, they smiled, shouted words of encouragement and cheered as he rode forth, the scene made all the more poignant by the frayed uniforms they wore and the trials that he knew would soon be upon them. He turned and waved as the gates began to close, and in the distance beyond the men who had crowded at the opening, he saw Fannin, alone, standing in the middle of the quadrangle watching him ride away.

CHAPTER FIVE

In Victoria Jim easily found the contingent from Fannin's command. They were diligently doing everything possible to get munitions and supplies brought up from the coast, as well as from the settlements to the east, and were well aware that shortages at La Bahía were growing more acute each day. There was little that Jim could contribute to the efforts already underway, so he took advantage of being in Victoria to address his primary purpose: finding reinforcements for the Alamo. Victoria had no more men to give, but being at the crossroads of activity as the crisis heightened afforded the likelihood that other volunteers, individually or in units, would come this way sooner or later.

As it happened, the detachment from La Bahía that Jim had found there was under the command of his good friend, A. C. Horton, who had been the principal organizer of the Mobile Greys. So Jim was able, without artifice, to explain to him the crisis looming in Bexar and secure his promise to pass word of the urgent need for volunteers at that post. Although under Fannin's command, Horton was of the same mind as Jim and, short of outright insubordination, promised to do all he could to help.

Leaving the local situation in his friend's capable hands, Jim was free to move on to other places—places where he might find military units forming, or already formed and standing by awaiting orders. He knew that Brazoria and Gonzales were likely spots for such activity, as both places had been the scenes of earlier actions as the Texians began to rid themselves of the Mexican yoke.

So, after passing but a single day in Victoria, he set out early the next morning for the long ride to Brazoria. Riding away in the cool morning of a day that promised to be near perfect, it suddenly came to him that it was his birthday: twenty-nine years old and still trying to make a place for himself. That notion crowded out all else for a moment but soon gave way to what was still uppermost in his mind: the meeting with Fannin at La Bahía. Jim really didn't know what to make of him. He knew that Fannin had made sacrifices in personal treasure and given of himself countless times in the cause of freedom for Texas. But now these alliances with rogues— this vacillation and inconsistency—to Jim, these actions defied explanation, except perhaps as manifestation of a kind of base ambition. Nevertheless, Fannin's words had caused Jim to acknowledge to himself some ambivalence in his own position.

Had he been too harsh in his judgment of Fannin? Perhaps being circumspect about the commitment of his command was the prudent course. But no, it was clear that events were overtaking them and indecision masquerading as prudence would not answer.

As he struggled with these thoughts, there came to mind the faces of the men he had helped to deliver to that troubled command. He thought of them with both admiration and concern. Brave men all, anxious to do their part, he wondered what lay in store for them. Their plight might be even more dire than that of the men in the Alamo.

He could not shake the picture of them from his mind. The Mobile Greys, still attired in the tattered relics of their once natty uniforms, lovingly sewn by mothers and wives, sisters and aunts. It brought to mind a brighter time eleven years before—almost to the day—when, as a cadet, similarly attired, he had marched in honor of General Lafayette. It had been on the occasion of the general's visit to Columbia as part of his triumphal and much celebrated return to the United States in the winter of 1824-25. Just as the whole country still idolized him and turned out in welcome wherever he went, so had the people of South Carolina.

The company of cadets to which Jim belonged had been formed at South Carolina College specifically to serve as honor guard during the visit. The cadets, like the Mobile Greys, had been splendidly turned out. They had drilled and prepared for weeks, and as the day finally arrived, were anxiously awaiting the general's arrival. They had formed at the outskirts of town on the Camden road in order to escort the official party into town. It had rained heavily during the preceding week and all of Columbia had been concerned that the festivities might be totally washed out. But the good Lord smiled on them and delivered a beautiful, spring-like day with clear air and blue skies, even heralded by the timely appearance of lighthearted chickadees.

Although their honored guest would be with them but for one day before moving on to Charleston, the town had been shut down for the entire week as elaborate preparations were completed. Even so, owing to delays caused by the rain, General Lafayette had been asked to remain overnight in a house some twelve miles away in order that final touches to the bunting and other decoration be completed on the morning of his visit. As a result, the old general, despite the rigors of the trip, was well rested and in fine fettle as he and his party finally came into view.

The cadets came to attention and presented arms as the general stood in his open carriage and acknowledged their presence with a salute. The cadet captain, mounted on a splendid gray stallion, was followed on foot by a color guard bearing the flags of France and the United States. He approached the carriage, briskly executed a salute with his saber and formally requested permission of a smiling Lafayette to escort the party into town where the official welcoming party headed by the governor awaited.

At a nod from their guest, the honor guard fell into marching formation, and the procession began—crossing the river and up the hill to the State House. It was heady stuff for the cadets. To a man, each of them was determined that the general, who had seen parades of the finest armies in the world, would truly be able to say that he had seen none finer than those who marched in front of him this day. They marched smartly and with precision up the road and into Columbia.

Never a line wavered, never an eye wandered—marching in perfect step, a military unit worthy of all the respect they had invested in the man who was a hero to them all. They passed thousands of people who had turned out for the event and finally arrived at the flag-bedecked podium, which would also serve as a reviewing stand. As the dignitaries took their places, the cadets stood at rigid attention. They began the ceremonies by passing in review, and finally forming ranks beside the stand as the great crowd cheered, they moved forward to the front of the podium.

Speeches of welcome were made, eloquent speeches

of a kind that flowed easily from the lips of South Carolinians: speeches extolling Lafayette's departed mentor, Washington, and speeches of reverence for his contemporaries Jefferson and Adams, who still lived, and finally—amid cheers—the great man stood to respond. Here he was, General Lafayette, hero of the War for Independence, hero of two worlds, returned to the United States, about to address yet another gathering of the Americans he loved so well.

His words were simple as he formally thanked his hosts and reminded the assembled crowd that South Carolina had been his first landfall in what was now the United States, and he expressed his particular pleasure at returning—rain and all—to find that the country had grown and prospered. To some degree, his words were perfunctory, but it was clear that they were also heartfelt and even modest as he disclaimed the extravagant praise that had been heaped upon him for his deeds in the War of Independence. Finally, he ended his speech. The governor, who had risen to present him a scroll commemorating the occasion, said, "Please, my dear General. The people of our nation are forever in your gratitude. You are much too modest. We can never thank you adequately!"

The aging Lafayette was truly moved. Although the visit to America had restored his dignity and a fortune depleted through a lifetime of standing on principle, it was these kinds of demonstrations of his continued rapport with the American people that meant the most to him. He turned and looked hard at the governor as he graciously accepted the document and the hospitality of the people of South Carolina with the words, "I assure you that modesty is not feigned in the presence of such an illustrious group."

The speeches ended, and he descended from the podium to conduct a ceremonial inspection of his honor guard. Unhurried and attentively, he walked along each rank of cadets. They stood rigidly at attention, ever mindful of other military units with which they would necessarily be compared, trying to be what they thought he expected, trying to be part of that great army that had defeated Cornwallis.

Suddenly, he was standing in front of Jim. Now eighteen years old and grown into an exceptionally handsome young man with black hair, over six feet tall and straight as a ramrod. His dark eyes sparkled with pride as he realized that he was the object of the general's scrutiny.

As were all his fellow cadets, Jim was familiar with most of the major events of Lafayette's life—not just his role in the American revolution and his having known Washington and Franklin, but as the man who had charmed the court of France, yet had been present at the birth of the French Revolution. He had endured years in an Austrian prison, even matched wits with Napoleon. Though not extolled in these precincts, he had taken a strong position against slavery.

But to Jim, the most compelling of the tales about the general took place in Virginia when Lafayette's artillery fired a fatal cannonball into the tent of the British officer, who years before in another war on another continent, had slain Lafayette's own father. Jim found this coincidence intriguing, all the more since his own father and grandfather had fought at Yorktown and might even have witnessed the incident.

When Jim finally found himself face to face with the celebrated general, it was as if he were at last meeting a storied relative or being united with an old friend. For a brief moment, the general's benign and smiling face seemed to confirm this illusion.

To the general's eyes, the splendid military figure before him, the forthright countenance, seemed to embody all of the best qualities with which he associated his lifelong admiration of Americans. He was moved to remark, "What a fine looking young man!"

He had not addressed Jim directly, but he felt obliged to say, "Thank you, sir!"

The general smiled and moved on, leaving Jim with the feeling that by briefly connecting with the general's consciousness, he had also and in some way connected with all of his history. For a moment, he had been part of Lafayette's world.

The general had reacted to a certain aura that Jim projected, not quite as if a light were shone upon him, but once noticed, a presence, a kind of bright-eyed cognizance, which could not be ignored. His quick mind and engaging personality were apparent without his speaking a word. These traits, combined with his great good looks and skill as a horseman, led to his being much admired by his peers who sometimes, only half in jest, compared him in the most extravagant terms with the knights of old. Like those mythical figures, he was also headstrong, often behaved as if he thought himself to be immortal, and frequently acted on impulse.

Growing up, Jim inevitably became involved in many escapades which, among his family and friends, had become legend. But most of these had taken place while he had been in Abbeville, completing his secondary education at Dr. Waddell's academy. Even so, his days there had marked the real beginning of his education and the beginning of the end of boyish pranks as well as the idyllic era at home in Edgefield.

Lafayette had thoroughly enjoyed his day in Columbia. Although crowded, the schedule was not overwhelming, and his warmth was returned by the citizenry everywhere he went, making it a delightful experience for everyone. Early in the evening, after a series of events throughout the town, a reception was held for him at the college. It included the entire faculty and all of the students, some one hundred strong. A highlight of the reception was the welcoming address delivered by a student who was a member of one of the literary societies, which took advantage of the occasion to induct the general as an honorary member. This set the tone of this more intimate event. As Lafayette rose to thank the students and faculty assembled, his demeanor was clearly less formal than it had been earlier in the day.

Nevertheless, in his opening remarks he delivered greetings to Dr. Thomas Cooper, president of the college, from Thomas Jefferson, whom he had visited earlier in the trip, and to the student body a remembrance from Jefferson's grandson, Francis Eppes, who had graduated from South Carolina College less than two years before. Many of the students were surprised to learn of Dr. Cooper's acquaintance with Jefferson. To them, Cooper was simply the *Old Coot,* a slang expression for a type of turtle he was said to resemble. And as they viewed him in this new light, they had learned that even old coots were not be taken for granted.

But there was more to Lafayette's speech. That evening, within the span of little more than twenty minutes, Jim and his friends were introduced to another level of discourse—different and exciting—and not at all the kind of oratory to which they were accustomed.

It was delivered by a man of the world, a man who had been exalted and humbled, but who had never abandoned his principles. Being neither pedant nor polemicist, in his remarks he sought only to stress to the students the importance of constancy and to help them to understand their places in the great unfolding drama of history. Although he alluded to events in his life that had profound impact on a fast changing world, he did not dwell on personal glories of the past. Rather, he drew upon a lifetime of experience—in the most exciting of times—to frame contemporary events and help form a view to the future.

Lafayette also captivated the audience with his manner; he was at once erudite and subtle, and somehow bespoke a deeper well of knowledge and experience, some of which came from places the students sensed they would not want to visit. As his words penetrated their consciousness, they, who had at first felt like bumpkins, became aware of the strength of their own intellects, and their view of this elderly man who stood before them changed.

With each sentence, the years dropped away until generational differences disappeared. They realized that they were sharing the essence of a dominant and unrelenting spirit—a true hero whose vision and continued dedication to truth and honor equaled their own youthful idealism.

Finally, the moment passed, the speech had ended, and an old general took his seat.

When the applause had ended and prior to his departure for the banquet being hosted by Governor Manning and the mayor, he moved among those assembled to exchange a few personal words of farewell. He went from group to group. As he approached Jim and his friends, Jim found himself anxious to establish rapport with this man he admired so much. He was struggling to find words worthy of the occasion when suddenly he realized the great man was once again in front of him, extending his hand and offering thanks to someone whom he recognized as having been part of his honor guard. As they shook hands, Jim blurted out, "My father was with you at Yorktown." Instantly, he felt embarrassed.

Rising to the occasion and understanding this young man's struggle to bridge the gulf between them, the general, remembering such times in his own youth, looked carefully at Jim.

"It is easy to imagine you there, as well," Lafayette said.

CHAPTER SIX

At the time of General Lafayette's visit to Columbia, Jim had been in his sophomore year at South Carolina College. Now, nearly two years later, John Quincy Adams had succeeded Monroe as president, and a patriarch of Jim's own uplands, John Calhoun, was vice president. People were looking forward to the elections of 1828, wondering if Calhoun might stand for election as president. Jefferson and the elder Adams had both died on the fourth of July during the past summer; a mystical and powerful reminder of the fiftieth anniversary of the signing of the Declaration of Independence. Lafayette was back in France, embarked on yet another crusade, and Beethoven had entered the final month of his life.

Clearly times were changing, just as Lafayette had said they would. The past was inexorably giving way to something new, but memories of the old heroes remained. One in particular, though only recently passed from the scene, still touched the students' daily lives in many ways. He was Jonathan Maxcy, the first president of South Carolina College. Serving from the time the college had opened its doors to students in 1805 until his death in 1822, his influence and memory remained strong.

Dr. Maxcy, like Lafayette, had accomplished much at a very early age. Acknowledged as one of the most gifted orators of his time, he had made his reputation not through force of arms or involvement in momentous events of history, but through the power of his presence, which reflected his transcendent nature and scholarship. And, of course, he was brilliant. He had been president of Brown University at age twenty-four. He had brought with him an approach to pedagogy patterned after the tradition of colleges in New England but modified somewhat to reflect his own move in the direction of the more practical applications of education.

Nevertheless, the academic curriculum was founded on the classics, and all students were members of one or the other of two literary societies, the Euphradian and the Clariosophic. These groups reflected the southern penchant for declamation and debate, but they also served as forums for the digestion and assimilation of the lessons of the classroom. Membership in the two groups was about equally divided and generally reflected the regional origins of the students: Euphradians tended to come from Charleston and the tidewater, while the Clariosophics were more representative of the uplands.

So it was that Jim, as an Edgefieldian, had become a member of the Clariosophic Society. He took seriously his participation in the group as he did the representation of a goddess on the seal of the society. She was Hope, the soother of the various distresses of life, and she held a bud just opening in her hand, promising something blooming and pleasing after the gloom and chillness of winter.

The students adhered to a rigorous schedule. Rising

at 6:30 in the morning—even earlier in the spring. They
began each day with morning prayer followed by their
first recitation of studies before breakfast. Throughout
the day they kept to a tight schedule until the mandatory hour of retirement, 9:30 P.M. The exactitude carried
over into their dress as well. They were obliged to have
their hair cut short, and wore uniforms consisting of
high hats, short-waisted blue coats with long tails, and
tight trousers. The seniors wore black gowns when
convened for college exercises or duties.

This Spartan pattern of daily life was overlaid with
a set of stringent regulations. The rules were comprehensive, indeed, with minor infractions exacting such
punishments as committing to memory Virgil's *Aeneid;*
while more heinous transgressions such as blasphemy,
dueling and fornication were cause for expulsion.

The close reins under which the students were held
notwithstanding, they were spirited and rowdy. Most
could quote at length from Tom Paine, and they took his
words to heart. The instinct to assert themselves was
great, in any case, and they often risked everything by
engaging in pranks from essentially innocuous escapades such as stealing turkeys and plucking them na-
ked before returning them to their owners, to sometimes more outrageous stunts, from which the faculty
was not immune.

On one such famous occasion, some of the students
spirited away Dr. Maxcy's carriage to a hiding place in
the woods miles from the campus. But having been
forewarned, he had secreted himself within and after
reaching the spot, stepped forth and had the culprits
complete the round trip while he enjoyed the ride. Not
exacting the maximum sanction by expelling them on
the spot was an example of the forbearance he found
necessary to balance the exuberance of youth with the
imperatives of order. It was a fine line, but an example
scrupulously observed by succeeding generations of

faculty as long as such infractions were clearly subordinated to the overall goals of the college.

In this same spirit, the students themselves exercised a rigid discipline within their own ranks, but according to their own lights, which allowed them to turn a blind eye to certain offenses yet impose sanctions on others, seemingly less serious. Within the Clariosophic Society and the Euphradian as well, fines were regularly imposed for such untoward behavior as wearing a hat in the hall or standing by the fire during a debate, as well as for the wonderful catchall, *impropriety*. There was little tolerance of any comportment that might demean or compromise the essential elements of a code to which they all subscribed.

Thus, pranks in hand with learning, the overall basis for their education was sound indeed. Almost to a man they were diligent in their work. Camaraderie was strong; they developed a strong sense of honor and held a fierce pride in their college.

Much of this spirit was in no small way a legacy of Dr. Maxcy. The students lived in an environment that he had created and were subjected daily to the product of his thought, as well as to anecdotes about him. Dr. Maxcy had to them become legendary. The idea of him captured their imaginations. By the time Jim arrived as a freshman in the fall of 1823, few of the students actually remembered him, yet Dr. Maxcy was a perfect example of all the things they held dear.

So it was that the Clariosophic Society undertook to erect a monument to his memory. Fired by the stories of those few members who actually remembered their late president, they set about raising money for the Maxcy monument. Although they pursued it zealously, it was an effort requiring the work of several years, and it had befallen succeeding classes of Clariosophics to carry on until the funds were raised. But finally it was accomplished. They were ready to realize the dream, and it was Jim's class members, who had never known their hero, upon whom it devolved to complete the project. To do this they turned to the architect, Robert Mills, who with Edward Clark had designed many of the original campus buildings.

But where to put the monument? Why, of course— the most prominent place on the campus, right in the center of the "horseshoe," that great open space, which was defined by the facades of Mills and Clark. It was where the students often assembled. Here the rowdy side of their nature often burst forth; they built bonfires, sometimes fueled from the steps of the surrounding buildings, fomented revolutions of sorts, exclaimed and declaimed endlessly. But it was an ideal spot for a monument to their not-to-be-forgotten mentor. Despite the boisterous uses to which it had often been put, the place would become the focal point of an architectural ensemble that was the epitome of serenity, scholarship and grace, an ever-present reminder of Dr. Maxcy's vision.

Raising the money had been only the beginning. Now they had to wait for Mr. Mills to prepare the design, and after that was completed, the actual construction. It was to be an obelisk standing on a marble base, reaching an overall height of about fourteen feet. It would be suitably inscribed in Latin with the eloquent words of George McDuffie, who had graduated in the peak years of Dr. Maxcy's tenure and was destined to become governor of the state.

But it would be the following December before the unveiling, and the seniors had no expectation of being present for the great event. No matter, they all drew enduring satisfaction from the accomplishment. They had faithfully carried forward the work of the Clariosophics and felt closer to their fellows, past and future, for having done so. With the project now in the hands of those who would actually execute it, they were free to turn to other things—such as complaints about the food.

Food was always a major issue, and every year, by spring, conditions at the commons surfaced as a source of ferment. This year of 1827 seemed worse than usual, so that it was only February when their dissatisfaction reached the boiling point. They struggled to put up with the fare in a manner consistent with the high blown philosophies and ideals of gallantry, which otherwise nurtured them, but the more revolutionary of those examples began to seem appropriate. They were after all young men with voracious appetites. They felt themselves genuinely aggrieved and, as South Carolinians, not about to endure injustice for very long!

Although strictly forbidden by regulations of the college, the students were given to formation of *ad hoc* groups, known as combinations, to deal with every manner of complaint. They would form one without hesitation in support of a just cause. The students were to an extent encouraged in this behavior by the example of Dr. Maxcy's successor, Dr. Cooper, who, friend of Jefferson's or not, had the reputation of being something of an iconoclast. If the *Old Coot* could rail against religion and write pamphlets questioning the "value of the Union," then surely they could take a stand to redress a serious and just grievance. What could be more serious or more justified than their outrage over the abominations that were regularly served in the name of food in Andersen Hall?

It was within Andersen Hall that the commons was located, and it was mandatory for the students to take their meals there. Just as the buildings around the horseshoe made up a sort of oasis that hid from view the shacks and muddy chicken coops that lay just behind them, the scholarly environment of the college overlaid some of the more rowdy impulses of the inmates. The requirement to dine in the commons was a manifestation of this and became a means of containment of the students who had to be kept under control and out of Columbia as much as possible, lest the excesses of their robust spirits get completely out of hand.

But there were other considerations. The college, having been in existence little longer than the lifetimes of its students and still struggling to make ends meet, had as its latest appointment as steward one Benjamin Williams. Under contract to operate the dining hall, provisioning, preparation, and service of the food were all his sole responsibility. But a crucial condition of that contract was that he be paid according to the number of meals served, and the college was under solemn obligation to require the students to take their meals there.

The budget for operation of the commons was always seriously underestimated, with the consequence that survival of the steward was clearly a question of critical mass. Only with full participation by the entire student body could Benjamin afford to deliver any meals at all, and the quality of the fare was not a priority, except for those who had to eat it. Most of them, already rebellious by virtue of their age and breeding, were at the point of taking matters into their own hands. There were, however, just enough students to whom the quality of the food didn't seem worth all the agitation. Both the steward and the administration saw little merit in the protests, and hoped the problem would eventually go away.

But it wouldn't. There *was* real merit to the protests. The young men, in thrall of idealism and focused as they were on fair play and righteousness, not to mention their own stomachs, were intent on seeing justice done. They knew that the college was in its infancy and felt they had to take a stand now for those who would come after them. Each meal fanned the flames of their indignation, and the unresponsiveness of the administration added fuel to the flames. Everyone was tired of it.

Like the others, Jim had grown weary of the problem as well. Having been away at college for nearly four years, he was looking to the future. While spending his summers helping with the operation of the plantations, he had realized that he was not cut out to be a planter. He also had a growing awareness of the world, which sometimes brought troubling thoughts, some of which involved the very idea of slavery. Lafayette's adamant opposition to it had set him to thinking.

Jim had grown up surrounded by slaves—taking them for granted really—and only gradually becoming fully aware of their condition. It was the way he had found the world, and that order of things seemed as natural as the air he breathed, but he had never faced the reality of it until . . . Lafayette. He knew that the economic order of not only the South, but a large part of the North, probably England as well, was built on cotton, and the cotton industry in turn was built on the institution of slavery. No wonder people called it *peculiar,* and seldom said its real name.

But what to do about it? Jim didn't know. He would never turn against his own, but he had decided to follow another calling. He was already planning how, after he graduated, he would move on to Abbeville and there, within the aura of John Calhoun, read the law.

But the problem with the food—that was different. And it was here and now. He could actually do something about it! Moreover, he was sick of it; the food, and the fussing about it. While for him it was fading as a priority, it remained unfinished business, and Jim, like his classmates, was in the frame of mind to settle it once and for all.

So it was, one brisk and chilly day at the noon meal when appetites were keen, Francis Pickens sat looking at the unappetizing mess on his plate. Judging by the pin feathers, it was fowl of some kind, but hacked up in such a way that it was not clear what part of it might be edible. A scrawny chicken to begin with, once the greasy skin was peeled back, nothing remained but sinew immersed in a watered-down, not-quite-white flour gravy. Stale bread, rancid butter, and a cold serving of long collards more brown than green completed the meal.

He contemplated it a few seconds longer, then looked up at his fellow diners, most of whom were in the same state of rejection. Jamison, who sat at his right, was making a game effort to extract something worth eating from the meat. Even Elliot was rearranging the greens, seemingly considering the consequences if he were to actually venture to taste them. Jim sat at the table opposite him with his eyes fixed at a point somewhere in the middle of the table, his gaze avoiding the plate.

Although the dining hall was not entirely silent, there was an impression of stunned silence, if not shock, as the students once again contemplated another disagreeable meal. Each meal unfolded in the same way: shocked silence, followed by increasingly vocal complaints until they took their leave of the commons resolving to find food elsewhere. And they did find all sorts of clandestine ways to satisfy their hunger. They shared provisions sent by their families, and sometimes, at great risk, found places to board at public houses in and around the town.

But these alternate arrangements off campus could be chanced only at night and were rare. Usually it was only within the privacy of their rooms that they were able to nibble at an odd assortment of carefully hoarded comestibles that had been obtained by all manner of means. But always, they complained.

As he looked at the unhappy faces around him, Francis finally became the first to resort to what had become their usual solution. Looking down the table, he called out, "Carroll, the *lick* if you please sir, but by all means, help yourself first!"

James Carroll was Jim's roommate. He looked up,

smiled as he took the clay pot from the table in front of him and dolloped a great spoonful of the dark brown, almost black, viscous liquid over the stale bread on his plate. *Lick* was sorghum syrup. A generous serving of it over stale bread and even butter that was rancid had the salutary effect of softening the bread, masking the cow taste of the butter, and making the whole concoction palatable. In fact, it could achieve the same end with any of the offerings of the mess hall. It was nourishing, of course, but very bad for the teeth and unacceptable as an attraction to the palate over very many successive meals.

As the pot made its way down the table, most everyone helped themselves, but when it reached Jim, he simply passed it across the table to Francis.

"What's the matter, Bonham, y'all waitin' for the baked ham?" laughed Francis.

"No, I've just had about all the lick I can stomach in one day, that's all!" Jim smiled back. "It covered up those green eggs pretty well this morning!"

"The color or the taste?"

"Both!"

A few chuckles, and then the students began rehashing the same complaints that by now were almost perfunctory. Finally, from his end of the table, Carroll spoke up.

"Well, what are we going to do about it? We have sat here month after month, some of us for years, watching this situation get progressively worse. Gentlemanly protests don't help. Our last petition seems to have been ignored." His voice trailed off as he sighed, and then continued, "I'm tellin' you, I can't—no, I *won't*—live on lick any longer!" In response to his roommate's solemn declaration of refusal to live any longer on the sugary staple, Jim spoke up.

"Are you saying you're *fed up*?"

"I am indeed, sir!" Carroll replied with mock formality.

"How can you be *fed up* when you claim to be so hungry?" Francis half shouted.

Even Carroll laughed, and after the third or fourth generation of *double entendres* had subsided, he turned, and called one of the *dubs*, "Tom!"

"Yas suh!"

"Is Mister Benjamin around?"

"No suh, he always leaves soon as da meal served."

"The meal? What meal?"

Carroll was about to continue, when he was interrupted by Jim.

"Never mind, James, we'll get no place with Benjamin anyway."

"I know, but a good thrashing might get his attention!"

Tom, still standing nearby, smiled at the thought.

"Tell you what; let's meet after classes this afternoon," Jim said.

Everyone understood what that meant—to congregate in the middle of the horseshoe at the place they were already calling "the Maxcy," even though erection of the monument had not yet begun. The idea seemed to satisfy their need to do something, to take some kind of action. As the meal continued, the conversation finally turned to other things like Professor Henry's impressive translation into Latin of the inscription for the monument and even things as far afield as speculation on whether the United States really would offer to buy Texas from Mexico.

When they met that afternoon, there was an air of *gravitas*, almost as if Jonathan Maxcy were there with them to assure that the discussion did not get out of hand. They began by citing the latest atrocities, a bill of particulars to justify the need for action.

Jim, intently listening, absorbed the words of his classmates and, as was often his wont, got caught up in the passion of the moment and stepped forward. His presence was always impressive. Taller than most of his peers, his intent expression underscoring his confident manner, everyone listened when he spoke.

"Gentlemen, let me tell you . . .," as all eyes turned toward him, he waited for the general babble to die down, "some of us have been going on about this for years and all this talk is wearing thin. We make the same complaints, but continue to be ignored year after year. It's time to really do something, or resign ourselves to the situation!"

"What do you want to do? Burn down the Andersen Hall? Nothing else has worked!" shouted Francis.

Even though the question was only rhetorical, everyone shuddered at the thought, and Jim only partially addressed it in his response.

"If we are going to resort to a rash act, it'll have to be constructive. We must move beyond foolishness."

"As constructive as when you threw the sheriff into the creek, Jim?"

Jim laughed with them and said, "I hope I'm past that, but no, we have to do something that is responsible, yet gets action."

"What then, Jim?"

Jim didn't know. But he knew they had reached a point where whatever course was taken would likely lead to serious consequences, and that whoever participated would have to be prepared to pay the price. Yet he wanted to avoid doing something that would be at once foolish and unproductive. And then, even without formulating it in his mind, he heard the words coming out.

"We need to threaten to quit the commons—and *mean* it !"

"*What*? Are you crazy? We'll be expelled!" were the expressions most discernible as a general hubbub ensued.

Then Jim shouted, "No, *wait!* Not all of us, just the seniors. We're about finished here anyway. We'll form a combination, submit our petition. If they won't back down, and we're forced to leave, then they will have some answering to do to the people of this state!"

All eyes were on the seniors who cast glances at each other as Francis spoke up again. "All of us?"

"Each person has to make that decision for himself."

Then Tom Mays spoke, "Wait a minute Jim, what if they do back down? What do we tell them we want—better food or what?"

"Who'll decide what's better? It won't work!" someone shouted.

"Not better food from commons; that would never happen—just the right to eat where we want! Who knows, it may force our friend Benjamin to improve the fare. Some of us may even want to continue eating there."

"No, no! " they shouted.

Mays, who was president of the Clariosophics and accustomed to enforcing parliamentary etiquette, was becoming uncomfortable with the increasingly boisterous nature of the meeting. Besides, it was getting dark, and he noticed that they were being observed by a group of professors who were standing on the steps of nearby Rutledge College. So he reminded them, "For a group of gentlemen who pride themselves on orderly discourse, we certainly resemble a rabble. We should continue this discussion in a businesslike way, but under the rules of order."

They all looked at him and the expressions on their faces told him that he had struck a chord, so he continued. "Besides, it's getting dark."

Thus the meeting ended, the students leaving in small groups talking in more temperate tones among themselves. But they did reconvene the next afternoon in the Clariosophic meeting room above the chapel, and in an orderly and parliamentary fashion decided that the seniors would indeed form a combination and call themselves the "blackshirts." Although they would represent the interests of everyone, membership in the blackshirts would be restricted to seniors, in particular those who were prepared to see it through, whatever the consequences. They would formally petition the administration informing them that effective March first, unless permitted the option of taking meals at places of their choosing, they would not return to the commons.

Some of them secretly thought that the *Old Coot* would find a way to support them. They believed that the decision taken by the blackshirts was closer to his attitudes than continued caving in to indifference would be. And to some degree they were right. But when finally confronted with the ultimatum, the faculty, realizing that the students were due a short holiday at the end of February and expecting that they would have cooled off and would return when classes resumed on the first of March, simply responded by stating the rule that any student failing to take meals in the commons would be dropped from the roles . . . and they refused further discussion of the matter.

So, at the end of February, Jim departed South Carolina College, never to return. As did twenty-three of his classmates. They were not expelled. They simply never came back. Only twelve remained for graduation, but there were no commencement exercises that year.

Jim accepted his college career having ended without the usual formalities, and he went off to Abbeville to begin his studies of the law. But this milestone in his life was not to be without experiencing some rite of passage.

For Jim it would be cruel, indeed, as the beginning of his adult life was profoundly underscored by the death of his younger sister Elizabeth. It happened in September when, like so many people of the time, she was taken suddenly. At age eighteen she was a beautiful young girl, full of promise one day and gone the next. The loss had particularly shaken Jim, but pulling himself up from the depths of sorrow, he resolved that Elizabeth, with whom he had been very close, would continue to live on through him. They had laughed and learned together, just as they had shared dreams of the future, and he knew her youthful idealism would always be with him. He hoped, too, that his mother might see this, and take some solace from it.

CHAPTER SEVEN

The sight of chimney smoke rising from Gonzales stirred Jim from thoughts of days gone by. Even as his meeting with Fannin at La Bahía had been disappointing, the reception Jim received in Brazoria had been good. Back in December he had decided to settle there and establish a law practice once hostilities had ended, so in a way he felt at home. More importantly, the response to his appeal for help for the garrison at Bexar was immediate and positive.

John Wharton, who with his brother had been one of the early proponents of independence for Texas, needed no urging. It was no surprise for him to hear that Santa Anna would soon be on the march. Word of Travis' concern had already reached him—and even before Jim's arrival, he had started organizing a local company of volunteers. But Jim's presence and his appeal underscored the crisis and confirmed what Wharton already believed—that conflict was more imminent than realized by many of the settlers in the relative calm of the settlements of east Texas.

So, with Jim's help, Wharton accelerated his efforts

and set about gathering munitions and other provisions. As a consequence of his regular movements between San Felipe and Brazoria, Wharton was able to make sure that the plight of the volunteers at the frontier and the implications for all of Texas were known throughout the region. After learning the outcome of Jim's meeting with Fannin, Wharton even approached some of Fannin's close friends who lived around Brazoria. He urged them to remonstrate with Fannin and use their influence to make clear to him that the political infighting, which had disrupted the government over the past two months, was being set aside for the common good, and that he should do likewise and cease looking to Lt. Governor Robinson and his splinter group for orders.

After two days of concentrated effort, Jim was heartened to realize that they were well along towards having a company ready to depart for Bexar. Volunteer ranks had swelled to nearly two hundred, and provisions and weapons were coming in. But on the third day an express arrived, and the news it brought could not have been worse. The Mexicans had arrived in Bexar on the 23rd (the same day Jim had arrived at Brazoria) and the Texian garrison was now besieged in the Alamo! The terse report was sparse in detail, but it made clear that what had been hasty, but deliberate and systematic preparations, now became desperate and urgent.

There was not a moment to lose. With mobilization of the Brazoria Company in the capable hands of John Wharton, Jim prepared for his immediate return to Bexar. Travis, Bowie, and the rest would be anxious to know of his meeting with Fannin, as well as what else was happening on the outside.

It would be a four-day trip, and it would take Jim directly through Gonzales, a natural place for the assembly of any forces that might be gathering to aid the men in the Alamo. Jim hoped to find some answers there; he even dared hoped for news that Fannin, having heard of the investment of the Alamo, might have had a change of heart.

* * *

Jim did not know what to expect in Gonzales, but owing to its proximity to the frontier and having the distinction of being the place where the first shots of the revolution had been fired, it had always been at the center of things. From the time he had first noticed the plumes of smoke until the town began to unfold before him seemed an eternity, but finally he was there.

The road had gradually turned into a street. It was even marked Water Street, and became straight as an arrow, pointing north and clearly leading into the town. Gonzales was being increasing defined by neat rows of buildings along the right side of the street. They faced the Guadalupe River on the opposite side. He could not help but compare the relative order of this scene with the sprawl of mostly makeshift buildings and the muddy river that had greeted him when first he saw San Felipe.

By contrast, the Guadalupe was pristine and clear, and a large sweeping bend seemed almost to converge with the street ahead. As he approached that point, he noticed several men entering a building that was adorned with two rows of large gold-trimmed green letters across the facade. The top row read . . . Thomas Miller . . . and below it, in smaller letters the words, General Merchandise. Only a young boy remained outside, and he turned as Jim approached.

"Good day, young man," Jim smiled.

"'Afternoon, sir."

"Might there be a livery nearby? I think my horse has earned a little rest."

"Yes sir. The main one is further up the street . . . Sowell's, but we've got one too, just across the square." He nodded toward the block just ahead. "I'd be proud to take care of your animal!" He spoke with obvious admiration as he looked at Sal.

"And I'm sure you'll do a good job, too," Jim said as he dismounted. "Suppose we just walk her over there."

"Yes sir! Just follow me." As they started walking towards the square, the boy added, "What's her name, sir?"

"Sal, and it's for sure she likes you!" Handing the boy the reins, he continued. "And what is your name?"

"Davy, sir, David Darst."

"Well, Davy, my name's Jim Bonham, and I'm pleased to make your acquaintance. And tell me, is there an hotel near your place?"

"Yes sir! Turner's, right on the square." After a moments hesitation, he added, "But we've got a room to let, too, if you want to stay near your horse."

"Well, that sounds just fine. I guess I ran into the right man when I met you!"

The boy returned Jim's words with a broad smile, barely concealing his pride at being able to carry off the transaction.

By then, they had reached the square and let Sal lead them to a nearby water trough. As they stood waiting, Jim saw that the true center of town was further to the east, away from the river. A feeling he had first noticed as he began his ride up Water Street, a sort of tension, returned. He supposed it was at least partially because he had seen so few people about. Could it be that some kind of military activity was the cause? Some units forming? Although he really saw nothing to suggest this, the feeling was getting stronger by the minute. Finally, he asked, "Is your father around?"

The boy, towheaded and freckle-faced—not more than fifteen according to Jim's reckoning—responded with pride and an undertone of anxiety.

"He's gone off with the others to the Alamo."

Jim's hope seemed to have been realized—*then a relief force has already been assembled. Thank God!*

"When? How many? When did they go?"

"They left Saturday afternoon. Should be there by now. Reckon there were twenty-five or more—all Gonzales men."

Jim's heart sank. They would need many more than twenty-five. Nonetheless, he felt a sense of gratitude and shared the boy's pride in the handful of brave men who had heeded the call. But he knew that unless substantial help was found quickly, this noble gesture would likely prove futile. Jim hoped that the boy did not read the concern in his eyes, and he did his best to sound encouraging.

"Are there any other soldiers here or on their way to Bexar?"

"Doc Sutherland and some others—about ten, I reckon, left the day before yesterday. I think they were going to join up with another bunch, but I'm not sure."

Once again Jim felt a spark of hope. He explained that he, too, was headed back to the Alamo. From the boy he learned that the people who could answer his questions, the Committee of Public Safety, were meeting in Miller's store, the building they had just left. Jim could hardly wait to get settled so he could return there and find out more about what was going on.

Sensing Jim's anxiety to get back to Miller's, Davy said, "That's our place on the corner over there. We can get you settled in no time!"

And as Davy promised, it took very little time at all. As they reached the house, Mrs. Darst appeared, a kindly looking woman, in her mid-thirties, Jim guessed. She was quick to confirm her son's promise of accommodations for man and horse. So, with Sal in the boy's good hands, Jim left with the promise of a hot bath, a good meal, and a warm bed when he was finished with the Committee. He was back at Miller's in minutes, and his luck again held, as all three of the town fathers who constituted the group were there. They sat at a table in a far corner and, although he was a stranger to them, they did not seem surprised to see him. Evidently, comings and goings of military types were common in Gonzales these days.

Introductions were over quickly as the spokesman for the group, Andrew Ponton, identified himself as the *alcalde*, and bade Jim shake hands with his colleagues, Adam Zumwaldt and David Burket. As Jim explained himself and his mission, they were heedful of the news he brought from Brazoria, but his earlier encounter with Fannin seemed to interest them more. They paid rapt attention as Jim concluded his account of that meeting.

"There's not much more I can tell you that you probably don't already know. When I last saw him, Fannin did not seem to want to budge! But maybe now. . . ."

The men all looked at each other, exchanging knowing glances. The one called Adam handed Jim a piece of paper.

"Here, read this," he said.

It was an express from Fannin. In it, he explained how the day after he had received news of the arrival of the Mexican army at Bexar, he had mounted a relief column that had bogged down even before clearing Goliad. Following a council of war with his officers, he had returned to the *presidio* of La Bahía (which he now called Fort Defiance) and was determined to remain there. As if to underscore his decision, Fannin had also sent later word of just having received news that Johnson's command has been destroyed at a place down the coast in a battle with a unit of the Mexican army. Apparently, only Johnson and a few men had survived and were expected soon at La Bahía. There was no word of Dr. Grant.

A gloomy silence ensued as Jim read the express, until finally, Burket broke the silence.

"But there's hope—other things are happening."

"Well, I just heard from the boy at the livery that there may be other help coming, but he was not too clear about it," Jim said.

"Well Jim, when Doc Sutherland and John Smith came ridin' in to tell us about the Mexicans being in Bexar, we all got ourselves movin' and have been doin' everything we can to spread the word. Meantime, we raised some volunteers here, twenty-five, and more were gonna' join 'em on the way. They've already gone to the Alamo," Adam said.

"Yes, I've heard. That's good news! It'll mean a lot!" Jim said.

"And Doc Sutherland and some others rode off expectin' to meet with Seguin and his men." As Adam saw the optimism begin to creep into Jim's face, he added, "There's a couple of other things you'll also be happy to hear."

Jim waited, but said nothing.

"You know Three-Legged Willie?"

"Sure, I met him in San Felipe when they were organizing the Ranging Force."

"Yes, well he's here—been here for days—and we're waitin' for him right now."

Jim wasn't sure of the significance of that news, but he took it as a good sign because there was no one more dedicated to the cause—nor a better friend to Will Travis—than was Willie. He was anxious to hear more.

"Why's he here?"

"Willie, Major Williamson that is, decided to make this his headquarters. Aside from our company—the Gonzales Company," he repeated with pride, "he's only got one other outfit right now."

"So the men from here who went to Bexar Saturday are part of the Ranging Force?"

"That they are."

"But where are the rest of his men? How many are there?"

"Seems like a lot more than we were able to get together. They're up in the north somewhere, but Willie feels like this is a good place to headquarter."

"I dare say he's right. But are his other men coming here to Gonzales?"

"We don't know for sure; that's what we're waitin' to hear. He should be here any time now, and he'll be able to tell us."

Jim's mind raced. *If Wharton can get here too, and perhaps even some help from Seguin, maybe there's a chance!*

Jim was suddenly overflowing with questions, but before he could ask another he noticed all eyes focused behind him. He turned; it was Three-Legged Willie!

Ponton called out, "Come on over Major!"

Williamson, his limp disappearing in the power of his presence, walked over to the group. Jim was elated to see him and hoped this meant that real help for the Alamo was finally at hand. Willie, his demeanor brisk and positive, greeted them all, and seemed both surprised and happy to see Jim.

"Jim! It's good to see you. I thought you were in the Alamo!"

"I have been on and off since Christmas—came out two weeks ago trying to get help from Fannin, then to Brazoria, and here I am," Jim said.

"And?"

"John Wharton won't be too far behind me, but time must be running short." The sight of Willie was as a tonic for Jim and it was evident as he continued, "...but seeing you here gives me hope. I understand that you have a formidable force of Rangers out there somewhere!"

"That's true, Jim, I do—about a hundred and twenty men under Captain Tumlinson, and I'm doing my best to get them in position to help. You know, we organized the Rangers to protect the settlers on the frontier, mostly from the Comanches, and none too soon. They've really had their hands full! But I've sent an express to Tumlinson explaining the situation at Bexar. I've asked him to try to get the settlers to evacuate their places and join together in their common defense at a few strong points to free up the Rangers to come on down here."

It was the best news Jim had heard in weeks—almost like a real cavalry unit!

"Do you think they'll be able to do it?" Jim asked.

"Tumlinson don't know the word can't. If anybody can find a way, he will. I've told them to assemble at Mina. From there we can move on Bexar," Willie said.

"Thank God! What good news! I just hope we can hold out long enough."

Leaving that observation unaddressed, Willie went on. "Meanwhile, we're grinding corn and drying beef." Then, without waiting for Jim to comment, he abruptly changed the subject.

"Tell me Jim, have you seen Fannin? Has he gotten over this notion that he should stay in La Bahía?"

"It's been the better part of two weeks since I saw him. It looks like he's changed his mind twice since then," gesturing with the express still in his hand, "and now is back to..." leaving unsaid what everybody knew.

"We'll bring him around. Don't worry."

"It had better be soon!"

"Now that Wharton is coming and with Tumlinson, too, he'll come around. We'll get him moving!" After a few seconds, which seemed like minutes as silence enveloped them, he continued, addressing the whole group. "What we need to do is send Fannin an express right away and urge him to bring his men here, join up with the others, and together we move on Bexar! What d'ya think, Jim?"

"Honestly, I don't know. I wouldn't want Wharton waiting around here for Fannin. It may be too late already!"

But no pessimist he, Willie was not so easily discouraged. "Well, it's worth a try, don't you think?"

"You're right, Willie, we need to do everything we can!"

Jim, normally the most optimistic of people, was concerned that everything they were planning took time. He kept thinking of how the numbers of the enemy around the Alamo must be mounting. What must it be like now? In spite of these feelings, he realized Willie was right. They had to keep trying. So he shook off his misgivings and helped draft the express to Fannin, trying to word it in a way that Fannin would find compelling. As they finished, Jim saw there was nothing more that he could do, other than return to the Alamo, relate the situation to his friends, and do his part in defending the place.

He rose and announced, "Well gentlemen, these matters are in your good hands. I'll be leaving at first light, and I need to get some rest."

"Where are you goin', Jim?" Adam asked.

"Back to the Darst's."

"No, I mean at first light!"

"Back to the Alamo. I've done all I can do out here."

All of them seemed surprised at this announcement. Their concern was voiced by Willie.

"But Jim, aren't you going to wait for the Rangers or Wharton? There's nothing you can do alone."

"I can tell them what's going on. I have experience with artillery. I can help."

"But Jim . . .," Burket began.

Jim interrupted. "I know you all mean well. I hope all this help comes, but I'll be going back in the morning."

Realizing there was no point in pursing the subject further, Adam said, "Well, why don't we go and have something to eat anyway? You must be hungry."

"Thank you kindly, Adam, but I'm already spoken for." He laughed. "Mrs. Darst has promised me a big supper, and I wouldn't want to miss it!"

"A dang sight better'n you'd get with us. Margaret sets a mighty fine table!" Adam laughed.

"You staying at their place?" Willie said.

"Yes."

"Well, I'm at Turner's, and it's hardly a stone's throw from there. I'm going to write a letter to Travis. OK if I drop by after supper and leave it with you?"

"I'll be happy to carry it, Willie." Looking at the others, he added, "And if there are any other messages or letters, maybe from some of the families to their men, I'll be glad to take them as well."

With that, Jim took his leave of the group and returned to the Darst's. Davy and his mother were anxious to hear what he had learned. Jim mightily wanted to be able to give them some hope that their husband and father would soon be returning safely to them. But on sober reflection and in good conscience, he could not. There was no telling when the hoped-for reinforcements would arrive, and it was clear that time was also becoming their enemy. The only real force that might make a difference was still Fannin's, and to Jim that was a closed book. The best Jim could do for the Darsts was to lay out the facts as he knew them, and let them decide for themselves on the chances of ever seeing the man of the house again.

As Jim spoke, he watched the boy listening intently. He saw his own experience of growing up with only the memory of his father about to be repeated in Davy. It touched him deeply.

"You know, Davy, your dad and the other men from Gonzales are very brave. It will mean a lot to us in the Alamo to have them there," Jim said.

"But I want to go back with you. I can fight, too! I was there when the Mexicans tried to take the cannon!"

By the look of pain that crossed the woman's face, Jim could see that she, too, was aware of the probable fate that awaited her husband, and Jim did his best to ease her mind by his response.

"I'm certain you can. But then who would take care of your mother? And the stable? In a war, everyone has a job; this is yours. You can be sure I will tell your daddy what a good job you are doing. He'll be proud of you!"

His words seemed to satisfy the boy, but Jim wanted to leave him something more to remember in the future. He walked over to Davy, put his hands on his shoulders, looked him in the eyes and spoke quietly, with perfect honesty and conviction.

"Did you know that right now, today, they're starting a convention back at Washington-on-the-Brazos and what they are doing is declaring Texas to be independent of Mexico! Do you know what that means?"

Davy, nodded, and Jim continued. "It means Texas is free. We still have to fight for it, but whatever good things happen to Texas in the future will be because of what your daddy and men like him are doing. He can only do it because he knows that he can depend on you being here and taking care of things."

"Will you tell him that I wanted to come?"

"Yes, for sure," Jim said.

Davy's mother, who had been patiently listening, finally interrupted. "My goodness, it's gettin' late, and I've got supper to finish! Davy, get your chores done and get cleaned up so you can help me."

Jim did indeed have a much better supper than if he had accepted Adam's invitation. It was better than he had expected, in a family atmosphere that was convivial truly enough, but still overshadowed by the empty chair at the head of the table. Jim enjoyed their company. Doing his best to lift their spirits, he also lifted his own. He even found himself telling tales of some of the events of his life, most of them serious at the time, but now remembered chiefly for the humor. Finally, he reached the story of the food strike at college. As he finished, the boy, who had listened with rapt attention spoke up.

"But what happened after you all left?"

Jim had never told that part of the story before, but now it gave him great pleasure to recount it to the lad. He leaned back and smiled.

"You know, Davy, although we weren't there to see it, we won after all. The next term, the college had a new rule: students no longer had to eat in the Commons," and then he added "but of course if the cookin' had been even half as good as your mama's, we'd never have had the strike in the first place!"

They all had a good laugh. The conviviality continued as Davy's mother countered with humorous anecdotes about her husband. Gradually, the tenor of the conversation changed as the little family told their story—how they came to settle in Gonzales, about their lives there, their hopes for the future. In the palpable absence of the father, Jim found himself becoming melancholy at such talk. So it came as some relief when Willie finally appeared, and he was able to excuse himself.

Willie was accompanied by a young man whom he introduced as David Kent.

"His daddy's one of the Gonzales Rangers. You'll meet him when you get back to the Alamo," Willie said.

"I've collected some letters for some of our men, and I have one here for my father too, if you don't mind," David Kent said.

"Not at all, I'm happy to oblige."

Before Jim could say more, Kent reached out, shook his hand firmly, thanked him with barely concealed emotion, and disappeared into the night.

"A fine young man," Willie said as he watched him leave.

"This town seems to be full of them!"

After Kent's departure, they went across the street

to the Luna, an unmarked grog house. Jim, not normally much of a drinking man, nevertheless welcomed the tot of sippin' whiskey that was placed before him. Jim thought that Willie seemed a little nervous as he finally handed him the letter for Travis, and his concerns were confirmed when Willie spoke.

"Jim, there's something I have to tell you about this letter…"

"What's that?"

"I've told Travis that Fannin is on his way."

"But Willie, you know that's not so—hardly a chance. You saw Fannin's express. Unless he's changed his mind since yesterday morning, he's not going!"

"That's just it, Jim. You said yourself, he's a man who changes his mind, and I intend to see that he does!"

"But Willie, it's just not true. It's false hope!"

"I prefer to think of it as just plain hope, and that's what Buck and those boys need right now!"

Jim could understand Willie's desire to encourage the men in the Alamo, but it was a deception he couldn't countenance.

"Listen Willie, I understand what you are trying to do, and I'll carry your letter. But I'm going to have to report to Will my appraisal of the likelihood of help from Fannin or from any other quarter, and I'm afraid it's a lot different than yours!"

"I know, Jim, but we're going to do our best." Then, after taking a long look at Jim, he said, "Tell that to Buck … and God be with you, Jim!" Then he got up and left.

Jim hoped that Willie's vision of the next few days would prove to be more accurate than his own, but sober reflection told him otherwise. Although Willie chose to encourage Travis with optimism founded more on hope than fact, Jim felt that Will and the rest deserved a more realistic report. He knew that with each passing day the Mexicans had to be growing stronger, even as the defenders depleted their meager stores. The time had probably already passed when there was any reasonable chance of breaking the siege, much less mounting a successful attack on the Mexican lines of supply.

Although the fires of hope always burned, however dimly, the likely fate of the Alamo was becoming clear. Jim was also haunted by the question of whether Santa Anna's lightning strike had doomed not just the Alamo, but all of Texas.

As he climbed into bed, these concerns followed Jim into a troubled sleep. Sometime during that short and restless night, his old nightmare returned. Eventually, he woke in a sweat, and in spite of the decidedly unpleasant prospects for the new day, he was happy to get up and be on his way.

He was soon ready to ride. Sal was rested and, if not fractious, close to it, prancing about in the crisp air, her energy infectious, and like Jim, clearly ready to go. Jim was anxious to leave this land of people who, difficult as it may be, could still envision a future. He was going somewhere else. Whatever it was in Edgefield that had been bred into him, now rose up. He was done with words and the insipid and dark arts of persuasion. He was ready to confront whatever it was that waited for him. So, farewells completed, his saddlebags full of hastily written messages, and his stomach full of Margaret Darst's ham and eggs, once again he set out for Bexar.

It would take well into the next day to get there. As he rode west, Jim could only imagine how the situation within the Alamo had changed during the fortnight since his departure. When he left, they'd been faced with shortages, sickness, and uncertainty. Now that the question of when the Mexican army would arrive had been answered, uncertainty would have a different focus, but he hoped that they had found ways to deal with the sickness and the shortages. He would soon know.

It had gotten much colder overnight as a norther blew in. As the day wore on, the winds diminished, still cold, but clear. The sun, weak as it was, felt good on his shoulders. Obviously, Sal felt it, too. If anything, her pace seemed to grow stronger with the passing miles, and the time went by quickly.

It was well into the afternoon when, without yet seeing anyone, Jim sensed someone approaching from the opposite direction. He reined Sal in behind a scrub holly. Moments later, his intuition was rewarded as a rider emerged in the road ahead. It was not a Mexican soldier as he had feared, but someone he recognized instantly—his old friend, Sam Maverick.

Sam, like Jim, was a South Carolinian, and they had both been young lawyers together in Pendleton. Although Sam had left Pendleton some months before Jim, both had moved on to Alabama and eventually to Texas. Living at opposite ends of the state and losing touch with each other in Alabama, it was not until they both reached Texas that their paths crossed again. They had both been surprised and delighted to find themselves meeting once again in Bexar.

Even more unimaginable only a few months earlier, they were to become part of the garrison in a tumbled down old mission, become a fort: the Alamo. But the time together had allowed them to enjoy some welcome diversion recollecting days gone by in Pendleton and Abbeville.

Now Sam was on his way to serve as one of two delegates from the garrison at the Alamo to the constitutional convention in Washington-on-the-Brazos. The other delegate, Jesse Badgett, has preceded him even before Jim had left for Goliad.

As the distance between them closed, Jim was the first to speak.

"Sam! I thought you'd be in Washington at the convention."

"Hi Jim! I know. The convention began yesterday, but I was feeling a little poorly after Jesse left, and when the Mexicans came, I wanted to stay as long as possible so I could bring the latest news to the convention. I'll get there before it's over."

"How is it in Bexar, Sam?"

"Not good; we're holed up in the Alamo, and Santa Anna's numbers increase every day. There must be thousands there now, and our supplies are really getting short." Jim shook his head as Maverick continued. "But there are less men on sick call, and I must say, it gladdened our hearts when those boys from Gonzales got in yesterday. People were feeling much better when I left this morning. And you, Jim—any help coming? What about Fannin?"

The expression on Jim's face answered Maverick's question, but he told him the full story anyway. Maverick grimaced.

"But it does sound like things are happening, although I don't know about the time. Santa Anna might be ready to storm the place any day now!"

"That's what worries me, Sam. He doesn't seem the kind who will tarry for very long. If he were, we wouldn't be in this fix now!"

"Yes, for sure, he's surprised us all! And truth to tell, even if help arrives, they'll have their hands full now dealing with the Mexicans. The time for making a difference may have already passed."

Maverick had confirmed Jim's worst fears, and at that moment Jim fully realized what his own fate was likely to be.

Remembering the days in Pendleton, Maverick looked at his old friend—strong and bright, impetuous, but always reliable. Loyal, yet restless, not enough of a plodder. He could see that this man, in the right situation, could do anything if he could but avoid subordinating his own interests to the instincts of a cavalier.

These thoughts passed through his mind in a flash and led him to speak very quietly.

"Jim, I take it you are going back into the Alamo?"

"Of course."

"Think about it, Jim, there's really not much hope left. Why throw your life away?"

"I have thought about it, Sam. I want to live, but I really can't do anything else. Will's expecting me. They're all expecting me."

Sam understood the values of their common heritage. He knew all too well the code of honor that drove Jim, so he simply smiled wanly, and said, "I know. Good luck, Jim!"

"The same for you, Sam!"

With that, the two men reached out and shook hands, waved farewell and departed in opposite directions to their respective destinies.

Jim continued on, making good time and finally stopping for a short night's rest in a tumbled-down cabin just off the road. He was now less than half a day's ride from the Alamo, and in the quiet of the evening he could occasionally hear the faint booming of cannon that told him his friends still held out. Even though his rough pallet could not compare with the comfortable bed in Gonzales, he hoped that the few hours of sleep he planned would be better than the night before. But he was not to be so lucky. Perhaps prompted by his encounter with Sam, the dream returned.

CHAPTER EIGHT

The dream that tormented Jim always began with an awareness of being imprisoned—locked up in jail, unable to go beyond the confines of his cell, which in his dream was always very small and existed in a place where there was no one to answer his calls. It invoked a sense of panic, an inability to protect himself if need be, helplessness, trapped behind a fence of steel bars at the mercy of unknown jailers. Sometimes these feelings became almost overwhelming. He would awaken in a cold sweat, heart pounding, his first thought being to confirm that he was, in fact, free, unrestrained, and able to exercise his own will. The frenzy of these dreams was so palpable that Jim sometimes wondered if such things, entirely fabricated in the mind as one slept, could induce heart failure.

As it happened, Jim had once spent three months in jail, but the situation was different. Among other things, the cell was bigger, and, owing to a strange set of circumstances, the cell door was never locked. But being locked up remained his secret fear; his worst nightmare.

Caning a fellow attorney for grossly insulting his client, a poor widow, had been justified, but threatening the judge had been rash, and as Jim had to admit to himself—stupid. Ninety days in jail! *My God! When will I ever learn,* he wondered. Jim had done many rash things in his life, but the consequences had never been so swift nor so drastic as this. He wondered how he would feel after the ninety days were up. The sheriff and the jailer, Isaiah, had both treated him not only with deference, but with admiration. Perhaps he had inadvertently settled some scores for them as well in this incident. Certainly, he felt no sense of humiliation. He continued to believe his action had been fitting, and he remained defiant. Nevertheless, here he was . . . in *jail!*

And he didn't like it. The instant the cell door closed, he felt a sense of panic like nothing he had ever experienced. The only thing that enabled him to keep his composure was that Isaiah did not turn the key in the lock.

"I'll just get you some soap, a towel, and a blanket, Mr. Bonham," he said as he disappeared down the hall.

Jim looked around. The cell was about twelve feet wide and somewhat deeper, about fifteen feet. It was one of six cells, three on either side of a central hall, which was empty except for an iron stove at the far end. As far as Jim could tell, his cell was the only one occupied. Except for the bars along the hall, the walls were brick, and high above the floor at the far side was a small barred window through which he could see a patch of blue sky. There were two simple iron frame beds with dirty sagging mattresses and no pillows, one wooden chair, and in the corner a rickety washstand adorned only with a rusty oil lamp. Not a very inviting place to spend the next three months!

He hardly had time to contemplate his new quarters when he heard a cacophony of female voices approaching in the hall. Almost immediately they were there, stunned into momentary silence as they stared at him through the bars.

He recognized Mrs. Gregg, wife of an older and very prominent attorney, and her Negro servant whose name he did not know. With them was another woman, familiar looking, but also unknown to Jim. She was obviously a friend of Melissa Gregg and seemed equally animated. Hot on their heels as they had come down the hall had been a somewhat bewildered Isaiah followed by a beaming sheriff. He was obviously honored to have his jail visited by such illustrious guests.

"My, my, Mr. Bonham, you do cause a stir!" It was Mrs. Gregg speaking. The last time she had seen Jim was at the Wardlaw's party celebrating the New Year. She had particularly doted on him as a sort of surrogate for his brother Simeon, who had long since married her goddaughter, Amanda Wardlaw, and spirited her away to Alabama.

As Jim sought to look as dignified as possible and not let his face betray the feelings he had been experiencing moments before, Mrs. Gregg also regained her composure. As she surveyed the dismal scene, she said, "This will never do!" Turning to the sheriff, she added, "Don't you have a larger, more comfortable . . . ah . . . *room* for Mr. Bonham?

"I'm afraid not, ma'am. This is all we got! We've only two wings, and they're both the same." And then as an afterthought, "We put the field hands in the other one!"

"How kind of you ladies to visit, but really, Mrs. Gregg, I'll be just fine," Jim said.

"Nonsense!" she retorted, and then in a softer vein she said, "After what you have done in defending the womanhood of Anderson . . . why, of all Carolina. We are not about to let you grovel about in this miserable . . ."

she finally let herself utter the word, "*cell* for the next three months!" Not knowing quite what she intended to do about the situation but totally amused, Jim could only smile.

Turning to her servant who had been holding a basket covered with a checkered napkin, Mrs. Gregg said, "Mandy . . ." and nodded toward the cell.

It being clear to everyone what was intended, and punctuated by a sharp jab to the ribs by the sheriff, Isaiah sprung forward and swung the heavy cell door open. No one seemed to take notice that it was not locked, and Mandy slipped quickly in, deposited the basket on the table, then returned to her position beside her mistress.

As Mandy was doing this, Mrs. Gregg turned towards her friend.

"Do forgive me, Mr. Bonham, this is my dear friend Annabelle Johnston."

"It's a pleasure, Mrs. Johnston, although I'm obliged to apologize for the surroundings!"

As her friend shrugged off Jim's remark and smiled in acknowledgment of the introduction, Mrs. Gregg continued.

"On behalf of the ladies of Anderson and hereabouts, we have come, not only to thank you for your courtly action on behalf of Mrs. Hager, but to see to it that while you are in this *place,* you will be as comfortable as possible—that odious judge! It is he and that quack lawyer you thrashed who should be spending the spring behind bars!"

Looking at the women and then at the basket they had brought, Jim was touched by their gesture.

"Why, thank you, ladies. How kind of you. I'm sure I will enjoy whatever it is you have brought me."

Looking at the basket, Annabelle spoke up.

"Oh, that's just a little somethin' to tide you over to

keep you from starvin' to death in here. She looked around disdainfully as the sheriff blanched, ". . . 'til we can get things sorted out!"

Not knowing exactly what they had in mind, Jim stammered, "Well, I'm deeply touched by your thoughtfulness."

"Never you mind, just enjoy your dinner. We'll be back!"

With that, the entire group that had been there only minutes, disappeared as quickly as they had arrived, leaving Jim to explore the contents of the basket. He realized that he was indeed hungry, and he was just uncovering the fried chicken when Isaiah returned. Jim's heart was immediately in his throat as he feared that the moment had come to turn the key in the lock. He did his best to appear nonchalant as he said, "Back again, Isaiah? More visitors?"

"No, I came about the lock."

Jim's heart sank.

"Sheriff says that since there's likely to be lots of comin' and goin' here. And you bein' a real gentleman and all, we can leave it unlocked. But I'm to tell you that you're on your honor not to leave!"

Jim felt as if a tremendous load had been lifted from his shoulders.

"Give my thanks to the sheriff, Isaiah, and of course he knows I'll honor his trust." He started to say more but decided that his short simple answer accepting the sheriff's decision as if it had been expected would better serve his—hidden and most vital—interests.

Jim's appetite returned with gusto as he sat down and savored the fried chicken, the potato salad, the apple pie, and the jar of cool sweet milk. This certainly had to beat any meal he was likely to be brought by Isaiah . . . and no recourse to a *combination* necessary, he thought as he smiled inwardly.

As he finished, Jim wondered what the ladies had in mind when they said they'd be back . . . more, even regular, decent food?

The next morning he found out what they had in mind. And it was more than he could have ever imagined. The first thing in the morning, Mandy returned. This time she was alone, but brought with her another basket. In it were biscuits with butter and peach preserves, sausage, and an orange. Where did they ever get that? And some hot coffee. Mandy retrieved the basket from the day before and with a big happy smile announced, "We didn't know how you liked your coffee, so we jess put little cream in it."

"That's just the way I like it, Mandy!"

Her smile broadened, and she left.

So, this might be a regular thing, Jim thought. Well that will surely help! Suddenly, he was aware that Isaiah was standing there, and as Jim looked up, he handed him a newspaper.

"Here's *The Messenger*. Sheriff thought you might like it...it's got all about you and the judge in it. Sez the judge is gonna keep you in here for the full ninety days!"

Jim received the paper, eager to read the story, but it would be hours before he had the chance. He had not even time to unfold it before two house servants appeared. They were carrying a large upholstered chair with two loose feather pillows. As they set it down in the hall outside the cell, the older servant said, "Where y'all want this, Mister Isaiah?"

Isaiah, who now seemed to know all about what was going on, took charge.

"Just set it there for a minute and let's get this cot out'a here."

Thus began nearly two hours of activity in which Jim's cell was transformed into a comfortable room, fit for a gentleman. Not only was he provided with a comfortable chair, but a footstool as well, a soft bed with two pillows, a table which would serve nicely as a desk, an upright ladder-back chair, a washstand with ewer and basin. They provided a small mirror, an open cabinet, two oil lamps, an oval throw rug, and even a pair of vases which, presumably, would eventually be filled with flowers. Just as the men finished installing about all the furniture the small room could hold, Mandy reappeared. This time she was carrying an armful of linens, which she used to make the bed and to complete fitting out of the washstand. As she finished, she and the two men stood and looked at their handiwork. Mandy nodded approval, again favored Jim with that sunshine smile.

"There now, Mr. Bonham, that's more like it," Mandy said.

Still in a state of surprise at what had been happening, Jim could only manage to say, "It is indeed, thanks to you all!"

Before he could say more, they disappeared, leaving Jim in amazement at the transformation of his quarters. He was soon joined by Isaiah and the sheriff who were equally impressed. The place had been remade, and it wasn't even noon yet.

By early afternoon, Jim was still getting used to his new surroundings when once again Annabelle appeared. This time she was accompanied by two younger women whom Jim was to learn were her daughters, Louise and Rachel. Accompanying them was her own mammy, an older but fit-looking women named Nora.

"Well, there you are again Mr. Bonham," Annabelle began. "We've brought some books and some other things, which you might find useful."

"Words fail me, miz Annabelle! I really don't know how to thank you and the other ladies for all of this." He looked around at his transformed surroundings.

"Feathers! We told you we would look after you, and we intend to keep our word. We mean to make your stay in this place . . ." she looked around as if she were in a leper colony, "not just something to endure, but a . . ." she searched for a word, "*pleasurable* experience." Then, realizing it could never really be so, or perhaps embarrassed at her choice of words, she blushed slightly, and added, "Well, at least as much as possible! Whatever books you want or favorite food, you just let us know!"

"Y' all are too kind, ma'am."

"Never you worry, Mr. Bonham, the ladies of this town will not forget what you have done! Tweakin' the nose of that horrible judge settled lots of scores you'll never know about."

"Well, I didn't actually tweak his nose, ma'am. I just threatened to!"

"Never mind! It's the same thing. You taught him a lesson. Why, it's the most excitin' thing that's happened 'round here since that heavenly display last November!"

She was alluding to a night when people from Niagara Falls to Augusta, maybe all over the world, had witnessed untold thousands of shooting stars within the space of a few hours. Jim, like most everyone else, had been wakened by the sounds of shouting in the streets and had watched in awe as the earth passed through the tail of a comet, creating one of the most awesome displays in living memory. It was—and many people so believed—as if some cataclysmic event, such as the end of the world, was about to take place. To Jim, it had been simply an extraordinary natural phenomenon, awesome, but nevertheless a sign of God's power.

"Why ma'am, you put my incarceration into a category it does not deserve!"

Ever the belle, she replied, "Why that was just to herald the judge gettin' his comeuppance, and you bein' the instrument of its delivery!" *Strange,* he thought wryly, *those heavenly fireworks and this bizarre incarceration!* And, as if reading his mind, she laughed.

"But it is almost as if the Creator got the venue of your reward confused!"

"I should certainly hope so," Jim joined in her laughter. *But no,* he thought. *He made no mistake. This is a crucible for learning the meaning of fear, no matter the fanfare that led up to it.*

Soon after, they left, and Jim, in the most unlikely surroundings imaginable, began to serve his sentence. True to their word, the good ladies of the town saw to every detail. His meals were brought in daily, his bed was made, and his cell kept swept and dusted. Fresh flowers and comestibles of all kinds were ever present, and he had only to make the slightest request for it to be fulfilled. Except for the bars and the ever present threat of actually being locked in, Jim's cell was among the most pleasant places in Anderson.

The ladies came and went, and their numbers expanded beyond just Melissa and Annabelle and their servants. They included women of all ages: eighteen-year-old belles with their mothers, youngish and middle-aged married women in groups, grandmothers with their slave women. Even widows sometimes were among the visitors. The parade of women through his cell left him in amazement. Some were stunning beauties and some blatantly flirtatious, but all provided charming companionship. They tended not only to his comfort and to his needs, but they seemed resolved that he should not be overcome by sadness or boredom.

It was as if the Amazons had captured a prince and were determined to make him so pleased with his lot that he would never think of escape. It was enough to turn any man's head, but the passage of time—wasted time—weighed heavily upon him. As he grew increasingly beholden to his benefactresses, he became more uneasy. They were all kind, all gracious, but their attentions caused him to wonder why he hadn't heard from Caroline. True, she lived some miles away in Pendleton, but his sister Sarah had found no difficulty in coming from Abbeville, a much farther distance. Certainly a few miles would not deter a visit if she really wanted to come. Then why hadn't she?

It was in Charleston where they first met. The crisis over nullification had led to his being there and commanding an artillery battery at Charleston harbor. The excitement was complemented by a social season made particularly dazzling by the presence of so many dashing young officers in their splendid uniforms. While all Carolina seemed to have convened in that graceful city for a confrontation, it was to happen for Jim with powder and smoke of a different kind.

It was at one such affair, a cotillion, that Jim, himself the object of many a sidelong glance from some of the most beautiful women in the South, first saw her. In an instant, the other women in the room disappeared. Caroline Taliafero was a rare beauty, indeed. To Jim it was as if a sunbeam shown on her, singling her out from all others. So overwhelmed was he that by the time they were finally introduced, he had reverted to being a stammering school boy with legs of jelly. He could hear his own voice mouthing banal phrases and was sure that his awkwardness had cost him any chance with her. But her impression of him was much different than he imagined. She found him handsome, dashing—the very picture of Southern chivalry—and barely took notice of his stumbling words. The attraction was mutual, and the romance began.

Everything went their way. Even as the nullification excitement subsided, leaving Jim to contemplate returning to his budding law practice in Pendleton, provi-

dence smiled on them in a special way. Caroline's father, as was the custom of many in Charleston who
sought to avoid the sickly summers in the tidewater,
had acquired a plantation in the more comfortable uplands as a summer residence. It was in Pendleton and,
by the most fortunate of circumstances, immediately
adjacent to Montpelier, the stately plantation home of
the Mavericks. It was easy for Caroline to persuade her
family to quit Charleston early and repair to the uplands to welcome the spring. With the benign contriv-
ance of Sam and his family, the romance was further
facilitated. It was a match that seemed destined for the
altar.

But as the days passed in jail, he wondered why
Caroline had never answered his note. Surely, she received it. *Has the attention of all these women made her
jealous? Is she embarrassed by my being in jail? Or perhaps
my rash act has revealed a side of my character that she finds
distasteful. Maybe Judge Richardson is close to her family.* He
did not know.

Although her absence at first had caused him some
anxiety, with each passing day it began to seem less a
concern—and this surprised him. He was concerned
that perhaps these daily visitations, which frequently
included some flirtatious distraction, had turned his
head. Had his feelings about Caroline been merely in-
fatuation after all? Had he, in his efforts to receive all his
visitors with the good humor and courtesy befitting a
glorified noble defender of womanhood, played the
role too well?

But wondering why he had not heard from Caroline
was not the only thing that occupied his mind. He
relived many times the incident that had caused him to
be here. He always concluded that he had been justified
in the beating he had administered to that blackguard of
a lawyer who had gratuitously insulted his client, a poor

widow who was overwhelmed by the abstruse workings of the law. But the letter he had written to the judge
threatening to tweak his nose the next time he showed
his face in Anderson—perhaps that was ill-considered.

He also remembered another day when he watched
two men standing back-to-back as they waited for a
command to begin the pace-off. Dueling was not that
unusual, but it was the only time Jim had ever participated in one, even as a second. His principal, the erstwhile Governor James Hamilton, Jr., calmly waited,
while his opponent sought vainly to suppress his ner-
vousness. And with good reason. Hamilton had never
lost a duel, and he had fought many. True, he had never
killed an opponent, but there was always a first time!

It had been in the heady atmosphere of practicing
law in Pendleton, the very center of John Calhoun's
world, that Jim had first met Hamilton. Kindred spirits
in many things, they became friends, and that relationship eventually led to Jim's being named a lieutenant
colonel of militia and aide to the governor as the nullification crisis heightened.

But on that day as Jim watched and waited for the
duel to begin, he knew that no matter how calm
Hamilton's demeanor, he was, in fact, placing his life on
the line in support of his *honor,* an otherwise hollow
word unless one was prepared to risk all for it. A man
who would do this would find no difficulty in taking
similar action in support of public grievances that cried
out for redress. The Boston Tea Party came to mind, as
did the Constitutional Convention. Then suddenly, almost before he knew it, the confrontation was over.
Hamilton stood for a moment, smoking gun in hand,
grimly regarding his wounded opponent, and then
strode silently from the field.

Threatening to tweak the nose of a judge is not the
same as facing a man with a pistol, but in Jim's case, the

consequences had proved more onerous.

He also spent large chunks of time reading. *The Charleston Mercury* regularly found its way to his cell, along with *The Hive* from Edgefield, and a wide variety of books supplied him by his benefactresses. And of course, he had other visitors. They kept him informed on other events, but it was his situation that was of the most interest to them. He was the envy of his male friends who, though circumspect in their comments, let it be known that they thought he was experiencing every man's idea of heaven. They didn't know about the minutes and hours ticking away, *or* the lock!

When these diversions failed to answer, Jim would fall into an introspective mood. Although this episode had made him a hero of sorts to some, he worried that eventually there might be a certain obeisance exacted from him before all would be right again with the local establishment. Being jailed as a matter of honor was no disgrace, but the attentions of all these women could be creating ill will among some of their men. In a broader sense, he could not but wonder what lay ahead.

News of the recent death of his hero, General Lafayette, reminded him of the passage of time and the uncertainty of life. It also led him to reflect once again on the life of Lafayette, whose five years in prison under infinitely worse conditions, had been endured while maintaining a steadfast adherence to his principles. Nor could Jim forget that one of the general's most cherished principles was opposition to slavery. Jim was no abolitionist, but he was growing increasingly uncomfortable with the contradictions that were ever present in his world.

He wondered about the future of his family. Thanks to careful management by Malachia and his mother, they had weathered the down years, but the family plantations faced a difficult future. True, the girls were

married, as was Simeon, and Luke would soon be gradu-
ating from South Carolina College near the head of his
class, but Jim could not escape a sense of foreboding.
The pressure from the great plantations in the west was
inexorable, and most of the underlying attitudes that
had exacerbated the nullification issue were unresolved.
Somewhere down the road, another crisis seemed inevitable.

Jim had no answers, but like it or not, he felt bound
to support the system, never mind that in the inner
recesses of his heart he had serious doubts. He sometimes wished that life could be simpler, but he understood he could not escape the fabric of the society in
which he lived. Jim knew that compared with most
men, he had everything; but he was not content.

And so the time passed . . . flirtations and introspec-
tion, laced with boredom and frustration in a setting of
creature comforts. Frightened at the reality of not being
in control of his life and counting every lost minute, he
became increasingly irascible and had to struggle to
maintain his composure and good humor when he
received visitors.

Jim learned lessons that otherwise would have been
impossible. Most of these insights were the product of
his pensive interludes, but some sprung from having
been humbled, albeit with the face-saving ministrations
of the ladies. He even learned a thing or two about
dealing with the women. Being in their company on
such an informal basis for so much of the time, whether
playing games of whist or simply engaging in conversation, exposed him to a broader range of their wiles than
he could ever experience within the unguarded and
straightforward relationships of his own family.

All of this internal churning notwithstanding, his
favorite time became the end of each day, when a book
would deliver him from his confinement. But before he

could sleep, he was compelled to test the door to be sure that it was not locked.

While these pursuits made it barely possible for him to endure confinement, his overwhelming interest was in resuming a normal life. He counted the days, and eventually the end was in sight. He was actually making plans again and his spirits were rising, almost with the passing of each hour. Feeling good already, he was even more pleased when Sam Maverick appeared at his door.

Sam was one of those who came regularly. While he had never offered any news of Caroline, his visits always left Jim feeling better. Two years older than Jim, he, too, was a lawyer, having graduated from Yale and taken up practice in Pendleton. Although his family had stood on the opposite side of the nullification issue, matchmaking between Jim and Caroline had strengthened their friendship.

On this day, somehow he was not surprised when Sam handed him a note from Caroline, a note which Jim avoided opening in Sam's presence, although Sam's expression seemed to indicate that he was aware of the news it brought. In the brief, awkward silence that followed, Sam adroitly changed the subject to some news of his own. This would likely be their last meeting, as he was soon to depart for Alabama, there to settle and look after a family plantation. As Jim absorbed this news, all the while wondering what Caroline had written, Sam hurriedly bade him farewell and was gone almost before Jim realized it.

Caroline's note was brief and, like plunging into an icy stream, confirmed Jim's dark premonition. Of all the reasons he had conjured up for her absence and her silence during his time in jail, it had never occurred to him that she had simply transferred her affections to someone else. He was shocked but curiously dispassionate about the prospect. It took him little more than a day to bring himself to reply. He wrote her a friendly, yet correct note, wishing her well and extending his continuing friendship. Except for a brief appearance at her wedding some weeks later, he was never to see her again.

By the time he said good-bye to the sheriff and Isaiah and walked out of jail, Jim realized that the experience had had a profound effect on him. He was now a different person, and extremely grateful to be free and away from the threat of the *lock.* His sister Sarah hosted a gala affair, which they laughingly called a coming out party, and to which the honored guests were his benefactresses. Caroline was conspicuous by her absence, and everyone assumed that having been jilted, he was crushed. Among the young women of the region, it made of him even more a prize.

CHAPTER NINE

Completion of his sentence did not put an end to the problems arising from Jim's defense of Mrs. Hager's honor. In going to extreme lengths to reverse the discomfort of his incarceration, thereby thwarting the intent of the court, the good ladies had inadvertently created a larger problem, one likely to have a much longer impact than the mere serving of a sentence.

So cordial and close had been his relationship with his benefactresses, that Jim was eyed with some suspicion by the fathers, fiancées, and even the husbands of some of the women—the more so for his having been jilted by Caroline. As first he was barely aware of the uneasiness manifested in the reserve with which he was treated by many men who were his friends. Only gradually did he come to realize that he was the object of—if not their jealousy—their doubt as to where some of the relationships might lead. His great good looks and easy manner with the women did not help to dispel this notion. He assumed that it would gradually subside and things would return to normal.

But as the weeks passed, he began to wonder if he

might not be permanently affected by this stigma. He also began to suspect than the suspicion was being sustained by something—or someone—else. Could it be that the man he had humiliated with a public beating was keeping things stirred up? He could not prove it, but the continued coolness of many of his former relationships with the ever present prospect of misunderstandings, even duels, and his own restive nature led him to seriously consider following Sam's example and begin life anew in Alabama.

Several members of Jim's immediate family had already been taken with *Alabama Fever,* as migration to that state was called. Julia, now grown and married to Sam Bowie, had settled in the area around Montgomery, as had brothers John and Simeon and their families. All had made the move and seemed quite satisfied with their decision. In letters home, they mentioned meeting other transplanted Carolinians such as Will Travis, Jim's boyhood friend, whose family had made the move years before. They had all even reported finding a place near Montgomery called Mount Willing. It seemed that not only people but places, or at least place names, were emigrating from Edgefield to Alabama. *Perhaps,* Jim thought, *this might be the place for me.*

Jim felt with his sister and brothers already established in the region, he could anticipate a ready-made network of family and friends, and it made the idea of emigrating to Montgomery attractive. It seemed a hospitable place for him to begin again. With the lessons of the past behind him, he could set about making his own niche.

As the decision crystallized in his mind—even before he admitted to himself that he would take this course—he began to feel unburdened. No longer would he have to be knight-errant to a group of women. The thought of being free of this was liberating. Finally a spring came into his step, and he actually found himself awhistling as he walked down the street. He was becoming his old self again!

He would miss his home ground and the heady atmosphere of the circle around John Calhoun. But he would be trading all of that for a newfound freedom, which seemed to fit his nature—a nature which he was to learn had other needs in order to be fulfilled. He felt confident that he was moving in the right direction. Although a sign of the times, the fact that the direction coincided with geographical west did not strike him as portending anything other than the natural order of things.

Finally the day came when he took his leave of Anderson and Abbeville and Pendleton, Columbia and Edgefield and the culture he had known all his life. His westward journey had begun.

The trip to Montgomery was arduous. The fall of 1834 was a time of heavy rains. After two weeks of struggling with his unfortunate horses through muddy roads and across swollen streams, he finally made the three hundred miles. Tired and frustrated, he arrived in early October and made his way to the inn operated by his older brother, John. Able to relax at last and joyously welcomed, he was made to feel at home.

Many other South Carolinians had made the move as well, and he soon felt himself to be among friends. But he was dismayed at the amount of sickness around him. Even though there was a kind of familiarity in that the region had some of the look of the Carolina uplands, Montgomery was close enough to the Gulf to be subject to all the diseases engendered by a subtropical coastal climate.

Nevertheless, he delighted in the family life of John and Sally and with his newfound niece and nephews. In a letter to his mother, he wrote:

". . . She has four children, three boys and one girl. You have heard much about Mary Bonham being a spoiled child, and disagreeable, but I have never been more agreeably disappointed in my life. She is a very pretty sweet girl and not more affected or spoiled than any pretty young girl would be. She has a strong favor of her Aunt Julia as you have heard and thinks the highest of her and talks much about her. Mary has a beautiful brunet complexion and not dark skin as said — eyes are dark hazel color—looking black at a little distance. Her disposition is cheerful instead of petulant, and her manners and address, especially with older persons, I think are good.

"Sally Bonham is much improved. She has been very kind.. . ."

Within days of his arrival, Jim and John made the trip down to Simeon's home near Camden. They passed through the new Mount Willing, and although it was nothing like the old homeplace of their grandfather, the reunion with Simeon was as warm as if it had been. Years quickly faded away as the three brothers joked and caught up on the news of their lives.

Looking at Simeon's four children, Jim felt a little envious and hoped the day would not be long in dawning before he would look into the eyes of children of his own. But he took great delight in Simeon's children, just as he had with John's. All of these nieces and nephews, however, again made him aware of the passage of time, and he wondered how he would feel when he would meet the children of his little sister, Julia.

As the brothers laughed and joked, he could not but notice that John seemed to be carrying some burden or concern. Seeking to keep him in the carefree mood of the moment, he said, "John, how did you let your little brother Simeon catch up with you? Amanda has had four little ones as well. They'll soon be passing you!"

"Don't you think eight more Bonhams is enough,

Jim? But you should talk! When are you going to settle down?" John asked, smiling.

"Touché, brother! I just haven't got the hang of it yet!"

Simeon's wife, Amanda, who had been watching the good-natured banter, spoke up.

"Don't you worry, Jim, we'll soon introduce you to more young ladies than you can shake a stick at! You won't escape much longer!"

With the memories of the Anderson jail still fresh in his mind, Jim winced, and only smiled in response.

Although John was soon obliged to return to Montgomery, Jim remained as a guest of Simeon and Amanda for a few days. It had been years since he had seen them, and he was pleased to find them happy and well satisfied with their new life, particularly as evidenced by Simeon's enthusiasm for his law practice. It was a reflection of his easygoing manner and his freedom from the restless nature that drove Jim. He wished he could be more like Simeon in this respect, but he feared it wasn't in him.

Just as he could not abide John's way of life as keeper of a public house, he was not sure he could sustain interest in what seemed the mundane concerns of staid community life, free of all the excitement that was ever the case in Edgefield and Abbeville. But he was resolved to settle down. During their conversations, Simeon even suggested that Jim might join him at the law office, and while the offer was attractive to him, Jim declined.

It was in the course of Simeon's efforts at persuading Jim to reconsider that Jim learned of Simeon's interest in politics.

"You know, Jim, I've gotten pretty much involved in politics. If I should succeed in being elected to public office, then that is another reason for you to be with me—to look after the practice."

Jim's interest was piqued. "Really, what office would you be seeking?" he asked.

"Well, actually it's not generally known yet, but a fairly strong group is going to put my name forward for nomination as a candidate for Congress."

"Congratulations! You'll make a fine congressman! But what prompted you to agree?"

"The times we live in, Jim—the opportunity to participate at that level seems too good to pass up."

Jim was mildly surprised. Perhaps the staid life was not for Simeon either. As he looked at his brother, trying to imagine him side by side with the likes of John Calhoun, Simeon too became contemplative, but finally continued on a slightly different tack.

"You know, it's funny the way things happen. It was the chain of events that led me to this decision that also brought me in contact with Will Travis. You remember when Amanda and I first came here I wrote that we had come across him?"

"Of course; but what's that got to do with politics? Didn't you also write later that Will went to Texas?"

"Yes, Will's in Texas, and during those years before he left I had no thought of standing for Congress. But still, there's a curious connection—maybe common denominator is a better way of putting it."

"Did you see much of Will?"

"Yes, for a while—quite a bit. His family had settled down in Conecuh County, not too far from here. I never told the full story in my letters, but about the time we arrived, Will was just starting to read the law."

"Will a lawyer! All of us—you, me, soon Luke," Jim murmured bemused and half-aloud as Simeon continued.

"Will lived in Claiborne and his mentor was a certain Judge Dellet who, by the way, also came here from Carolina. You'll meet him soon. But by coincidence, Dellet was the very man to whom I had been referred by

Amanda's brother, David. Curiously, the judge, too, was graduated from South Carolina College. He was there before the Wardlaws, but like David and Francis, had been valedictorian of his class. I guess there must be some affinity among those who achieve that honor. *Ha!* But anyway, they've been friends over the years, and David insisted I get in touch with him."

"Now that you mention it, I believe I have heard his name mentioned in Abbeville or Pendleton. So that's how you came across Will?"

"Just so! And as it happens, the judge is as prominent in legal and political circles here as the Wardlaws are back home."

"So I suppose that with your law practice and political ambitions, you must see the judge regularly. But what's that got to do with Will? He's been in Texas for some time now, hasn't he?"

"Indeed! But I thought you would be interested in knowing how I first encountered Will."

"What's Will like as a grown man?"

Simeon went on to explain that Will had been unsuccessful in his law practice and had tried publishing a newspaper in Claiborne, which had also failed.

"Nothing really seemed to work for him," Simeon continued.

The news saddened Jim. "Too bad!"

"There's more. Will is married, and they have two children, a boy and a girl."

"Well, that's some compensation for hard times."

"Yes, but Will has left them. He disappeared one night and the next thing anyone heard, he was in Texas."

"But why did he leave?"

"It's a mystery. Of course there were debtors, but otherwise, only rumors and gossip. No one really knows. And the judge is now legal counsel to Will's estranged wife!"

Jim sought to reconstruct Will in his mind's eye. He

remembered Will as a spirited, gangling, young boy with reddish hair, and for a time almost like a cousin to him and his brothers. He had liked him and was disturbed at what Simeon was telling him.

"What about the rest of his family—his parents, are they still hereabouts?"

"Yes, there are lots of them around, and I'm sure they must hear from Will from time to time."

". . . and the judge?"

"Yes. Well . . . as I said, the judge now represents Will's wife, Rosa. He seems not to have forgiven Will his shabby behavior, not only with Rosa but in leaving the way he did. The situation keeps the judge more or less abreast of Will's activities in Texas and, in spite of everything, I think he still seems to care about Will."

"What makes you think that?"

"I don't know. Perhaps it's the way he speaks of him, even when he's denouncing him as a scoundrel. But it may be—and this is what you will be happy to hear—because Will has turned his life around since he went to Texas. Apparently, he's actually become quite prominent and plays a leading role in affairs out there. I think the judge may be secretly pleased to see his original appraisal of Will vindicated in spite of the trouble with Rosa."

"That *is* something! Good for Will! But his wife and children—what's going to become of them?"

"I really don't know, Jim."

"Does the judge say anything about what's going on in Texas?"

"Not much. But as you know, they seem to be on a course of breaking away from Mexico," Simeon said.

"Well, the next time you see the judge or any of Will's family, you can tell them to let him know that his old friend is in Alabama. Please remember me to him!"

"I will, of course, but I've digressed. Mention of Judge Dellet leads me back to my political aspirations and to some of the problems I'm anticipating with my law practice. Campaigning takes time, and if I'm fortunate enough to be elected, then what happens? It seems to me that you could join me at the law office and . . ."

"I understand," Jim interrupted. "It sounds mighty attractive, and I'm certainly sensible to your thoughtfulness in suggesting it. But what if you don't win? Then I might end up just being in the way, and you'd never tell me. Besides, I'm not sure yet that this is where I really want to be."

"What do you mean? Don't you like it here, Jim?"

"I'm not ready to say I don't like it, but it seems a sickly place—everybody struggling just to stay well."

"That's true, but you came at a particularly bad time. It can be wonderful here. Really, Jim, you should be able to be happy anywhere. It's what you make of a place. Give it some time."

"I know. I have a restless streak in me. But I'm getting older. I want to get it right."

And so began Jim's life in Alabama. He settled in Montgomery and, though Simeon didn't push him to join the practice, it was thanks to the many referrals and introductions from him that Jim's prospects soon became very promising. He met the illustrious Judge Dellet, who extended not only hospitality but encouragement. And there were others of Simeon's acquaintances who were similarly helpful.

One of these was a state representative from Greensboro, A. C. Horton, who would figure greatly in Jim's future, and whose vitality and energy were infectious and did much to help Jim come to grips with this new place.

Being in Montgomery, Jim spent a good deal of time with John and his family. He took a particular liking to Mary, who reciprocated with exuberance and delight at the sight of her Uncle Jim, and soon put him on the same pedestal with her Aunt Julia.

He enjoyed the role of favorite uncle not only with her but with all of his nieces and nephews whose parents indulged him cheerfully as he spoiled them. Jim continued to have difficulty with the idea of John operating a public house but after all, he reasoned, their grandfather Absalom had been an innkeeper after the war. Perhaps John was simply following in his footsteps. But Jim often sensed some preoccupation or dissatisfaction in John. Was his worry over the inn or perhaps his health? Maybe it was simply a product of being too conscientious, the family curse about which Jim and his brothers had joked for as long as he could remember.

Am I the same way — too introspective — always worried? But no, that can't be the case. Jim felt himself to be a happy person. He loved life too much to go around wearing a long face. But he was concerned for his older brother.

Christmas was quickly upon them and cause for a weeklong family reunion at Julia's culminating in a New Year's ball. It was a memorable and joyous occasion for all of them and, true to her word, Amanda had conspired with Julia to find a girl for Jim.

The ball was a gala affair reminiscent of similar events Jim had experienced in Charleston and Abbeville, not the same size nor as elegant, but carefree and great fun nevertheless. For Jim the splendor of those past days was eclipsed the moment he set eyes on Lila Sue. Jim and his brother-in-law Sam were standing near the punch bowl when he first caught sight of her entering the room with an older couple he guessed were her parents and followed by another younger man he hoped was her brother. At the sight of her, he completely lost track of his conversation with Sam and fell silent. As Sam turned to see what had caused this reaction, Jim became aware of his lapse.

"Please forgive me, Sam, it's just that . . ."

"She is striking, isn't she?" Sam smiled.

"Who are they?"

Before Sam could answer, Jim saw his sister greet the new arrivals effusively, and then watch, his heart in his throat, as she escorted them directly towards him. They were upon them in a moment. Jim, trying to maintain his composure, heard Julia saying, "Jim . . ."

As he fumbled through the introductions, Jim fought to avoid staring as he learned her name was Lila Sue. So smitten with her was he, that he felt the entire room was watching him, reading his mind. He found himself offering cups of punch, which were gratefully accepted by the parents and her—*thank God*—brother Volmore, but graciously declined by the young lady who had, in an instant, captured his heart.

An awkward silence ensued. Seconds seemed like minutes, until Jim finally heard himself saying, "Miss Madsen, with your father's permission . . ." he glanced towards her parents, "would you favor me with the next dance?"

At that moment their eyes met, and although Jim did not hear her answer, he knew it was, "Yes."

He offered her his arm, turned and bowed to her smiling father, who with the others, stood there in awe as they watched Lila Sue being swept away.

It was an auspicious beginning for the new year. For Jim, Lila Sue was everything he sought in a woman. Not only was she beautiful, but from the first moment there was an ease of communication between them, a kind of comfort, as if they had known each other forever.

When first he kissed her, it was sweeter than ever he could have imagined. It was a kiss he was never to forget. It unlocked a part of him that until then, he had not known existed. Ever after, words failed him when he sought to explain to himself the magic of that kiss. Perhaps it was the purity and truth of it, which told him in a way that no words could that she truly loved him. But whatever the explanation may have been, he knew that nothing he could ever do, or anything he could ever experience, could surpass the pleasure of that moment.

Now, all of his former discontent with Montgomery disappeared. The beautiful pine trees glistened in the crisp winter air, the redbirds were redder, even the muddy river sparkled. It was, suddenly, a better place; every aspect of life was brighter.

The romance ripened, and it was not long before he and Lila Sue decided to be married. The news, though not surprising, was welcomed by both families. They began to plan their future as Jim buckled down and began to build his practice in earnest.

The days passed quickly, each one happier than the last, and Jim's only concern was of being too happy. It was all too good to be true, but he ascribed the vague feelings of apprehension to a holdover from the events that led him to Montgomery in the first place. Things have a way of evening out, he reasoned. Each day he grew more confident that he was winning the battle of place. Simeon was right—you can find happiness any-where.

So it was with a good deal of surprise that in the middle of March he learned that his new friend Horton, the man who had helped him to become reconciled to life in Montgomery, was himself chucking it all in Alabama and heading for Texas. It seemed that the lure and challenge of that storied place had won another disciple. Although it puzzled him a great deal, Jim had no opportunity to question his friend on what lay behind his decision. There was only time to bid him farewell and ask to be remembered to Travis, should Horton encounter him in Texas.

It was only a few days later, on a fine clear evening with hints of spring in the air, when suddenly and unexpectedly, Jim's life changed again. He was return-ing from what had been a fine dinner and thoroughly enjoyable evening with Lila Sue and her family. Riding slowly and taking in the balmy breeze, his thoughts had returned to Horton and his sudden move. He was still pondering it when he came across John's houseman, Jonah, standing in the road waiting for him.

"Please Mister Jim. Mister John is took ill." With a look of genuine misery, he added, "Please hurry, da missus need you!"

The apprehension he had been feeling for weeks now took form. Jonah had come on John's horse, and Jim quickly decided to use the animal himself to get to the inn as quickly as possible, leaving Jonah to saddle and bring his own horse back.

When he arrived, the long faces of Sally and the children, made sallow by the single flickering oil lamp, were the pictures of despair. At the sight of Jim, Sally burst into tears, ran and threw her arms around him as the children gathered around. He did his best to calm them, saying, "What's the situation? Where is John?"

Mary sobbed, "He's in bed. The doctor's with him now."

"Well, what is it?"

It was one of several maladies, which collectively were known to the people thereabouts simply as *the fever*. Use of the article *the* and the tone of voice in which the expression was uttered always connoted something very serious and all too frequently, deadly. John lingered only one day and died the next evening.

It was a blow to all of them. In his own grief, Jim remembered how much John had been almost a second father to him. He was thankful that he was there and able to help Sally and the children through the ordeal.

He remained with them for several weeks after the funeral, pitching in and learning more about innkeeping than he ever cared to know. But it was cathartic for all of them, and occasional smiles were even beginning to return to the faces of Mary and the other children, when he received more bad news. Lila Sue had fallen ill. He had seen her only twice during the fortnight since John's death and, preoccupied as he was, did not notice anything amiss with her. His first emotion on receiving the news was panic, as he thought, *my God I'm not going to lose her, too!*

He rushed to her side. While it was clear that she did not have *the fever*, she was, nevertheless, quite ill. A lingering kind of thing, with long days somehow turning quickly into weeks. It was a battle that lasted through the spring and turned into a summer of anxiety. But Lila Sue was a fighter, and under Jim's watchful eye, her health would gradually improve, only to ebb, and gradually begin the cycle again. Jim felt that his own will would save her—and surely it did—but the wedding had to be postponed indefinitely as she valiantly fought her way through a tenuous convalescence.

By now Jim was thoroughly convinced that her illness sprang from the damnable climate—*this sickly place*—and he sunk back into the negativism that he had fought so hard to put behind him. But it was not just his imagination. Even the doctors had said that a change of climate would probably be necessary to a lasting recovery for Lila Sue. Jim once again confided in Simeon.

"I tell you, brother, I'm just not sure I can make a life here. I was beginning to feel better about it, seeing the good things about the place. But with John—and now Lila Sue—my apprehension has returned. Sometimes, it is close to overwhelming. I know it's because of all this illness, but, still..."

"Don't let it get you down, Jim. In spite of what I've said in the past, maybe this place is not for you."

"I've been fighting that feeling, you know I have. I thought I had it beaten. But now, I don't know. . . ."

"It would be no disgrace to go back to Edgefield. Why don't you think about it? You could take Lila Sue, and . . ."

"I wouldn't think of it as disgrace," Jim interrupted,

"but Simeon, I just can't spend my life moving from place to place. Next year I'll be twenty-nine! I've got to settle down!"

"But maybe not here, Jim," Simeon said with the calm smile that had always come when he wanted to stop his brother from doing something rash. "Perhaps you're one of these people who goes to Texas. I hear there's much opportunity out there, and it's a different kind of place: lots of land, more open. Somehow it seems it might be brighter and fresher . . . more challenging." Jim was musing on these words as Simeon continued. "Funny, just the other day I got a secondhand message from Will Travis. He said to tell you 'hello' as well, and that if Alabama didn't suit, then come on to Texas!"

He must have run into Horton, Jim thought; then aloud, "What's he doing in Texas, Simeon?"

"Practicing law—a little bit of everything, I gather . But now he seems mostly with the military, trying to break away from Mexico."

"Well, it might be interesting, but running from pillar to post is not an answer. You were right when you told me that a man has to take a stand and deal with life as he finds it. That's good advice, and before I ever move again, there will have to be a very good reason!"

As he uttered these word's, the vision of his poor Lila Sue struggling to regain her health came back to mind. A healthier climate, the doctor had said. Nevertheless, Jim was intent on continuing the new life he had started. He buried his concerns somewhere deep inside himself and fought to regain his natural optimism, *not to flinch.* But there were days when it was difficult indeed.

Until finally, as mid-July approached, the galvanizing event overtook him. The dog days were already upon them, and late on a hot, sticky morning, Sam came through the door into Jim's office, his countenance betraying the most abject tragedy. Jim felt his blood rush to his head as he steeled himself for the bad news.

"Jim, it's Simeon. He died last night!"

Simeon! My God, how can it be? Then, with an instinctive calmness that in no way reflected the torment and anguish rising inside him, voicing the words, "How—what happened?"

"He got *the fever* a few days ago and just like that—he was gone." Then trying to fill Jim in with what few facts he had, Sam continued, "They said it didn't seem bad at first, but Julia's on her way there now."

Jim's thoughts immediately went to his mother—his poor mother. *First John, then Simeon, both in the space of a few months. Will I be next?*

Simeon's death following as closely as it did John's produced an anguish and a sadness unlike anything any of the family had experienced. The only consolation to Jim was having been able to spend a good part of his brothers' last few months together. Close to overwhelming, the grief at last became bearable, but another milestone had passed, and a new life was beginning for all of them. Jim knew that for him and Lila Sue, it would not be here. No longer would he suppress his instincts or hang on from day to day, waiting to see what fate had in store. He had regained confidence in his inner voice.

In the days following the funeral, he talked at length with Judge Dellet, and it was in one of these conversations that the subject of Will Travis again arose. Although the judge avoided the personal issues which had caused the rift between him and Will, he spoke at length about Texas and the things going on there.

Once again, even though indirectly, the idea of Texas was thrust upon him. And then, within days, as if ordained by fate, Jim received two letters in the same post: one from Horton and the other from Will Travis. Horton, his expectations apparently fulfilled, announced his intention to return to Alabama before the end of October to recruit volunteers in the struggle for independence now intensifying in Texas. Will's note, though less specific, urged Jim to come and participate in the exciting times, the promise of a new life implicit in his words.

That did it! It was then that Texas really did beckon him. In an instant he saw it clearly, a new, bright place where he could go and make a niche for himself and Lila Sue. If Horton could get settled there in a matter of months, so could he. It would not be long before he could return to fetch his bride.

But first he had to return to Edgefield. Not only was he intent on consoling the family, but there were documents that had to be transmitted to David Wardlaw, who was one of Simeon's executors. And he wanted to tell the family of his plans for the future. Lila Sue, her health gradually improving, was excited at the prospect, but also apprehensive.

"Jim . . . are you sure this is the right thing to do? I fear we may be separated forever!"

"Dearest, without you, life is nothing to me. And I must get you out of this place—this sickly place."

"But how do you know Texas will be any better? Besides there's about to be a war."

"I've heard what everyone has heard, and I believe it must be a wonderful place, a good place to start a life. And if there's a war, then we'll win it!"

The dream was affirmed by the hope in her eyes.

"But I promise you, war or not, win or lose, I'll make a place for us. I'll come and fetch you and by this time next year we'll be together!"

"I hope so, Jim. I pray that it will happen."

"It will! You concentrate on getting well. Keep that preacher standing by and time will pass before we know it!"

"I'm sure it will."

CHAPTER TEN

As September turned into October, the days became perceptibly shorter, and autumn was in the air. Usually, it was a welcome season, but this year the finest of days were being lost to a shroud of gloom that hung over the house. Even the afternoon sun had not been enough to take away the chill as Sophia sat in the kitchen aimlessly shelling peas while Louisa, feigning work, kept a watchful eye on her mistress, looking for little ways to lift her spirits. She had never known Sophia unable to shake off misfortune, but this time was different, and Louisa was taking advantage of every opportunity to strike a spark that would bring the old light back into Sophia's eyes.

They spoke of the good old times, the times when the house was full of children. Though this talk sometimes brought a nostalgic smile to Sophia's lips, it would soon fade, leaving Louisa to search for a new subject. Inevitably, when all the small talk and neighborhood gossip was done, the conversation turned to the Bible. Sophia and Louisa were co-religionists in a real sense. Sophia had made it possible for Louisa to become a member of her own church, acknowledging Louisa's equality in the eyes of the Lord and thus providing her an escape, of sorts, from slavery. So they would wile away the hours, shelling peas or peeling potatoes, and speaking of Job and the misery he endured, and Abraham's readiness to sacrifice Isaac—and what it all meant.

Sophia's melancholy had been brought on by the recent deaths of John and Simeon. Working her way through the grief raised many memories of loved ones long gone, as well as her recently departed sons. She could not be distracted from her bittersweet reminiscences, and even with the support of Louisa, overcoming the pain was something she had to do alone. Sophia had faced losses before and, with faith in the Lord, had been able to spring back. With His help, she believed, she would do so again. But still, the empty feeling lingered, and it was only with the greatest difficulty that she was able to go through the motions of daily life.

Her greatest solace came from memories of the days with all of the children around—often hectic, but good days, any one of which she would give almost anything to relive. She knew that she could not linger in this kind of nostalgia for long. She would rouse her thoughts and try to think about the present. Her daughters were gone and happy in their lives, but what of her three surviving sons? She sensed that Malachia was getting stale with the responsibilities he had shouldered all these years helping her to operate the plantations. James Butler was gone, searching for his place in life, and only her youngest son, Milledge Luke, seemed truly satisfied with his place here in Edgefield.

Luke was her youngest, and by now had grown into a handsome young man. Like Jim he had gone to South Carolina College, but unlike Jim, he had graduated. That silly food strike—it brought a smile to her lips—and it almost moved her to tears to remember how Milledge had idolized James Butler, following in his footsteps in the Clariosophic Society. But she was thankful that he had not followed him to Alabama. Enough Bonhams had gone to Alabama.

And so it was this day—the talk with Louisa had waned, and Sophia's thoughts spun on as the afternoon dragged by. As she sat there, unshelled peas in her apron and looking out the window at the long road up that hill over which so many dear ones had disappeared, she suddenly became aware of a rider coming down the road. She watched him with interest thinking that perhaps it might be Milledge returning a day early, or one of her cousins who often came for an impromptu visit. But there was a difference. The figure was familiar, but it was none of them. Her interest heightened as the rider came closer. *My,* she thought, *he sits a horse just like James Butler.* A moment later she said out loud, "It *is* him!"

Sure enough, there he was, unmistakable in the saddle now urging his horse into a trot as he grew nearer to the place he loved so well. Two distraught spirits were about to heal each other.

After several days, Sophia and her strong tall son had just about talked themselves out—mostly remembering John and Simeon. They even found themselves laughing as they recounted long forgotten anecdotes. It became a sort of catharsis, almost making it seem as if they weren't gone. And a new element was added when Jim told his mother of Lila Sue. It gladdened Sophia's heart to hear that Jim had finally found someone to share his life. She smiled inwardly as she noticed he could scarcely leave reference to Lila Sue out of any conversation.

Within a few days the gloom was lifted from Red Bank. Luke had returned, and Malachia had come over from Flat Grove. And so what began as a time of poignant remembrance became a happy reunion for them all.

Inevitably, the subject of Jim's future plans arose. Although they had hoped he would remain in Edgefield, his news of Lila Sue and the enthusiasm with which he described their plans to settle in Texas made it all palatable, the more so since Jim seemed in no hurry to leave. He was anxious to get on with his life, but this was part of it. The visit was good for them all. Though they knew that sometime soon he would be leaving, it would not be until the time was right.

That is not to say that they did not make an effort to persuade him to stay. It fell upon Luke to be the spokesman for the family; to convince Jim to think carefully about Texas, and to remember that he could make a life here in Edgefield.

Somewhat circumspect, Luke spoke first of practical issues. But to no avail. Jim had thought it through. However, in the course of their discussions, Luke discerned more than he had ever realized, the underlying restlessness in his brother's nature—something that Luke, himself free of such tendencies, could not fully understand. Although he respected his brother's views, he continued the discussions, making the case for building on what one is given in life, for permanence and continuity within the family.

For Jim, having to deal with the logic of Luke's arguments was a good test. It forced him to bring discipline to his thoughts as he explained himself to Luke. They talked on and off for several days when finally, one bright Sunday morning after church, they walked out by the creek. Luke skipped a rock over the water, all the way to the bend, just as Jim had seen him do countless times before.

"Jim, I hope you'll forgive me, and I promise I won't continue to press you, but are you really sure about your decision to go to Texas?"

"As sure as I can be Luke, and I take no offense at your concern!"

" I'm sure you know, but it must be said, there really is a place for you here. There's room for us all!"

"I know that brother." After hesitating for a moment, Jim continued, "Listen Luke, I know you mean well, but Texas is not China. Ships come into Charleston and Savannah. I'll see y'all again."

"All of the family wants only what is best for you, and I'm doin' my best to understand."

"I know, but let me see if I can make in clear to you. Do you know why I went to Alabama in the first place?"

"Well, yes." Luke then wondered if he did, but continued, "You soured on Pendleton, couldn't stand to see Caroline married to someone else."

"To some extent that's true, but there's more. Being in jail all that time, three things happened; I was treated like a hero by the local ladies, and I must say that was most enjoyable." He smiled at the thought of it. "But, being locked up...." Jim went on to explain his feelings about imprisonment and his panic at the thought of the lock clicking. "But there was one good thing that came from all that frustration and wasted time. I was able to assess my life and see things just a bit more clearly. Nothing like a blinding revelation, you understand," he laughed, "but perhaps some insights I might not otherwise have had." He paused again, then finished, "In any case, I certainly hope so!"

Luke had listened with great interest, and when Jim grew silent, he asked, "And the third?"

"The third?"

"Yes, you said there were three things."

"Ah, yes. Well as pleasant as the good ladies made my incarceration, it also led to an untenable situation after I got out."

Luke was surprised, and finally smiled. "Why Jim, you mean you became entangled?"

"No, but lots of people thought I might be. Lord, if I were guilty of all the suspicion that was cast towards

me, I'd have to be three people! I never dreamed there
were so many jealous suitors, even husbands! I left
before it got too bad and, you know, Pendleton is not
that far from here."

"Jim, this is ridiculous. You can't let a situation like
that drive you from your home!"

"No, of course not. That's not it really, but I wanted
you to understand some of what brought to the surface
this restlessness. There's really more to it than that,"
seeing the look of surprise still in Luke's face he continued, "believe me!"

"Of course, I do." But the quizzical expression remained.

"Listen Luke. There are other things."

Luke waited attentively, pleased to be learning at
last what drove his brother.

"The idea of starting fresh, not just with my life, but
with everything, free of our *peculiar institution*. It can't
go on this way forever, Luke." Luke was even more
surprised.

"Well, Alabama was hardly the place to get away
from slavery. Does it really bother you that much?"

Jim reflected on Luke's question. "It's always been
part of our lives. You know I can't abide the abolitionists
and the high-handed way they go about everything—
using it as a cover to achieve their political goals. But
just the same, sometimes when I look it in the face and
think about the stand taken against it by people I admire
—like Lafayette—I find it difficult to abide. It's really
not a condition any human should have to endure. I
guess, along with our acceptance of it, we all know
down deep, it can't go on forever. The whole situation is
like death. You know that some day you'll have to face
it, but not now!"

"I understand, but what can we do about it? We're
caught in it. We're slaves to it just as much as the Negroes,
and if it collapsed tomorrow, everybody would suffer."

"I know, but you can understand freedom from it, without becoming a Yankee . . ." he laughed, "is part of the attraction of being in a new place starting over unencumbered by an institution which . . ."

Luke interrupted, "Jim, there are devils everywhere."

"Surely brother, you are correct. That's what Simeon said. I suppose all I really want is a niche, a place to be comfortable with myself."

"But, you've got it—here"

"I know, and maybe it was just those three months in jail, but the idea of starting afresh, really fresh, not as in Alabama, but in a really new place like Texas—it appeals to me more each day!"

Luke was silent, waiting for Jim to continue, but he could not hide the skepticism from his face.

"I know it may seem impetuous, but it's not that; it's more a matter of impatience. I do things out of impatience," Jim said, responding to Luke's skepticism.

"What do you mean?"

"Maybe it's more about time. That's something else I learned in jail—the value of time. I used to think I had all the time in the world, but now I know that I don't. Think of all the plans that John and Simeon must have been making. Time is passing and I want to find a place that feels right." He thought for a moment. "It's like looking for the best place to fish in a creek. I can't relax and just fish until everything is right with the place. You remember; you and Simeon used to kid me about it. I'd pass up the most promising holes, spots that most people would settle on in an instant, looking for just the right place. Then I'd get nervous about the time it was taking to find it.

"In a way, that's how it is now; time is passing. It sometimes weighs heavily, but I want to get it right! I guess, at the bottom of it all, that's what attracts me to Texas. It seems as if it just may be the fishing hole I've always been looking for!"

"And what if it's not? What makes you think you will find it in Texas, or that Texas will even win her freedom from Mexico?"

He didn't answer Luke's question directly but brought the conversation back to a more practical level.

"Do you remember when we were boys—my friend, Will Travis? They lived just over yonder. He used to meet us at the crossroads on the way to school."

"Yes, I think I do, but they moved away, didn't they?"

"Yes, moved to Alabama."

"Did you see him in Alabama?"

"No, he had gone from there to Texas by the time I arrived. But Simeon saw him many times. Early on he had come to know a Judge Dellet, who had been a sort of mentor to Travis, and that's how they made the connection. Besides that, Will sometimes corresponds with people back there, his family and others. In fact, when he heard I was there, he wrote to me telling of the great things happening in Texas: land practically for the asking, industrious people and, according to him, only a matter of time 'til Texas will be free from Mexico. It seems like a new country, starting on a new foot and, if necessary, worth fighting for!"

Watching Luke's reaction carefully and trying to anticipate any unspoken objections that Luke might still have, Jim continued.

"You know Luke, I'm not a vagabond, but what I want was never in Alabama. I truly believe that the good Lord only sent me there so I could find Lila Sue and be with John and Simeon at the end."

"And to learn of Will Travis' exploits in Texas?"

"Yes, that, too."

"But Jim, you can leave your imprint here as well. You are already a man of substance. You need only to build on what you already have. You can make of it what you will."

"That's true, but what I really already have is inside me, and somehow it doesn't fit the role I would fill here. It would be playing a game that might destroy me. More and more this seems to me like someone else's world. There's something else out there waiting for me. Something I want a hand in making and besides I guess I have to say," he laughed, "it's boring here!"

"Boring!" Luke laughed too. "Tell that to the hotheads around here! Nobody has ever accused Edgefieldians of being boring!"

"No, of course not. Not *really* boring, but maybe too routine for me." Becoming serious again for a moment, he looked hard at Luke. "No, Luke. I don't really know what I'll find out there, and maybe you're right. But I've got this feeling—although I really didn't know it at the time—I also went to Alabama so I could find my way to Texas!"

As Luke observed Jim's enthusiasm speaking of a new beginning, he realized that his brother was, indeed, cut out for another kind of life. At that moment, although he did not voice it, all his objections to Jim's plans vanished, and he resolved to do all he could to help his brother realize his dream.

The conversation ended when they were interrupted by Mercy's little boy, Josh, who came to fetch them for Sunday dinner. And what a dinner it was! Appetites had returned and Louisa was happy. It was almost like old times and as if informed by an unseen voice, Jim's imminent departure became an accepted fact and the conversation turned to practical matters. They spoke of his forthcoming trip, first to Montgomery and Mobile, then on to Texas, how long it might take, and even when he might return for his bride, and how he would bring her back to Edgefield for a visit—perhaps returning to their new home in Texas by sea from Charleston or Savannah. The talk around the table made everybody feel better, confirming as it did that Jim remained part of the family and making his going not seem so final.

The next few days were spent in preparation for the long trek to Texas, Luke helping in every way. As the time for departure neared, he disappeared early one morning, saying only that he was going to Mount Willing. It was late in the afternoon when he returned and asked Jim to step out into the yard in front of the house.

"Just stand right there, Jim." He motioned as he disappeared around the end of the building. Amused and curious, Jim did not have to wait long before finding out what it was all about.

Luke soon emerged from around the corner of the building leading a magnificent horse—a beautiful dove-colored mare, fifteen hands high, with classic configuration—a powerful chest and a head that brought to mind drawings of Etruscan statues. With flowing mane and large intelligent eyes, alert sensitive ears which seemed almost like semaphores—all taken together, communicating the finest breeding.

She was, Jim thought, the finest looking horse he had ever seen. The only ones that came even close were the steeds in his boyhood imagination. As he looked at her, she whinnied, almost as if she remembered him from those days.

As Jim stood transfixed, Luke said simply, "Jim, she's yours. Her name is Saluda."

So it was, one bright morning a few days later, astride Saluda and with his packhorse alongside, Jim began the ride up the long hill from Red Bank. Nearing the top, he stopped, turned and waved good-bye to his family still gathered in the road at the foot of the hill.

Chapter Eleven

November 15, 1835

My Dear Mother,

I hope this letter finds you and all of the family well. It is only now that I have reached a point in my journey, that I have had the opportunity to write you. Perhaps it was because today provided such a memorable experience that it finally raised me from the day to day concerns of travel. Of course, all of you, and the wonderful time we had together during my visit, are never far from my mind. I also think with concern of my poor nieces and nephews, having lost their fathers, and cannot help but remember how their situation compares with what their fathers experienced as boys. However, the good Lord has blessed them with good mothers, just as he did all of us.

You will be happy to know that I saw them all when I returned to Alabama, and they seem to be doing well. They were most appreciative of the gifts you sent and asked to be remembered to their grandmother—

although, I am sure you will be hearing directly from them. Amanda was particularly pleased to learn that things worked out so well with Rolf and Cisey—as Simeon had impressed her so much with your attachment to them.

I was also able to see my dear Lila Sue who, like you, has reconciled herself to the restive side of my nature. But of more importance, her health seems to be improving—all the more reason for me to hasten becoming established in Texas, so that I can return for her—and bring her to a bright new life in a bright new place. You (and she) will find that my restlessness will leave once I have made my place!

I am also happy to report that things worked out well with Mr. Horton. I found him in Mobile, just as we had planned! Within only a few days, we were able to recruit a number of volunteers for the struggle in Texas. They all seem to be well motivated and, shedding humility for a moment, I will tell you that the example of my own commitment may have been persuasive to some of them. Although many of them are not from Mobile, they, nevertheless, call themselves "The Mobile Greys." They number about thirty, and have all departed for Texas, most of them by ship, excepting a few who are traveling overland, with me. So you see, I am not alone, and subject to the foul deeds of various highwaymen along the way! Quite the opposite, some people look at the group of us as we ride along, and I'm sure must wonder if we are not brigands of some kind. But there is a lot of immigration to Texas along this route, and most people properly place us, some even want to join us. But so far that has not happened.

Traveling conditions are about what I expected. More bad than good, but over all tolerable. Occasionally we find a good meal, but of course nothing as good as the worse day at Red Bank. In fact they put me in mind of the Commons at college, but along this road, a food strike would count for nothing!

The scenery is magnificent—mile after mile—makes me appreciate the grandeur of our land. I wish you could have been with us this morning. As we rode along it occurred to me that for some time, perhaps an hour or more, I had been vaguely aware of something, a pervasive presence, that was all around us. Invisible, yet there, undeniable and inescapable. But, I could not place it! Perhaps, I thought, I had been too long in the saddle; my mind was playing tricks on me, but I didn't really think that was it. Sal was restless too. It was not fearful, but still it was there, and powerful, and it made me feel uneasy.

I believe we were all in an unearthly, almost dreamlike state, and as I rode along I began to realize that we were coming closer to whatever it was. We had just passed across fields that had recently been cleared and, moving up a grassy slope, were just coming to realize that a new ingredient had been added; sound — when, through a break in the trees at the top of the slope we saw it. The Mississippi River!

And let me tell you mother, what a sight! Swift and powerful, broader than I could ever have imagined, the spectacle was breathtaking. I don't know how long we sat there, staring in amazement, until finally one my friends spoke up, and it was if we all had been in a trance. We laughed—and we sure learned why they call it 'the father of waters'!

I can tell you—like that incredible shower of shooting stars a few years back—it was a sight I'll never forget, and it raised my spirits. I truly felt the power of the Almighty and somehow it made me able to live with all the terrible losses we have suffered—Elizabeth, and Daddy too—and I thought that having me write you about it might help you too—a demonstration of the mystery of God's creation. Now we have to cross it! We have moved on up the river to a landing near Natchez, and are settled in here for the night. We expect to take the ferry in the morning, and then on to Texas! I will write you once I am there and settled.

Before closing I must ask you to pass on to Milledge my enduring thanks for all the help he was to me as I took my leave, but most of all for the gift of Saluda! She is easily the most wonderful horse I have ever encountered . . . she is strong . . . rides smoothly . . . is good natured and intelligent. I have never known a horse so strong, nor have I ever seen her reach the limit of her endurance. My companions' horses (not to mention our pack animals) are always well spent while Saluda seems as if she could go on forever. It is a pleasure to have such an animal, and I will be ever sensible to Milledge for giving her to me. I've come to calling her "Sal"—I wonder what Aunt Sally would think of that!

I am told that there is a post which moves down the river to New Orleans, and that you may have this letter in as little as two weeks time! I hope so, but whenever it reaches you, please pass along my remembrances to everyone.

Your affectionate son,

James Butler Bonham

CHAPTER TWELVE

The cold, dreary rain had persisted for days. It turned San Felipe into a sea of mud, in which little islands of weathered wooden buildings seemed to merge with the gray landscape of oncoming winter. Even the dusky Spanish moss added to the gloominess. Yet, the dismal surroundings did not dampen the spirits of Jim and his companions as they finally reached their destination, and they were not dismayed by what they found.

Feeling more comfortable traveling overland, they had made the trip on horseback in a kind of impromptu race with the main body of the Greys who were coming by sea. All along the way since they had left Mobile, they had heard nothing but talk of Texas and the rebellion; the situation in Texas seemed everywhere to have piqued the popular interest. Throughout their journey they had fed upon it, so that by the time they finally crossed the Sabine River into Texas, it was as if a great crusade had reached the Holy Land. Their anticipation had heightened with every passing mile. Every obstacle, every river—the Sabine, the Neches, and finally the Brazos—only served to spur them on. It would take more than mud and rain and a grimy little town to dampen their enthusiasm.

The short ferry ride across the Brazos had not only marked the end of their journey but had deposited them close to the center of town. As they rode in, they attracted little attention. New arrivals were common. Adventurers, land speculators, and volunteers all made up a steady stream which had come to be taken for granted. They were naturally drawn toward the central plaza clearly visible a few blocks distant. As they moved through the muddy streets passing stores and taverns, stables and houses, it was soon clear that San Felipe was indeed a busy place. The dreadful weather notwithstanding, people were coming and going as if driven by a sense of common purpose. Wagons were being loaded with goods, and it seemed that everywhere small groups of men stood engaged in animated conversation. An air of excitement was palpable.

Texas seemed to be living up to their expectations, and these men were anxious to become part of it. But first, they had to find lodgings and tend to their animals. Asking directions of a man who had given them a friendly nod, they were told of an encampment just downriver which had become a sort of assembly point for some of the volunteer groups. For the Greys this seemed like the most obvious place to begin their search for Captain Burke, and the others.

But Jim had his own interests. He was intent on finding Will Travis if he could, but in any case, taking the first steps towards making his new life in Texas. Besides, the idea of another night in a makeshift encampment held no attraction for him. What he wanted was a proper place to stay. So he and the Greys went their separate ways, agreeing to meet later in the day at one of the taverns they had just passed.

Jim was not long in finding lodging. Peyton's Hotel was neatly identified by a sign hanging from the lampost in the front yard. It was a large rambling house painted white and offering the shelter of a broad covered porch. The house was in such sharp contrast to what he had seen of the town that it almost could have been in Mobile. But the best thing about it was the promise of comfortable accommodations, and a dry and warm stable for his horses as well.

He felt fortunate to have found the place so quickly, but even more so as he dismounted and was greeted by a young man who told him that there were rooms available. He was told that this would not have been so, had not many of the *regulars* been on duty at the frontier. Even so, there was no telling how long he could keep his room, because these *regulars*, whoever they were, might return at any time. Long since used to living from moment to moment, the temporary nature of the lodgings bothered Jim not a whit. The idea of a hot bath, dry clothes, and a comfortable bed that night crowded out all other concerns.

To store his gear, he was directed to a tack room in a building between the stable and the main house. Connected to it was a storeroom in which he could safely put the bulk of his belongings as he unburdened his horses. One end of the room was divided into bins and within each bin was wood shelving against the rear wall. Each of the bins were full, and they seemed to have been assigned to various individuals, probably the *regulars*, because makeshift signs, presumably the names of the owners of the contents of the bins, were affixed to each one.

Jim read the names: J. W. Fannin, John Wharton, R. M. Williamson, Jim Bowie . . . *that's certainly a familiar name* . . . and continued down the row until finally, he found an empty space. Just above it, on the wood itself in letters now barely legible, was the name W. B. Travis —Will Travis! Had he found Will so easily? Was he a *regular* at the Peyton's? Clearly, the bin had not been used in some time, so Jim cleared the cobwebs and filled it with his belongings, covering them as best he could with an extra saddle blanket.

By the time Jim found his way inside, the young man who had at first received him had disappeared. However, Mrs. Peyton herself appeared. Younger than Jim had expected, she was friendly and outgoing, and might have been Sally welcoming a traveler to the inn in Montgomery. But the thought of Sally faded as he heard Mrs. Peyton repeating the warning of a possible claim on the quarters she was about to assign to him. Taking his nod as an understanding of the terms and accustomed to dealing with new arrivals, she hastily showed him around the premises, led him to his room, and announced that she had already set someone to heating bathwater. It was the most welcomed reception that Jim could imagine, and in response to her parting question as to whether she could be of any more help, he asked about Will.

"Why yes, indeed, Mr. Travis used to stay with us from time to time, but he has his own house now, just a short distance from here." Anticipating Jim's next question, she continued, "You'll have no trouble finding it, but he won't be there. He's out at the frontier fighting the Mexicans at Bexar and those places. There's no tellin' when he'll be back." And after a pause, "Are you a friend of his?"

Jim explained the relationship.

"Well, I'm sure he'll be mighty happy to see you. I'm sorry I don't have any more information, but you know . . . your best bet might be to ask George Huff or his son down at their store. George is a good friend of Buck's, that is, Mr. Travis, and he'd probably have as good an idea as anybody when he might get back."

After settling in, Jim's first order of business was to pay a visit to George Huff. He found the storekeeper to be a friendly and helpful man, but he had no more idea than Mrs. Peyton as to when Will—*Buck* as he was apparently known to his friends hereabouts—might be returning. So Jim went out, hoping to meet up with the Greys again, but in this too, he had no luck.

However, his search yielded other information. In waiting at Allen's Tavern, he learned that indeed he and the Greys had arrived at a time when the conflict seemed to breaking out in earnest. He heard accounts of a battle at Gonzales, a place somewhere to the west where the settlers had routed the Mexicans whom they were now confronting at San Antonio de Bexar—Bexar as most of the people in Allen's called it. It sounded as if decisive battles had taken place, or were about to. Walking back to Peyton's, Jim wondered if the revolution might already be over.

For the first night in weeks, Jim had a room, a real bedroom, to himself. After a sound sleep, he awakened eager to be out and about. Mrs. Peyton laid out a good breakfast—for Jim the best he'd had in weeks—but he was in no mood to tarry. He wanted to find out more about Travis and see if there was any news of the Greys.

Though he finished breakfast quickly, Jim lingered over his coffee a while longer, wondering just how he might go about connecting up with Will. Then, just as he was finishing, he became aware of someone standing beside the table. At first he thought one of the Greys had found him, but looked up to see a strange face. The man was impeccably groomed, his balding forehead shining in stark contrast to the mutton chop sideburns which framed the sharp features of his face. His countenance bespoke correctness, but little personal warmth. He was slight of build and wore a well-tailored suit of dark blue. It seemed to Jim that he might be a banker or a college professor . . . *if there are any hereabouts . . . or hell, maybe even a lawyer. Everybody was a lawyer!*

"Mr. Bonham?" the stranger began.

"Yes."

"Sir, my name is James Fannin," he paused and smiled. "Mrs. Peyton tells me that you were asking after Captain Travis."

So Will's a captain, Jim thought. "Why yes, I was. Are you a friend of his?"

"A comrade in arms. And yes, a friend as well." His manner casted doubt on whether, indeed, he was a friend of Will's. "And you sir, a friend?"

"Well, yes. We were boys together, but I haven't seen him since. It's been many, many years. I'm not even sure I would recognize him."

"He's hard to miss!" Fannin laughed.

Not knowing quite what Fannin meant by his remark, but continuing in the same lighthearted vein, Jim also laughed. "But it appears I have." And then realizing that Fannin was still standing, "But please excuse me, sir." Jim rose and beckoned to the chair across the table. "Have a chair, won't you? Have you had your breakfast?"

Without answering Jim's question, Fannin sat down. "Then you've come from Alabama?"

"Well, of late I am. I lived in Montgomery for most of this past year. I came here with a group from Mobile, but really I'm from South Carolina." Seeing the puzzled look on Fannin's face, Jim continued. "Will's family lived near us when we boys, but they moved to Alabama. I haven't seen him since. It was only through an unlikely coincidence that we came to be in touch with each other, and partly as a result of his urging I now find myself here!"

"Ah yes . . . well, I'm from Georgia. We must have been neighbors, too!" He laughed.

"Yes, I suppose we were. Our home's in Edgefield. Georgia's hardly a stone's throw away!"

Fannin went on to draw Jim out, eventually finding out about Jim's role during the nullification scare, and finally telling him of his own military background, including attendance at West Point for two years.

"So you commanded an artillery battery in Charleston Harbor! I passed through there at that time. We could have bumped into each other. In fact, you seem familiar to me. I wonder if we met in Charleston?"

The recollection of those days, which now seemed so long ago, brought a smile to Jim's face.

"I suppose we could have, sir, but I must confess, I do not recollect it. It was a busy place in those days!"

"Just so! But that's all past. Now we have a challenge here, which is not likely to end so peaceably."

It was hard for Jim to think of the nullification business as "peaceable," but compared to what seemed to be brewing in Texas, he had to admit to himself that it was. So he nodded as Fannin continued.

"Well, welcome to Texas Mr. Bonham. It seems all roads lead here." Then, looking over Jim's shoulder, he asked a servant who was standing nearby for a cup of coffee. They sat in silence as the coffee was poured and, watching Fannin take a careful sip from the steaming cup, Jim asked again about Will.

"Do you have news of Will? Mrs. Peyton said he was off at the frontier with the army."

"I've just come from out there myself a few days ago and yes, Travis was there."

"Did he come back with you?"

"No. He was still there when I left in an action somewhere to the south of Bexar, but I imagine he'll be back soon. We're at a standoff with the Mexicans, and things are getting fairly confused. A lot of the men are leaving."

"Leaving?"

"Yes, they want to get home. They're tired and want to get ready for planting. Everybody needs a breather while we get together a government and a real army."

"But what of the Mexicans?"

"The only real troops they have left in Texas are in

San Antonio, and they're not strong enough to do much. It'll be spring before any major force can get up there from Mexico."

"So the war is not really joined yet. From the talk at the tavern last night, it seemed as if . . . "

"It depends on who you talk with. Many of the settlers assume the Mexicans are as good as beaten, at least for now, but volunteers are coming from everywhere, looking for a war." He eyed Jim knowingly. "That's why I say things are confused, and that's why I'm here now."

"Where do you think it's all headed?"

"Well the die is cast now. For sure we've broken away from Mexico, and there's no doubt it'll take some fighting before we can make that stick with Santa Anna. He's sure to come with a real army. But by spring we'll be ready for him, maybe even cut him off before he can get back up here."

"But how are you going to get an army together? You say it's breaking up."

"It is, but that's what the Consultation was all about." Fannin explained to Jim how within the past few weeks the settlers had convened a group to address the business of forming a provisional government. They called it the Consultation and named one Henry Smith as governor and Sam Houston as major general, commanding the army. The Consultation had dissolved only days before, but not without naming a Permanent Council to carry on with their work. The Council was presently in session in San Felipe. Almost each day a pronouncement of some sort, usually addressing fund raising or organization of the military, issued forth from their deliberations.

Listening to Fannin's explanation, it seemed to Jim that in the course of the Council addressing the essential issues, there had to be a good deal of political maneuvering going on. And of course, it was not surprising.

Jim wondered where Travis might stand in all of this, and his political instincts once again flowing, Jim posed the question in an obtuse way.

"But where does that leave the forces out there in Bexar and those other places"?

Fannin didn't answer him directly, but continued, "Command is being changed, the whole thing is being reorganized."

It was clear to Jim that the conclusions suggested by the talk at the tavern the night before were ill-informed. By no means was it almost over. It was only just beginning! He had indeed arrived in Texas at a crucial time. And it was also clear why Fannin had made it his business to be here in San Felipe now. No doubt about it, the common goals of the colonists notwithstanding, factions would be forming. Jim wondered if one day soon he would have to choose sides. But bringing his thoughts back to the more immediate subject, Jim stated the obvious.

"It would seem then that the Council's deliberations must be completed quickly, if an effective army is to be put in place."

"Indeed! And I must say with your military experience, Mr. Bonham, there certainly should be a place for you in that army!"

"I came here to settle, but not without the expectation of doing my part." He then went on to explain his involvement with the Greys and concluded, "I'll certainly appreciate any suggestions you may offer."

"As a volunteer, or would you join the army?"

"I'm prepared to *volunteer* to join the army," Jim laughed. "What's the difference?"

"We make a distinction. Volunteers come and go, but when you're in the army, the commitment is more permanent."

Jim thought the distinction too finely drawn, but did not pursue the subject. In any case, he had come to

Texas to make a new life, and to him, participating in a struggle for independence seemed the natural thing to do. Nevertheless, he took from Fannin's words an understanding of the need to establish himself as a citizen lest he be considered solely an adventurer. He could see that once independence had been achieved there would likely be a strong differentiation between the settlers, the actual citizens, and the adventurers. He found it amusing that, under the present circumstances, there already seemed to be such lines being drawn although presumably, most everyone shared the goal of independence from Mexico.

Jim's ruminations were belied by a twinkle in his eye and a half smile that both puzzled and, in a way, intimidated Fannin. Picking up on Fannin's comments, Jim continued.

"Well, Mr. Fannin, however one might categorize it, I intend to seek a commission in the army *and*, when this is over, settle down hereabouts." Looking at Fannin with what he thought was a friendly smile, but which Fannin took as a kind of benign forbearance, Jim said, "Perhaps you'll be kind enough to direct me . . . "

Jim's expression and his lighthearted indifference to the distinction between joining the army and volunteering for it, created an impression in Fannin that Jim may have relegated him to the role of a petty functionary. Fannin had seen that look before during his ill-fated career at West Point, and he didn't like it. Nevertheless, he was not a man to let simple irritation get in his way, particularly since it was clearly unintended. He recognized Jim as a man of substance, moreover one from the old South who might prove useful to him in the future. Adopting a tone of cordiality, he interrupted. "Of course, of course, you can be sure that your services will be most welcome!" Fannin paused for a moment and then continued. "You should meet the governor. I'll be pleased to introduce you."

"I'd be much obliged, sir."

Then the conversation turned to more practical matters. Fannin explained that the Council met on Sundays and, therefore, the earliest opportunity to meet Governor Smith would be Monday. Had Jim but known it, he could have been entering the governor's office that very moment with Captain Burke who had indeed already arrived in San Felipe and was being received with no fanfare. But since his immediate focus was on finding Travis, the idea of meeting the governor on Monday suited him just fine. It would give him the better part of two days to get the lay of the land, particularly in what might be a complicated political landscape, and to decide what course he should pursue—he hoped with the counsel of Travis.

By the time they parted, Fannin had little more to offer as to the whereabouts of Travis except to provide a more solid base of recent information to support the belief that Will was, indeed, likely to appear in San Felipe soon. But Jim was grateful for his offer of a letter of introduction to the governor and agreed to meet him at army headquarters Monday morning to pick it up.

Jim made good use of the intervening time. San Felipe was small, and he was able to familiarize himself with the town quickly. Although the rain had subsided and some sunshine was beginning to break through, his impression of the town did not improve. The same stores, taverns, and muddy streets radiating from the boat landing, and a scattering of mostly nondescript houses—that was it. Peyton's Hotel and a few other permanent-looking buildings stood out in sharp contrast to their more shoddy neighbors. Nevertheless, the sense of energy remained, and Jim found it infectious and stimulating. The people he met were drawn to him as well. His presence was like a magnet. He was personable and, although naturally reserved, communicated a friendliness that put strangers at ease and encouraged free-flowing conversation. He had heard as much from Fannin, but he was nevertheless surprised to discover the depths of the political maneuvering evidently in progress, and even more, the frequent questions about his position on slavery.

As a Southerner, and one who was obviously of a class likely to hold slaves, his opinion seemed a lighting rod to those who were strongly partisan on both sides of the issue. Slavery was illegal in Texas, and he found opinion sharply divided as to whether it should be introduced once independence became a reality.

To him, it was a tiresome issue. He had heard it all before, had left it behind, in spirit as well as practice, and he did not want it to complicate his life or his future. To Jim, it represented the past, and although he had lived his entire life in its shadows from his boyhood days at Flat Grove to his law practice in Montgomery, he saw it as a moribund institution, certainly nothing upon which to found the economy of a new nation.

Notwithstanding his strong convictions in favor of States' rights, he found the idea of fighting for *independence*, in order to introduce *slavery*, incompatible. Nonetheless Jim would never have considered aligning himself with the abolitionists. So he adroitly sidestepped the issue whenever it arose, living with his ambivalence, and resolving to come to grips with that question at another time. All the same, he could not help but observe that the practice of indentured servitude, which *was* legal in Texas, was as a practical matter, little different than slavery.

* * *

Early Monday morning, Henry Smith, the first governor of Texas, rose to welcome Jim as he came in. He saw before him just the kind of man he hoped would be attracted to Texas and to their cause—intelligent looking, but toughened by God knows what, with a manner about him that suggested strength of character, enthusiasm, and determination. After exchanging greetings and shaking hands, Smith spoke.

"So you're a friend of Fannin's," he said as he looked at Jim carefully.

"We met each other the other day, the morning after I arrived, and he was kind enough to write that note." Jim smiled as he nodded at the paper the governor was still holding.

"But he says here that you are a friend." Smith seemed mildly puzzled.

"Well, we *do* come from the same part of the country." Jim continued to smile, but he was uneasy at learning of Fannin's gratuitous shading of the truth, and it was clear that his reply had not impressed the governor. *Not a good beginning,* Jim thought, but he continued in a lighter vein. "Then again, I make friends easily." Seeing that the governor was only mildly amused at his attempt at humor, Jim adopted a more serious attitude, and continued. "He was probably doing his best to stand in for Will Travis, whom I've not yet been able to contact."

At the mention of Travis, the governor's attitude changed visibly. More relaxed, he asked, "Then it is Travis who is your friend?"

"Well, I hope they both are." Then he explained his relationship with Travis and how he had come to be in Texas. As he was speaking, Jim began to be distracted by the expression on the governor's face—*no, not just his expression*—his very countenance; something familiar, but puzzling. Then it struck him. Jim stared at the governor in disbelief. He was staring into the face of his *mother*! The likeness was uncanny; the governor's name was Smith. *Could it be?*

Jim was stirred from his preoccupation with the governor's features as he heard him saying, "Yes, I understand you came in with some of the Mobile Greys. Captain Burke and two of his friends called on me the other day. They were most anxious to get back to Velasco and reunite with the others! Indeed they are probably there already."

Jim was relieved to hear this news, and he listened attentively as the governor explained how the Greys, like so many other volunteers, had landed at the port of Velasco, which lay at the mouth of the Brazos. Leaving his men encamped there, Burke had immediately ridden to San Felipe to officially volunteer the services of the Greys. He had also been fortunate in connecting with Jim's traveling companions on the same night they had arrived. Meeting with the governor the next morning, he had received an immediate assignment—*return to Velasco, assemble the unit and proceed to Bexar, there to report for duty to the commanding officer of the Texian forces!* Jim was happy for Burke and the others, and his feelings were evident.

"I know they will acquit themselves well, sir!" Jim said.

"I'm sure they will—they are much needed." Smith's voice trailed off. Then he began a discourse on the importance of volunteers from the United States to the cause of Texas, and the urgent need for financing. But once again, the governor's resemblance to Sophia distracted Jim to the point of losing the thread of the conversation. He heard himself giving perfunctory answers to the governor's questions about attitudes towards Texas back East and his motivation for coming to Texas. Only gradually was he able to once again focus on Smith's words.

"You say you came to Texas to start a new life. Most of us did, but now we have to get from under the Mexican yoke, or there'll be nothing here for anybody."

Jim listened, attentively now, as Smith explained with surprising frankness some of the problems he was facing. "You know we're not as united in this struggle as I would like to see, or as we need to be. Things are near chaos. There are all kinds of people here with all kinds of interests: settlers who for a long time just wanted to be left alone, but now are ready to fight; land speculators, circling like vultures; adventurers; and volunteers and good people from everywhere who have come with the loftiest of motives. Thank God for them!" He looked at Jim as if assigning him the latter category, and then, shaking his head and speaking almost to himself, he continued.

"I have to keep them all pulling together, but sometimes it's hard to remain patient. Even now, the issue is in doubt at Bexar. If we can whip the Mexicans now, it will give us the time we need, but people simply must realize that *this* is the moment to act!" He focused more directly on Jim again, and then added, "I'll tell you this, your friend Travis sees things clearly!"

As Smith went on, Jim, unfamiliar with the people and the situations being described, could only observe, "From what I've heard in the town, it certainly seems as if everyone is together on the idea of independence."

"Yes, it seems that way, but in all candor I must tell you some of them seem to have strange agendas motivated by who knows what. Nevertheless, we have to press forward and quickly! Just look at all these volunteers; they're arriving daily, with great expectations but being met with a situation full of uncertainty, unstructured. We can't even get all the units together, as with your friends. We absolutely cannot allow them to become disillusioned, or we are truly lost!"

Even though the governor seemed a bit pessimistic and even intemperate in his manner of speech, Jim could relate to his lack of patience. It was an emotion familiar to a son of Edgefield District. Moreover, the governor's words rang true, and Jim admired his singleness of purpose, a quality, Jim felt, which would serve the Texians well in the ensuing struggle. As it was clear the interview was nearing an end, Governor Smith, more relaxed now, rose, and extended his hand.

"We're glad to have you. You should offer your services directly to General Houston, and be sure he keeps me informed of your assignment!"

Jim nodded. "I will indeed, sir, and thank you!"

As he was about to turn to leave, he realized that there was something still on the governor's mind. For a moment the two stood looking at each other in silence. Then inexplicably, Smith said, "Mr. Bonham, you keep looking at me as if you'd seen a ghost." Now it was his turn to joke. "I'm not *that* intimidating, am I?"

"Forgive me, sir. It's just . . ."

"Perhaps you were expecting George Washington?" Smith laughed.

Jim joined in the laughter, and thinking, *oh, what the hell,* blurted it out.

"It's just that you bear a very strong resemblance to my mother. You could be her brother!"

"That's not likely," Smith said, surprise showing on his face, "but, who knows? Maybe we're connected somewhere in the past."

"My grandfather's name was Jacob Smith. He was from Virginia." Jim waited to see if this information struck a chord with the governor.

Smith thought for a few seconds, and then responded, "Well, I grew up in Kentucky, but you know, my father was born in Virginia. He was a minister." He thought a little longer. "But, I never heard of a *Jacob* Smith, and you'll have to admit Bonham, Smith is not exactly an uncommon name!" Both men smiled, and as Jim turned to leave, Smith said, "Well, kin or not, we're in this together now. Welcome to Texas!"

Moved by Smith's infectious enthusiasm and by nature sharing his directness, Jim somehow felt a kindred spirit, if not a kinship. His spirits rose much higher than could be discerned from the simple words he spoke as he took his leave. "Thank you, Governor; I'm truly happy to be here." And he was. Already, this place was getting under his skin. He felt he belonged here. Though in some ways it defied logic—being part of a revolution; helping to build a new country. Perhaps this was the place he had always been seeking.

Watching Jim leave, Henry Smith's own spirits lifted. The arrival in Texas of people the likes of Jim Bonham, was to him a source of great encouragement. He could sense that Jim had understood him, and he felt that he had gained a loyal ally, one who could help not only to win independence, but to build Texas afterwards.

The next day, in the same spirit in which Lafayette had volunteered to George Washington, Jim wrote a letter to Sam Houston, offering his services.

San Felipe
December 1, 1835

General S. Houston,

Permit me, through you to volunteer my services in the present struggle of Texas, without conditions. I shall receive nothing, either in the form of service pay, or lands, or rations.

Yours with great regard,

James Butler Bonham

P.S. Will you, if you please, do me the kindness of showing this letter at any leisure moment, to his Excellency the Gov.
J.B.B.

Was he *volunteering* or *joining* the army, he wondered. *Oh well, let Fannin make the distinction,* he thought as he smiled to himself.

December first was a Tuesday, and Jim's letter was read to the Council the following Thursday morning. His offer was promptly accepted, although the Council, then in the process of organizing a permanent army, was not immediately specific as to what his rank or position might be. But that was soon resolved by his first meeting with Sam Houston.

As the two men met—one younger, ever idealistic and clearly resolute, and the other a bit more canny and tempered by the years—a sense of mutual regard quickly developed. This came easily as each recognized the many values they shared, but it was their common friendship with James Hamilton, Jr., erstwhile governor of South Carolina which, when discovered, cut through the reserve normal to such meetings.

Hamilton had been a mentor to both of them: Jim as his aide during the nullification crisis, and Houston when serving under him on a committee of the Congress. Thus, it soon seemed that they were not strangers to each other, but old friends with a ready-made basis for mutual trust and loyalty. This lead Houston to ask Jim immediately to undertake recruiting duties around San Felipe.

Though he had no official standing yet, Jim began these duties. He was mildly surprised to learn that not all of the people who were flowing into Texas were readily amenable to volunteering for the army. Many came to settle, but not to fight, and of course there was more than a smattering of land speculators and opportunists of all kinds. As Jim learned more of the despotism Texians had endured over the last few years, his zeal grew. There was no doubt in his mind that he had enlisted in a just cause.

He approached his assignment with natural verve and infectious enthusiasm and soon found himself, not only becoming familiar with a broad cross section of the nascent army, but enjoying a growth in his own influence as well. His activities led him down to Velasco and Brazoria and, in the course of his movements between San Felipe and the coast, he came to know many people who would be part of his life in the coming days.

Among these were Robert Williamson, a close friend of Will's, busily engaged in organizing a mounted ranging force to patrol the frontier, and John Wharton, who with his firebrand brother would have been right at home in Edgefield. Here in Texas they had been leaders in the move for independence. Indeed, Jim and John became friends. Largely as a result of listening to John extol the virtues of Brazoria, Jim decided to settle there at the earliest opportunity.

Although he had not yet received a commission, many of the people Jim met came to call him Colonel, in deference to his past service in South Carolina, he supposed. But in fact, rank meant little to him, certainly not to an extent that it would lead him to attempt to negotiate a prestigious position for himself. All of his life he had disdained the idea of grubbing for recognition. It was to him unseemly, and he came to observe that tendency in others with a sort of benign tolerance, an attitude which, although unconscious with Jim, was sometimes mistaken as being patronizing. Nevertheless, in his day-to-day dealings with people, particularly those who had their own demons under control, he was well-liked and trusted.

Before the month was half over, news reached San Felipe that on the tenth the Texian forces which Ben Milam had rallied at Bexar, had driven the Mexican General Cós from his final redoubt in an old mission, now a fortress: the Alamo. Milam didn't survive to see the victory, but Cós and his command, having ignominiously surrendered, had been given parole and were on their way back to Mexico.

There was now no Mexican army in Texas! It was great news, and to many, it seemed the war was over; at least postponed. Certainly the sense of urgency was gone, and the settlers who had comprised a good part of the Texian military force could get back to their farms. Many had been gone for long periods of time; Christmas was coming, and spring planting would soon be upon them.

For a while after hearing the news, Jim, too, entertained the idea of a quietus. It represented an opportunity to tend somewhat to his long-term interests. He thought perhaps with Cós now sent packing back below the Rio Grande, the army structure becoming more stabilized, and a new Mexican army not likely before spring, there may be a chance to, if not practice law, at least establish a presence in Brazoria. Maybe he may even be able to have some encouraging news to send to Lila Sue. But even before the general sent for him, he knew Brazoria would have to wait.

Please report to me at your earliest convenience . . . the message had read. So now, as Jim sat across the table from Sam Houston, the pleasantries having been quickly finished, the general began.

"I'm sure you realize the victory at Bexar is at best a much needed breather. It gives us more time to better organize the military and to form a workable government. But there is no time to waste!" Jim nodded as the general continued. "As you know, Stephen Austin and others have been sent to the United States to raise funds and to recruit more volunteers, while ironically, we will soon have our hands full keeping together those who are already here. That is one of my principal concerns at the moment. We simply cannot allow these men to become restless and drift off for lack of leadership!"

Again, Jim nodded. "Yes, indeed . . ." waiting for Houston to continue.

"For example, those men whom you helped recruit in Mobile—they, and others like them, are now at Bexar, awaiting orders, but no doubt watching most of the militia disband as the settlers head for home, and all the while wondering what their own role will be."

"I'm sure that must be the case, sir."

"Well, there's more to it." Houston sighed. "At one time I put forward the idea of sending an expedition down to the south coast—under Bowie, but I haven't heard from Bowie. Now the moment for such action has passed. What we must do now is consolidate our forces, add to them, and build a real army. We may just have time to do it before the Mexicans come back, this time with a large army, and probably under the command of Santa Anna himself. Our survival depends on being ready, and let me tell you Jim, Santa Anna may not be our only problem!" Jim could only listen attentively as he waited for Houston to explain. "There's local politics afoot here; cockamamie schemes being hatched right and left. We've got little camps of people right here in the Council, anglin' for their own interests, and God knows where it will all lead!"

"General, I've been witness to this sort of wranglin' all my life. I saw what it did to Calhoun, even Hamilton, so I'm mindful of what you're saying! What can I do to help?"

"Well Jim, as soon as you can, I want you to get over to Bexar. You can go with one of the express riders, and *re-recruit* those men over there. Not just the Greys, but anybody else who will listen. Officially, you're still a civilian, so there won't be any conflict with Colonel Johnson. He's the commandant now. It's just that I want somebody I can absolutely trust to let those men know that they should stand fast, wait for my orders, and not go striking out on some fool's mission.

"Just quietly pass the word, and use your consider-able powers of persuasion. That's all. I've seen how you handle yourself around here, so just go there, follow your instincts, but do what you can to hold those men together."

"Of course, sir, I appreciate your confidence, but what then?"

"Just wait 'til you hear from me. If I have not contacted you by the end of the month, you are free to return here, or to Brazoria, as you choose. However, it is more likely that you will hear from me before then. I am intent on mobilizing the army as quickly as possible, probably at La Bahía, and I would want you there."

Though loosely formulated, Houston's orders were nonetheless clear. Jim understood well what needed to be done. As he rose to leave, he smiled.

"A tricky proposition, sir, but certainly with enough ambiguity to make it just the cup of tea for a Carolina lawyer!"

Laughing aloud, Houston responded. "Well said, Jim! I know you'll be sensitive to all the nuances of the situation. And for sure, there will be no road maps. I also want you to know that I truly appreciate what you've done in the short time you've been here." He held out his hand as he added, "And I'm well aware that you have not yet received your commission. There's a lot of politics going on, but it should be announced very soon!"

Indeed the very next day, the selection of field officers was announced. Among them were appointments of James Fannin as colonel of artillery and Travis as major. Though Jim had no expectation of being included among those higher ranks, it was a strong sign that he, too, would soon receive his commission, just as Houston had said. Jim also hoped that word of the appointments would finally bring Will to San Felipe, although by now he had little hope of seeing him before he left. Nevertheless, he was enthused at the idea of going to Bexar and looking forward to departing as quickly as possible.

But first, there were details to attend to. He had made arrangements for an announcement of his new law practice to appear in the Brazoria paper in early January, and though he was happy to set those plans aside in favor of his new assignment, he was now obliged to postpone moving his goods. Indeed he, too, would now maintain *in absentia* a storage bin at Peyton's. And of course, there were the usual preparations for the trip itself. This would keep him fully occupied with little time to speculate on Will's whereabouts.

Late the next afternoon, nearly finished with his preparations for the trip, Jim returned to Peyton's and was in the barn among the pantheon of storage bins when he turned at a noise behind him to see Fannin approaching. It was the first time he had seen him since his appointment, and the sight of Fannin already in the uniform of a colonel was an added surprise.

"Congratulations, Colonel!" Jim greeted him as Fannin stopped beside him, his face beaming.

"Thank you, thank you!" Fannin replied, hardly able to restrain his pride.

To Jim, he seemed like a new man, animated and with purpose; diffidence had been replaced with self-assurance, but Jim wondered what had brought him here. He was not long in finding out. After a few words of greeting, and confirming Houston's concerns, Fannin got right to the point.

"Now that the Mexicans have withdrawn, there is some sentiment in the government for taking the initiative and moving on Matamoros at the mouth of the Rio Grande. We can occupy the place and make it more difficult for them to move an army up to our frontier."

"How might that hold them at bay?"

"The fear of being outflanked . . ." he began as he went on to explain the strategy behind the idea. Jim listened quietly until Fannin finally concluded. "I thought you would like to be aware of this, in case you and your Alabama friends might be looking for action."

Was the recruiter being recruited? It seemed clear to

Jim that he was, so he drew Fannin out with a question, "Is this something the general wants to do ?"

"It was he who first advanced the idea, although I'm not sure where he stands at the moment."

Jim's silence mirrored his skepticism of the idea, and finally Fannin said, "Well, it's not set yet, but you might think on it." But that was not all that was on his mind. He feigned to leave, then stopped and said, "Oh, by the way, may I ask, Mr. Bonham, do you have a plantation back in Carolina?"

"My family does."

"Slaves?"

"Of course." Jim's defenses were going up.

Sensing the tension growing in Jim, Fannin smiled and asked casually, "Well, are you going to plant here?"

"I'm a lawyer, Colonel; I intend to practice the law when things settle down."

Fannin eyed him coolly. "As a lawyer you know that slavery is illegal in Mexico, but this won't be Mexico! We'll need slaves. If you or your family are interested, there'll be a real market here. I know some people . . ." Fannin stopped. What was this look of disdain on Bonham's face? This was not the kind of reaction he had anticipated from a Southern aristocrat, particularly one who had been ready to fight for nullification. Then Fannin grew silent, waiting for a reaction from Jim.

So that's his game, Jim thought. *If only . . .* he was not about to temporize with this man, but eyeing him coolly—and he hoped correctly—replied simply, almost pleasantly, "We're not in that business, Mr. Fannin, and besides, from what I've seen of Texas, it seems as if a newer way of life is in store here."

An awkward silence ensued as both men stood staring at one another, but it was quickly relieved by the entrance into the room of another man in slightly more dashing garb, not military but dashing nevertheless. Fannin turned, and welcomed the newcomer, "Why Buck! You finally made it!"

Chapter Thirteen

To Will Travis it seemed his life was entering a new phase. The revolution was a reality now. There could be no turning back. A final campaign was certainly ahead of them, but with Cós having been beaten at Bexar, the Texians busily forming an independent government, and a divorce behind him, he felt he had time and reason for taking stock of his affairs. Things all seemed to be coming together at a sort of milepost as he faced the future finally free of the marriage that he had left behind in Alabama five years before.

Now, with Rosa out of his life for good and his little son with him here in Texas, he could get serious with Rebecca Cummings. Almost since the day of Jim's arrival in San Felipe nearly three weeks earlier, Travis had been at nearby Mill Creek resting after the campaign at the frontier and planning a future with Rebecca. But the interval soon passed as events led him to repair to San Felipe. The time had come for him to look after his interests and to define his role in the coming struggle. A new army was being formed, an army organized to some degree along the lines that he himself had put forward. When news of the appointments reached him, he was chagrined to learn that he been commissioned only as first major of artillery, below James Fannin who was named lieutenant colonel. Of all the military occupations he might have had, he was least suited to that of artillerist, nor did the thought of serving as Fannin's subordinate sit well with him. He immediately drafted a letter respectfully declining the appointment and set off for San Felipe to deliver it to the governor personally.

It was only when he stopped at Peyton's Hotel that he learned of Jim's arrival in Texas; not only had he arrived but was at that very moment out in the storage shed. A pleasant and most welcome surprise! He had heard that Jim had followed Simeon to Montgomery, and when he learned from A. C. Horton that Jim was apparently none too happy there, he had written him a brief note, extolling the virtues of Texas and inviting him to come and take part in building the new country.

Jim had responded, expressing pleasure at hearing from his old friend again but indicating his intention to remain in Montgomery. Then, in letters from his family, Will had learned the sad and shocking news about Simeon and John, but had heard nothing more from Jim. It was only when Will learned that Horton was planning a recruiting trip back to Alabama that he suggested Horton contact Jim to see if he had changed his mind about coming to Texas.

Although he had finally received a short letter from Jim indicating a change of mind, he knew nothing of the Mobile Greys or when his old friend might arrive in Texas. Even though he expected one day to see Jim again, it was, nevertheless, somewhat of a surprise to find him here now only a hundred feet away.

As Will entered the shed, he was surprised to see Fannin. The tall stranger who was talking with him he knew must be Jim. As he approached, the stranger turned. Travis saw a search for recognition in his eyes.

"Jim ?"

"Will?"

"Of course!"

As the two exchanged a hearty handshake, Fannin took the opportunity to excuse himself and was quickly gone, almost without notice by the two men who had been boys together at Red Bank creek.

There was something familiar about Will, but Jim did not recognize the face from so long ago. Yet there was some elusive quality that had told him this was indeed Will Travis. He looked at him and saw nothing of the little red-headed boy, headstrong and dauntless in such feats as vaulting fences and splashing across creeks, deadly accurate at throwing rocks, and as Simeon had recently reminded him, unusually attentive at Sunday School—maybe even one of the more model students ever to attend the Red Bank Baptist Church. He was sure that were he to pass Will in the street now, he would almost certainly fail to recognize him.

Now he saw a man, not as tall as somehow he had expected and hair not red as he recollected but more brown. The young boy who resided in his memory had become a man whom he did not know. But still, there was that familiar quality . . . *what was it*? And then it came to him—*the eyes*—the look when taking aim with a rock. With this insight, the gates of memory opened further. As his imagination took over and peeled away the years, he saw more clearly the boy who had played along the creek—Will and him in their games of war, pitching horseshoes, shinnying up hickory trees, and all the other adventures that had filled their lives.

Now as grown men, they were to each other as blank pages. Although both were prepared to think the best, neither knew what the other had become.

While in Montgomery, Jim had learned that Will had become a lawyer, and had also had a fling at publishing a newspaper. Of course, he heard the stories

about Will's wife and family and his mysterious departure for Texas. Jim knew all these things, but also knew
that they were best left behind.

In the three weeks since he had arrived in San Felipe,
Jim had learned that hardly anybody called him Will
now. He was *Buck*. He spoke in a vernacular familiar to
Jim and, like Jim, seemed toughened by the road he had
traveled. He had a direct, engaging personality and, as
his letters back to Alabama had revealed, was totally
absorbed with the idea of Texas becoming an independent republic.

Will knew even less about Jim. To Will as a boy, Jim
had been bigger than life, and he seemed that way now.
Clean-cut, earnest-looking, and strong; he would have
imagined him as nothing less. But he wondered what
had really brought Jim here. Was it merely to distance
himself from the pain he must have experienced over
the last months, or a quest for adventure? *That would be
consistent with the Jim I knew as a boy*, he thought.

But Will's own experience had taught him that there
are many reasons a man may be ready for a change. No
matter, seizing common ground left over from times
gone by, Will's first words after their greeting were,
"Jim, I was terribly saddened to hear about Simeon and
John. I wish I had known them as men."

"Thank you, Will. They were, both of them, good
men, and they left behind fine families."

Will discreetly asked a bit more about Simeon's life,
but as far as Edgefield and South Carolina were concerned, he really seemed to have little interest other
than hearing the prevailing attitudes about the events in
Texas.

Jim responded as closely as possible at a level of
detail corresponding to what he gauged was the extent
of Will's interest. Then he began to question him about
Texas. He carefully avoided questions about Will's life
in Alabama, or why he had left there. But he found

Will's description of the last five years of his life in Texas to be animated, colorful, and totally absorbing. In listening, he found himself at one moment shocked at hearing of some outrage inflicted by the Mexicans and, in the next, succumbing to side-splitting laughter at some rustic tale of the frontier.

Will's narration, while deft, had also been concise. While serving the purpose of breaking down the reserve between them, it had also proved to be a great help to Jim in understanding more clearly what was going on in this chaotic place called Texas.

As they talked, both were surprised and delighted to find that—perhaps springing from their roots—they had much in common and instinctively understood each other. Though obscured by time and different life experiences, the like-mindedness was real. As they worked their way through the inevitable reminiscences of boyhood pranks and the hard benches in church, Jim came to realize that, passage of time or not, the early years in old Edgefield had forged a bond that would always be there.

In a short time, they did much to close a gap of years, seventeen crucial years in which they had traveled vastly different roads in turning from boys to men. But the afternoon was beginning to wane, and both had to get on with the business of the day. By means of drawing the conversation to a close, Will asked, "What are you doing now Jim? Are you going somewhere . . ." then adding, somewhat tentatively ". . . with Fannin?"

"No, he seems to believe that I may be some sort of patrician planter and have an interest in bringing slaves to Texas." Jim let his comment hang, and Will's failure to respond answered the unspoken question as to whether Fannin was close to Will. Changing the subject, Jim said, "I'm leaving tomorrow for Bexar."

"Bexar?" Will seemed surprised.

Jim told him how he and Horton had recruited the

Greys. He told of his long trip and activities since arriving in San Felipe, and finally of Sam Houston's determination to maintain them and others like them as cohesive units. Will listened with interest, but a look at the lengthening shadows outside the door led him to cut short the conversation.

"Then you must have as much yet to do today as I do. Suppose we meet again at supper."

Supper proved to be an even more interesting event than either had expected. They were joined at Mrs. Peyton's table by John Wharton and Jim Bowie, who had just arrived in San Felipe from Bexar. Jim had become friends with Wharton over the past several weeks, but meeting the famous Jim Bowie was an unexpected pleasure.

Bowie, a tall muscular man sporting slightly graying mutton chop side whiskers, possessed a strong presence and a high level of intelligence signaled by his hazel eyes. He reminded Jim of a merchant rather than the rough-and-tumble character he was reputed to be. He was extremely gregarious and openly held forth on all manner of issues, treating Jim as if they had known each other for years. Moreover, Bowie's observations made sense, and Jim instinctively liked him. The feeling seemed to be mutual. It was not very long into the conversation before they discovered that Sam Bowie, Julia's husband, was related to this very same Bowie, this renowned Indian fighter who sat across the table from him. The discovery called for another round of drinks and further animated the conversation. But they did not linger long on reminiscences or speculation about family ties.

Things were happening fast around San Felipe, and there was a good deal to discuss about the current situation. Will and Bowie gave detailed accounts of recent actions at the frontier, comments which both informed and fascinated Jim. Finally the subject of an expedition to Matamoros came up, the same idea to which Houston had alluded in his meeting with Jim. It was then that Bowie, having heard Jim describe the mission on which he was about to embark, sagely observed that a certain Dr. Grant had come to San Felipe seeking support for the Matamoros idea. He noted that Sam Houston, probably smelling a rat, was anxious to consolidate what troops he had before they were sent off on what all at the table considered to be an ill-advised adventure.

Bowie would not learn until the next day that Sam Houston had originally intended for him to lead such a force. And though the general had abandoned the idea, the seeds had been sown and would soon sprout a thorny fruit. Indeed it now seemed that support or nonsupport of the expedition might become a manifestation of the differences within the Council. The men at the table were all well aware of the internal strife that was developing as a new government struggled to emerge. So it was with some satisfaction that they embraced the camaraderie that developed as their paths briefly crossed over supper that night. If sides were to be taken among the Texians, each knew that they were all brothers in the camp of Governor Smith and Sam Houston.

Eventually, drink and the lateness of the hour took their tolls, and the conversation turned to less weighty matters. It ended as John Wharton made a toast to Jim as the newest Texian among the group. He told the story of how he had to guarantee that the fish would bite and the mosquitoes wouldn't, in order to persuade Jim to one day soon set up his law practice in Brazoria. They all had a hearty laugh.

"You have to watch these Wharton boys; once they get their minds set on something, they never quit," Will said.

Never at a loss for words, Jim said, "Something tells

me I'm in the company of more than one person with those talents. I'll try to measure up!"

The good humor and conviviality, which remained with them as dinner ended, told Jim that he had found friends and comrades with whom he could fight a war and build a country. He slept well that night.

CHAPTER FOURTEEN

Will's accounts of recent events were still in Jim's thoughts as he made his way toward Bexar. Between these and the cryptic, almost ominous, orders from General Houston that had set him out on this journey, he had much to think about. But his speculations led nowhere. He would simply have to follow the road and see where it led. Meanwhile, he was fascinated by the changing countryside. He had never seen land like this. The eastern part of Texas and San Felipe had much the same look as the places he had always known. But as he and Joe Barnes, the express rider, moved west, the changing terrain increasingly filled his consciousness.

The forests gave way to more open country with longer vistas, and the streams became narrower and clearer. At first there were rolling prairies dotted with live oaks, and moss disappeared from the trees as they began to be smaller. Then the land gradually became rockier and more hilly, and the vegetation began to include cactus and mesquite.

At night the near-full moon seemed fuller. It was getting colder. Even the air changed; it was fresher, and altogether appropriate to the grand expansiveness of it all. Jim could feel a rising sense of adventure, almost as intense as in those boyhood days with his brothers and Will. Although nothing like the woodlands inhabited by the Lady of the Lake, and certainly like nothing else that had ever made its way into his imagination, the land was having a strong impact on him.

Jim found exhilaration in just being there. He found himself repeatedly stifling the impulse to urge Sal into a mad dash across the open land for the sheer fun and freedom of it. He knew he had found the kind of place he had always sought.

Eventually they came to the crest of a small hill, and there, spread before them, was a town different than any Jim had ever seen. His pulse quickened as he realized that he was looking at San Antonio de Bexar. Smaller than he had expected—perhaps by comparison with the scale of the natural surroundings—it was a real town nonetheless. It was dominated by the towers of a cathedral, and though many of the buildings were little more than mud huts, the entire scene had a look of stone, almost as if it had been carved out of the landscape . . . or grown there.

Unlike the shantytown look of decaying wooden buildings in San Felipe and other settlements in the east, it conveyed a sense of permanence, of being as one with its setting. After all, he reminded himself, it was an historic bastion, the principal foothold of Spain and then Mexico in Texas for over one hundred years. There certainly had been time enough to develop a presence in the landscape.

Exotic to Jim's eyes, or maybe because it was Christmas Eve, the calciferous patina of the place made Jim think of how Bethlehem must have looked. *An odd thought*, it seemed, *if only we had arrived at night under the stars.*

"What are you smiling at, Jim?" Barnes asked.

"Oh, nothing," he replied instinctively; then feeling obliged to formulate words to explain where his train of thought had led him, he added, "I was just thinking, tomorrow is my brother's birthday."

"I had no idea you came from such a well-known family!" Barnes exclaimed as he laughed aloud.

Jim laughed, too, as he thought of Luke who would now be twenty-two, and how Christmas had always been special at Red Bank, where irreverent jokes of celebrating two birthdays had long been part of the tradition.

As they moved down the road toward town, Jim noticed a walled compound, which they would soon pass. At about the same time as he began to realize what this must be, Barnes, as if reading Jim's mind, spoke up.

"That there's the Alamo. It's probably where your friends are."

"I expect you're right, Joe!"

As this point, the two said their farewells. Barnes continued on across the nearby river into Bexar, and Jim nudged Sal towards the Alamo.

Passing through the gates of the old mission, he could see why it had come to be used as a fort, albeit one in great need of repair. The walled perimeter and the heights of the old chapel, as well as the commanding views in all directions, suited such a purpose. But there was less activity within the walls than Jim had anticipated. A few groups of men, obviously Americans, some horses, some Mexican women going about various chores, and in the distant reaches of the compound even a few tents.

The men turned indifferent faces to the newcomer, while the women ignored him completely. The resident horses, however, showed a great deal of interest, whinnying and snorting as he approached. Indeed some of them seemed familiar and all were most certainly intent on welcoming Sal. The entrance to the chapel was at his right, and beyond it loomed the end of a long building that extended away from them and seemed to be the center of what activity there was.

The nonchalance of the men nearby gave way to interest at the commotion with the horses, and then to excitement as one of them shouted, "It's Jim! Jim Bonham!" Whereupon two other men joined the man who had recognized Jim and came running. As it happened, these were the same Greys who had ridden with Jim from Mobile. As they gathered around, the reunion was soon in full sway, punctuated by handshakes all around and much conversation. They soon attracted the attention of everyone and brought smiles even to the faces of the women.

From within a building, which extended along the perimeter wall at the left of the compound, there emerged a man of perhaps thirty who looked friendly but harried. Slight of build, with sandy-colored hair and hazel eyes, he wore a uniform but with no insignia of rank. He flashed a homespun grin that came easily, and speaking as if to an old friend said, "Welcome! Would I be right in guessing that you're Colonel Bonham?"

"Indeed I am, sir, and you are?"

"Lieutenant Colonel William Neill." He was the same Colonel Neill who barely a fortnight before had played a major role in the defeat of General Cós in this very fortress, and now found himself second in command of the garrison of Bexar. After introducing himself, Neill continued, "I've heard tales of your ride from Alabama, so I feel like I know you."

"Lord knows what those boys told you, but I'm happy to be here!"

"Well, we've got quarters right here, and I can have someone tend your mare." Neill turned to signal a man standing nearby, but Jim interrupted.

"Thanks, Colonel, but I'll settle her down myself, and I do appreciate your offer of quarters!"

"Then follow me." Neill smiled as he led Jim to the gate of the nearby corral.

It was only a matter of minutes before Sal was unburdened and sharing the water trough with her old friends. Jim and Neill watched silently for few moments. Then they walked the short distance to the stairway, which led to the small room Neill had assigned him. Pausing there and thinking Neill was about to take his leave, Jim turned to thank him for his hospitality. By then Neill's grin was fading and his continued cordiality barely concealed an underlying anxiety, a restlessness that was confirmed by his voice as he spoke.

"So, Mr. Bonham, do you have any news for us?"

Jim wasn't sure how to answer the question, and as he pondered where to begin, Neill continued.

"Captain Burke and his men have been wondering what became of you, but they all seemed to think that you would eventually find your way out here!"

Jim briefly described his activities since arriving in San Felipe, and how he came to be in Bexar. Neill listened to his story with great interest and seemed to be considering carefully what his next question might be. But Jim saved him the trouble.

"General Houston is most anxious that the Greys and other volunteer units remain together and available to be assimilated into the new army. I suppose he felt that owing to my association with the Greys, I could help David Burke keep them together."

"Then you'll be with the Greys?"

"No, I'm not really a member of the Greys, but I helped organize them, so I guess they're stuck with me until things become a little more clear."

Clarity is what Neill wanted too, and he listened

attentively as Jim continued. "As to myself, my status is uncertain. Earlier this month the Council accepted my offer to serve, and as I explained, I've been helping with recruiting in San Felipe ever since. I suppose this assignment is part of it but, as of now, I hold no rank, although I suppose they will get around to offering me a commission soon.

"But for the present, as I told you, I've been asked to do whatever I can to persuade newly arriving volunteers not to wander off. The general asked me to remain here until I hear further from him. If no such word arrives by the end of the month, I'm free to return to San Felipe. Actually, I'll be going to Brazoria, because I've decided to set up my practice there. I'm a lawyer."

Neill seemed somewhat relieved as he responded, "Well Mr. Bonham, I'm pleased to hear that General Houston recognizes that there is a problem. Let me say that you may find your task with the Greys and the others a little more difficult than you might have expected." Then addressing the questioning look on Jim's face, he said, "You will find . . . in fact I'm sure Captain Burke has already discovered . . . that there is a great deal of pressure on the men—all kinds of promises of booty and adventure—to join in an expedition to Matamoros. If they do so in any substantial numbers, it will leave this place essentially undefended!"

Matamoros again! But all Jim said was, "Pressure? By whom?"

Neill did not answer Jim's question directly, but continued, "Since the Mexican army left, many of our people have assumed that this is over for a while, but let me tell you—it is *not*! General Cós is Santa Anna's brother-in law, and Santa Anna will not let his disgrace go unavenged, much less allow the revolution to succeed. He'll return —and soon. And when he does, he will bring a powerful army. Just ask the locals. They know!"

"I've heard about this Matamoros expedition, and I know it's causing some concern."

"Indeed! The volunteers are stewing in their own juices. Most of them, like the Greys, came from the United States and have no place to go. In fact their numbers continue to grow, and hanging about amidst inactivity and indecision does not suit them. They are ripe for recruitment into any seemingly attractive scheme that comes along!"

"But who would lead them?"

Neill looked uncomfortable, as if he were squirming to get out of his skin.

"Well, it's being pushed by a certain Dr. Grant. In fact, he is in San Felipe now seeking approval of the Council to lead the expedition. That leads me to ask if you have any news of what level of support might exist for it back there."

"I'm afraid I can be of little help. I have heard mention of Dr. Grant, but that's about all. As to the level of political support for the expedition, I have no way of judging it, but I suppose there's enough to cause Sam Houston to give me this assignment." After a pause, Jim continued. "I can tell you that San Felipe is beset with all sorts of politicking and jockeying, not to mention the activities of land speculators and others who seem to have no interest in fighting. They smell opportunities everywhere.

"Generally though, I would say the idea of independence is strong, and most everyone realizes there's no turning back. Even so, I suppose internal conflicts are to be expected. But amidst all this, I can assure you that both Governor Smith and General Houston recognize the need to quickly consolidate the army and establish a comprehensive plan to pursue the campaign. It's hard to believe that either of them would countenance leaving the frontier undefended. Wouldn't you agree Colonel, that my mission seems to confirm that conviction?"

"Indeed it does, and I'm pleased to hear it. But there's another aspect to all of this."

"What do you mean?"

Again, showing his discomfort, he said, "I'm sorry to say it, but I fear that our commanding officer, Colonel Johnson, is in league with Dr. Grant, in which case it will be most difficult to resist any action he may take in support of the scheme. I even feel disloyal mentioning it."

The whole situation became immediately clear to Jim. Colonel Johnson, being close with Grant, would himself embark on the expedition, taking with him both men and materiel from Bexar. If that happened, Bexar would be almost defenseless against a Mexican army which was sure to come. It was not a long leap for Jim to conclude that Sam Houston's concerns had been well founded. He sympathized with Neill whom he took to be an honorable officer. But Jim felt no constraints in questioning such action by Johnson.

"You do indeed seem to be in an untenable situation, Colonel. But I am not subject to Colonel Johnson's orders, and I assure you I will have no hesitation in doing everything in my power to persuade the Mobile Greys and anyone else who will listen to me to remain here and wait to hear from General Houston!"

Neill was relieved at Jim's declaration but was uncomfortable in further speculation about what Colonel Johnson might do. As it was clear to Neill that he and Jim were like-minded, he was satisfied to leave matters at that. He felt no threat when finally, in observance of the formalities, Jim asked, "Is Colonel Johnson about? I really should pay my respects to him."

"Of course, but you won't find him here. His headquarters are in the Plaza Santa Ynez at the end of Potrero Street over in the town. It may be better for you to find him on your own, and it will be no trouble. Plenty of our men are in town, and everybody knows the place."

"Well, I suppose I'll find him one way or another."

"I agree you should try, but if you miss him, don't worry. He's hosting Christmas dinner here tomorrow, and certainly you will be welcome!"

Just then Burke, who had gotten word of Jim's arrival, appeared, and a second reunion ensued. As the greetings and small talk subsided, Neill took his leave. Within minutes, Burke suggested that they cross the river and go into Bexar. Soon, they were walking along catching up on the news and trading impressions of Texas.

For Burke, it was a welcome opportunity to unburden himself. He revealed that his men had indeed been approached by none other than Colonel Johnson, and several had found the idea of pressing on to Matamoros an attractive prospect. But Burke was satisfied that he had squelched the idea and readily pledged to Jim that he would be able to hold the Greys together and await the orders of Sam Houston.

Within the town itself, there were not only more people but a heightened sense of excitement, even tension. Was it because Cós was gone? Or because the people knew there would soon be retaliation? Jim could not tell. Maybe it was simply because of Christmas. Whatever it was, it was mildly intoxicating. It was a refreshing change from the austere life of the last several months, even the languid mood within the Alamo, and certainly the political intrigue in San Felipe. Perhaps it was the obvious cultural difference, manifested in everything around him. Nevertheless, Americans were everywhere, and they seemed to be readily accepted by the local population.

Almost immediately Burke spotted some of the other Greys down a side street, and at Jim's insistence went off to join them. He knew that Burke would prefer to avoid the meeting with Johnson, and Jim, too, felt it might be better to meet the commandant alone. As he made his way down the street, he did not go unnoticed, particularly by some of the young women to whom this tall and handsome stranger was as exotic as he found them. More than one of them caught his eye, and he was reminded that a good deal of joy and laughter had been missing from his life for some time now. Until that moment he had not realized how the separation from Lila Sue and the deaths of John and Simeon had overshadowed all else in his life. But now, in the streets of Bexar, the clouds had lifted. He felt he belonged here, and the struggle for Texas was his.

It being Christmas Eve, Jim was not surprised when he found that Colonel Johnson was not at his headquarters. He was happy not to have to deal with him this evening. After his conversation with Neill, he felt that his meeting with Johnson would be strained. In any case, he was anxious to explore the town on his own.

The nearby plaza opened into an even larger main plaza, which was beginning to fill with people. As evening approached, fires began to spring up, little spots of warmth in the growing crispness, and perfuming the air with the distinctive smell of mesquite embers. People cooked or merely tried to stay warm as they began the Christmas vigil before celebration of midnight mass in the cathedral, which dominated the plaza.

It was quite different from the customs he knew. Except for this gathering and what seemed like an extraordinary proliferation of candles everywhere, there was little evidence of other observances of Christmas throughout the town.

He lingered in the plaza for a while, taking it all in, enjoying the strain of guitars from various quarters, all somehow in concert with each other. Occasionally he exchanged greetings with various Americans; there were all kinds from everywhere. Some of them he had met in San Felipe during the last few weeks.

But even the ubiquitous presence of his countrymen did not prepare him for the surprise which awaited him. Coming down the street towards him were two Americans, by now a common sight. He hardly took notice of them, but as they approached, one of them became increasingly familiar. Then suddenly, for a brief moment, he thought he was back in Pendleton. It was Sam Maverick! They recognized each other at about the same time and rushed forward to exchange greetings. Sam's companion was Bill Casey, a young lieutenant who introduced himself as Colonel Neill's adjutant. The surprise and pleasure of seeing such a familiar face lifted Jim's spirits all the more. He and Sam both found themselves standing there laughing while Casey looked on in amusement.

Meanwhile the street was becoming increasingly noisy, and conversation was out of the question. They ducked into a nearby cantina. By the time they were half finished with a second drink, Casey had left, and they had pretty much caught up with each other's lives since Pendleton. As the conversation moved to the present, it was not long before Sam confirmed the concerns which Jim had heard expressed earlier by Neill. Although he, too, had volunteered to serve with the military, Sam's reason for being in Bexar was as a settler, and a most committed one at that. Even though the next day was Christmas, he was eagerly anticipating consummating a purchase of land.

For the moment he was a free agent, and like Jim, not subject to Johnson's orders. Unrestrained by the inhibitions exhibited by Neill, he painted a much more sinister picture of the mischief being hatched by Dr. Grant and Colonel Johnson. As they finished a final glass, Jim laughed as he summed up their resolve: "Two Carolina lawyers ought to be able to find a way to frustrate these two scoundrels."

"Amen brother!" Sam laughed as they made their way back out into what had become a cold Christmas Eve. "Do you have a place to stay Jim? You are welcome at my house."

"I would accept your offer Sam, but under the circumstances, I'd better stick close to the Greys in the Alamo. In fact, I should probably find their captain soon, before he gets totally drunk, and get him back over there!"

"You're right, Jim, but old friend, I'm happy that you're here. Merry Christmas!"

"And the same to you, Sam!"

As they parted, Jim continued on down the street, his only mission now to find David Burke. And find him he did, just a few doors away in another cantina, where the level of celebration was a bit more intense. Although the laughter and music beckoned, Jim realized he wanted nothing now more than some rest. It had been a long day, and he was happy to find that Burke was similarly disposed. They decided to call it a day and made their way back to less festive environs of the Alamo.

Christmas day dawned clear and mild. Save the sense of a certain stillness echoing from the town across the river, it seemed like any other day. But the serenity suggested by the silence was not to be. Early on, Burke and the captains of some of the other volunteers met and drafted a proclamation in which they officially expressed their unwillingness to turn over their weapons and supplies to requisition by anyone. Their loud remonstrations left no doubt of their uneasiness with the situation. But the action of the commanders put Johnson in a bad mood, and Christmas dinner that afternoon proved to be an unpleasant affair, beset with tension to the point that the only thing good about it was that it eventually ended. It gave Jim a chance to meet Frank Johnson, however. He took an instant dislike to him, feeling that such would have been the case even had there been no prior discussions with Sam and Neill. Johnson seemed full of pretensions, took on airs in his manner of speech, which fell far short of being supported by the content. He boastfully assumed much of the credit for the victory over the Mexicans earlier in the month and spoke openly of the rewards and strategic necessity of marching on Matamoros.

Listening to Johnson, Jim was more than ever convinced that a Matamoros expedition could only be the worse sort of folly, and that he and Sam were right in their vow to do whatever they could to discourage the men from joining it.

The next day also proved eventful. Late in the morning an express arrived in which Jim received a message from Travis. It was short, but along with it was an important document. It was notification of Jim's having been commissioned a lieutenant of the legion of cavalry in the Army of Texas. Not the artillery, but the cavalry! Obviously, his fine horse and his horsemanship had not gone unnoticed. The document was dated December 20, the same day he had departed San Felipe. Within it was also news of several other appointments, including William Barret Travis as lieutenant colonel of cavalry.

So now it was official: Jim was in the army! . . . *and Will is my commanding officer!* In his note, Will congratulated Jim on his appointment and passed along a message from Sam Houston, in which the general asked that Jim remain in Bexar pending further orders, and vigorously continue in the assignment that had brought him there. Jim took this as a sign of increasing turmoil within the Council, and in light of what he had learned since coming to Bexar, it seemed likely that Dr. Grant's presence in San Felipe may well have had something to do with it.

So Jim set about his task with an increased sense of urgency. The next few days were spent in a kind of maneuvering every bit as Byzantine as that taking place in San Felipe. The loyalists were identified—Sam, Casey, Jameson—the indefatigable engineer who would come to be a good friend, of course Burke, and others. They did all they could, short of outright mutiny, to support the idea of the garrison remaining intact at Bexar awaiting the orders of General Houston.

All the while, Johnson continued to elaborate more on the Matamoros expedition. While he often seemed to vacillate, sometimes proclaiming his concurrence that it made little sense, he was clearly enamored with the idea and anxious to learn the outcome of Grant's efforts in San Felipe. Politics had indeed arrived at the frontier.

Relief for Jim finally came when, on the thirtieth of the month, he received a direct message from Sam Houston. In it, the general explained that he had directed Johnson to make known to the captains of all lately arrived volunteer companies that they should assemble their units and proceed at the earliest opportunity to the *presidio* of La Bahía in Goliad, where a general mobilization of the army would soon take place. Jim was to informally assure that the word did indeed reach the volunteers. Then he was to proceed to La Bahía, there to await the arrival of Houston and do what he could to rally other straggling forces he might encounter.

Johnson wasted no time in spreading the word among the volunteers, and it gave Jim hope that Johnson might be giving up on Matamoros. Though Houston's plan would inevitably lead to a reduction in the size of the cadre at Bexar, Johnson did not seem troubled at the prospect, and Neill accepted it in the spirit of being for the greater good of the cause. Burke and the Greys were heartened by the news, and with some others of the volunteers, were ready to depart within hours. They, with Jim, left for La Bahía the very next day.

CHAPTER FIFTEEN

The *presidio* of La Bahía had been established by the Spaniards over a century before as they made their way up the San Antonio River from the coast. It could be reached in less than a day from Copano Bay and became a sort of gateway to a large part of Texas. A sound fortress located between Bexar and Copano Bay, its military significance increased as the Texians prepared to fight for their independence.

The town of Goliad had grown up nearby. Like Bexar, some ninety miles to the north, Goliad was on the northerly edge of the great desert that separated central Mexico from the settlements in east Texas: places like Nacogdoches, Anahuac, and San Felipe, populated mostly by Americans. To them, Goliad and Bexar were the frontier. Although Bexar was more important strategically, La Bahía, because of its proximity to the coast and to the relatively secure towns along the eastward thrust of the coastal bend, was a more suitable place to assemble an army.

As they arrived at La Bahía, Jim and the others were met by Captain Philip Dimitt, commander of the garrison and a man whose *bona fides* in the revolution were well-established. Dimitt had played a key role in the assault against Cós in Bexar in December and also in provisioning the Texian army during the siege leading up to it. Moreover, he also held the distinction of having designed the flag, which some were to call the first flag of independent Texas—an arm holding a bloody sword. That flag flew over La Bahía as Jim and the Greys rode in. They found what seemed a viable and cohesive force under Dimitt, and he received the Greys as a welcome addition to the garrison.

But they had not been there long before discovering that many of the men assembled in La Bahía had heard of the Matamoros expedition and were anxious to join it. Nor would they have long to wait for the opportunity, because within days of the arrival of the Greys, Dr. Grant and his force arrived.

An arrogant man, Dr. Grant presented himself as the duly appointed senior officer of Texian forces and proceeded to commandeer horses and supplies of all kinds for his march to Matamoros. To avoid open conflict between his men and those following Grant, Dimitt acquiesced to these demands. But with the help of Jim and Burke and others loyal to Smith and Houston, Dimitt was able to persuade most of the volunteers then at La Bahía to remain there.

But many followed Grant, and as he departed, he left in his wake doubt and confusion. Disgusted, Dimitt rallied the remains of his own original force and withdrew to the east. He left what remained of the garrison under the command of P. S. Wyatt, captain of another volunteer unit from Alabama that had preceded the Greys to Texas.

But Wyatt's command was fragile indeed. Confusion abounded; direction was lacking; rumors were rampant; there was no money to pay them. The situation was complicated by impending shortages of all kinds. Thus, the only impact the Matamoros expedition was ever to have was the disruption and depletion of the Texian forces on the frontier.

Under these circumstances, the confidence of those remaining at La Bahía was severely strained. Many were close to leaving, but even amid the confusion and anxiety, it was clear to all that the *presidio* remained the focal point for assembling the army, and no one could deny a sense of impending action was palpable. Something was going to happen, something *had* to happen *soon*.

Jim reinforced this feeling among the men by forthrightly sharing with them his own orders from Sam Houston and by using all of his lawyerly skills to make the case for patience and loyalty. Most of the men agreed with him and believed that they could look forward to seeing Sam Houston himself in La Bahía very soon. But with the passing of each day, the situation became more difficult. Even Jim and Burke and the others who were working hard to hold the force together were beginning to wonder if the revolution were falling apart.

Thus it was a source of great relief and encouragement when one day Jim Bowie rode into the fortress. He had come from San Felipe, and his reputation alone made his presence a positive event. Moreover, he confirmed their hopes that things would soon change. He assured everyone who would listen that the governor and General Houston were addressing the issues of supply and pay, and that General Houston himself would soon arrive to take charge of the situation.

Bowie's arrival relieved the sagging confidence of the men. His words proved to be prophetic as, only a few days later, Sam Houston arrived in La Bahía. Everyone was heartened at the sight of the general, although they could not but soon notice that he was in a state of high dudgeon.

It was a difficult time for Sam Houston. The political struggle in San Felipe was intensifying just at the time when his presence with the army was essential. His absence from the center of political activity further encouraged mischief by enemies of whom he was then only barely aware and, as a result, the nascent republic was very much in danger of being stillborn. It had been only while en route to Goliad that he had discovered Grant had actually embarked on the Matamoros expedition.

This was the first of a series of even more distressing revelations he would experience in the coming days. Nor was he long in waiting for the next. An express from Colonel Neill finally caught up with the general at La Bahía, and from it he learned of all that had happened since Jim and the Greys had departed Bexar. Johnson, too, had gone off to join Grant, and between them they had taken many of the men and most of the weapons, ammunition, and other goods from the Alamo. They had left the place with only a handful of healthy men and very few supplies. Moreover, Neill reported, he had received what he considered to be reliable intelligence that Santa Anna was well-along towards mobilizing an army and would soon be marching into to Texas. Neill needed reinforcements and supplies of all kinds—and quickly!

Sam Houston liked to keep his options open as long as possible, but now he had to act. Neill needed immediate reinforcement, and it was evident that the garrison of La Bahía had to be quickly consolidated and supplied as well. He also had to determine whether both the Alamo and La Bahía were defensible over the long run. While he could see the conditions in La Bahía and around Goliad for himself, he needed to know more about the situation in Bexar. So he ordered James Bowie to form a relief force, proceed to the Alamo, and report his assessment of the viability of that post as quickly as possible. Not only were Bowie's skill and loyalty unquestionable, but the general trusted his judgment. He had but one reservation: concern with Bowie's health. And without drawing too sharp a point on it, he addressed that concern by asking Jim Bonham to accompany the detachment.

The men liked and respected Jim, as did the general, and he was confident that should unforeseen problems arise, the Carolinian would know what to do. His only orders to Jim were to "accompany Colonel Bowie and do whatever you can to assist him and to consolidate the forces in Bexar. You understand the situation." Not much of a brief, but all that Jim needed.

Only thirty men were available to join the detachment. As General Houston watched them leave, he wondered how many Mexican troops at this moment might also be marching in the direction of Bexar, and how long before they would arrive. It was then mid-January, and he reckoned that he had at least two months.

But meanwhile, mischief was being wrought in San Felipe. It would only be during the coming fortnight after he returned to his headquarters at Washington-on-the-Brazos that Houston would be able to know fully what had happened, and be able to sum it all up in a letter to Governor Smith.

Municipality of Washington
Jan. 30, 1836

Sir - I have the honor to report to you that in obedience to your order under date of the 6th instant, I left Washington on the 8th, and reached Goliad on the night of the 14th. On the morning of that day I met Capt. Dimitt, on his return home with his command, who reported to me the fact, that his caballada of horses, the most of them private property, had been pressed by Dr. Grant, who styled himself acting commander-in-chief of the federal army, and that he had under his command about two hundred men. Capt. Dimitt had been relieved by Captain P. S. Wyatt of the volunteers from Huntsville, Alabama. I was also informed by Major R. C. Morris that breadstuff was wanted in camp, and he suggested his wish to remove the volunteers further west. By express I had advised the stay of the troops at Goliad until I could reach that point.

On my arrival at that post I found them destitute of many supplies necessary to their comfort on a campaign. An express reached me from Lieutenant-Colonel Neill, of Bexar, of an expected attack from the enemy in force. I immediately requested Colonel James Bowie to march with a detachment of volunteers to his relief. He met the request with his usual promptitude and manliness. This intelligence I forwarded to your Excellency for the action of government. . . .

The general then went on to recount his continuing activities, and then returned to the subject immediately at hand.

. . . I found much difficulty in prevailing on the regulars to march until they had received either money or clothing; and their situation was truly destitute. Had I not succeeded, the station at Goliad must have been left without any defense, and abandoned to the enemy, whatever importance its occupation may be to the security of the frontier. Should Bexar remain a military post, Goliad must be maintained, or the former will be cut off from all supplies arriving by sea at the port of Copano.

On the evening of the 20th, F. W. Johnson, Esq., arrived at Refugio, and it was understood that he was empowered by the General Council of Texas to interfere in my command. On the 21st, and previous to receiving notice of his arrival, I issued an order to organize the troops so soon as they might arrive at that place, agreeably to the "ordinance for raising an auxiliary corps" to the army. A copy of the order I have the honor to enclose herewith. Mr. Johnson then called on me, previous to the circulation of the order, and showed me the resolutions of the General Council, dated 14th of January, a copy of which I forward for the perusal of your Excellency.

So soon as I was made acquainted with the nature of his mission, and the powers granted to J.W. Fannin, Jr., I could not remain mistaken as to the object of the Council, or the wishes of individuals. I had but one course left for me to pursue (the report of your being deposed had also reached me) which was, to return and report myself to you in person inasmuch as the objects intended by your order were, by the extraordinary conduct of the Council, rendered useless to the country; and, by remaining with the army, the Council would have had the pleasure of ascribing to me the evils which their own conduct and acts will, in all probability, produce. I consider the acts of the Council calculated to protract the war for years to come; and the field which they have opened to insubordination and to agencies without limit (unknown to military usage) will cost the country more useless expenditure than the necessary expense of the whole war would have been, had they not transcended their proper duties. Without integrity of purpose, and well devised measures, our whole frontier must be exposed to the enemy. All the available resources of Texas are directed, through special as well as general agencies, against Matamoros; and must, in all probability, prove as unavailing to the interest as they will to the honor of Texas. The regulars at Goliad cannot long be detained at that station unless they should get supplies, and now all the resources of Texas are placed in the hands of agents unknown to the government in its formation, and existing by the mere will of the Council; and will leave all other objects, necessary for the defense of the country, neglected, for the want of means, until the meeting of the Convention in March next. . . .

The letter continued with a dissertation on the dilemmas posed by the actions of the council, then returned to the subject of Matamoros.

... After the capitulation of Bexar, it was understood at headquarters that there was much discontent with the troops then at that point, and that it might be necessary to employ them in some active enterprise, or the force would dissolve. With this information was suggested the expediency of an attack on Matamoros. For the purpose of improving whatever advantages might have been gained at Bexar, I applied to your Excellency for orders, which I obtained, directing the adoption of such measures as might be deemed best for the protection of the frontier and the reduction of Matamoros. ...

After summarizing why he had at first proposed, then abandoned, the idea of a Matamoros expedition, Houston then returned to the subject of his chagrin with the Council.

... members of the Council were engaged in writing letters to individuals in Bexar, urging and authorizing a campaign against Matamoros, and that their recommendations might bear the stamp of authority, and mislead those who are unwilling to embark in an expedition not sanctioned by government, and led by private individuals, they took the liberty of signing themselves members of the Military Committee; thereby deceiving the volunteers, and assuming a character which they could only use or employ in the General Council in proposing business for the action of that body. They could not be altogether ignorant of the impropriety of such conduct, but doubtless could easily find a solid justification in the bullion of their patriotism and the ore of their integrity. Be their motive whatever it might, many brave and honorable men were deluded by it, and the campaign was commenced upon Matamoros under Dr. Grant, as "Acting" Commander-in-Chief of the Volunteer Army— a title and designation unknown to the world.
... Then who is Dr. Grant? Is he not a Scotchman who has resided in Mexico for the last ten years? Does he not own large possessions in the interior? Has he ever taken the oath to support the Organic Law? Is he not

deeply interested in the hundred-league claims of land which hang like a murky cloud over the people of Texas? Is he not the man who impressed the property of the people of Bexar? Is he not the man who took from Bexar, without authority or knowledge of the government, cannon and other munitions of war, together with supplies necessary for the troops at that station, leaving the wounded and sick destitute of needed comforts? Yet this is the man whose outrages and oppressions upon the rights of the people of Texas are sustained and justified by the acts and conduct of the General Council.

Several members of that body are aware that the interests and feelings of Dr. Grant are opposed to the independence and true interests of the people of Texas. While every facility has been afforded to the meditated campaign against Matamoros, no aid has been rendered for raising a regular force for the defense of the country, nor one cent advanced to an officer or soldier of the regular army, but every hindrance thrown in the way....

More vituperation expressed by the general, then,

It now becomes my duty to advert to the powers granted by the General Council to J. W. Fannin, Jr., on the 7th of January, 1836, and at a time when two members of the Military Committee, and other members of the council, were advised that I had received orders from your Excellency to repair forthwith to the frontier of Texas, and to concentrate the troops for the very purpose avowed in the resolutions referred to. The powers are as clearly illegal as they were unnecessary. By reference to the resolutions it will be perceived that the powers given to J. W. Fannin, Jr., are as comprehensive in their nature, and as much at variance with the Organic Law and the decrees of the General Council, as the decrees of the General Congress of Mexico are at variance with the federal constitution of 1824, and really delegate to J. W. Fannin, Jr., as extensive powers as those conferred by that Congress upon General Santa Anna; yet the cant is kept up, even by J. W. Fannin, Jr., against the danger of a regular army, while he is exercising

powers which he must be satisfied are in open violation
of the Organic Law. J. W. Fannin, Jr., is a Colonel in the
regular army, and was sworn in and received his commission on the very day that the resolutions were adopted
by the Council. By his oath he was subject to the orders
of the commander-in-chief, and as a subaltern could not,
without an act of mutiny, interfere with the general
command of the forces of Texas; yet I find in the "Tele-
graph" of the 9th inst. a proclamation of his, dated on the
8th, addressed, "Attention, Volunteers!" and requiring
them to rendezvous at San Patricio. No official character
is pretended by him, as his signature is private. This he
did with the knowledge that I had ordered the troops
from the mouth of the Brazos to Copano, and had re-
paired to that point to concentrate them. On the 10th
inst. F. W. Johnson issued a similar proclamation, announcing Matamoros as the point of attack. The powers
of these gentlemen were derived, if derived at all, from
the General Council in opposition to the will of the
Governor, because certain purposes were to be answered,
or the safety and harmony of Texas should be destroyed.

Col. Fannin, in a letter addressed to the General
Council, dated on the 21st January, at Velasco, and to
which he subscribes himself "J. W. Fannin, Jr., Agent
Provisional Government," when speaking of anticipated
difficulties with the commander-in-chief, allays the fears
of the council by assuring them, "I shall never make any
myself," and then adds: "The object in view will be the
governing principle, and should General Houston be
ready and willing to take command, and march direct
ahead, and execute your orders, and the volunteers to
submit to it, or a reasonable part of them, I shall not say
'nay,' but will do all in my power to produce harmony."
How was I to become acquainted with the orders of the
Council? Was is through my subaltern? It must have
been so designed, as the Council have not, up to the
present moment, given the official notice of the orders to
which Colonel Fannin refers. This modesty and subordi-
nation on his part is truly commendable in a subaltern
and would imply that he had a right to say "nay." If he
has this power, whence is it derived? Not from any law,

and contrary to his sworn duty as my subaltern, whose duty is obedience to my lawful commands, agreeably to the rules and regulations of the United States army, adopted by the consultation of all Texas. If he accepted any appointment incompatible with his obligation as a colonel in the regular army, it certainly increases his moral responsibilities to an extent which is truly to be regretted.

In another paragraph of his letter he states: "You will allow that we have too much division, and one cause of complaint is this very expedition, and that it is intended to remove General Houston."

He then assures the Council that no blame should attach to him, but most dutifully says: "I will go where you have sent me, and will do what you have ordered me, if possible." The order of the council, has set forth in the resolutions appointing Col. Fannin agent, and authorizing him to appoint as many agents as he might think proper, did most certainly place him above the Governor and commander-in-chief of the Army. Nor is he responsible to the council or the people of Texas. He is required to report, but he is not required to obey the Council. His powers are as unlimited and absolute as Cromwell's ever were. I regard the expedition as now ordered as an individual and not a national measure. The resolutions passed in favor of J. W. Fannin, Jr., and F. W. Johnson, and their proclamations, with its original start—Dr. Grant—absolved the country from all responsibility for its consequences. If I had any doubt on the subject previous to having seen at Goliad a proclamation of J. W. Fannin, Jr., sent by him to the volunteers, I could no longer entertain one as to the campaign, so far as certain persons are interested in forwarding it. After appealing to the volunteers, he concluded with the assurance "that the troops shall be paid out of the first spoils taken from the enemy." This, in my opinion, connected with the extraordinary powers granted to him by the Council, divests the campaign of any character save that of a piratical or predatory war.

The people of Texas have declared to the world that the war in which they are now engaged is a war of principle, in defense of their civil and political rights. What effect will the declaration above referred to have on the civilized world when they learn that the individual who made it has since been clothed with absolute powers by the General Council of Texas, and, that because you, [as governor and commander-in-chief] refused to ratify their acts, they have declared you no longer governor of Texas? It was stated by way of inducement to the advance on Matamoros, that the citizens of that place were friendly to the advance of the troops of Texas upon that city. They no doubt, ere this, have J. W. Fannin's proclamation, (though it was in manuscripts) and, if originally true, what will now be their feelings towards men, who "are to be paid out of the first spoils taken from the enemy." The idea which must present to the enemy, will be, if the city is taken it will be given up to pillage, and when the spoils are collected, a division will take place. In war, when spoil is the object, friends and enemies share one common destiny. This rule will govern the citizens of Matamoros in their conclusions and render their resistance desperate. A city containing twelve thousand inhabitants will not be taken by a handful of men who have marched twenty-two days without breadstuffs or necessary supplies for an army.

If there ever was a time when Matamoros could have been taken by a few men, that time has passed by. The people of that place are not aware of the high-minded, honorable men who fill the ranks of the Texian army. They will look upon them as they would look upon Mexican mercenaries, and resist them as such. They too will hear of the impressment of the property of the citizens of Bexar, as reported to your Excellency, by Lieutenant-Colonel Neill, when Dr. Grant left that place for Matamoros, in command of the volunteer army.

The letter went on in that same vein, until finally Sam Houston concluded it;

The evil is now done, and I trust sincerely that the

1st of March may establish a government on some permanent foundation, where honest functionaries will regard and execute the known and established laws of the country, agreeably to their oaths. If this state of things cannot be achieved the country must be lost. I feel, in the station which I hold, that every effort of the Council has been to mortify me individually, and, if possible, to compel me to do some act which would enable them to pursue the same measures towards me which they have illegally done toward your Excellency, and thereby remove another obstacle to the accomplishment of their plans. In their attempts to embarrass me they were reckless of all prejudice which might result to the public service from their lawless course.

While the Council was passing resolutions effecting the army of Texas, and transferring to J. W. Fannin, Jr., and F. W. Johnson the whole control of the army and resources of Texas, they could order them to be furnished with copies of the several resolutions passed by that body, but did not think proper to notify the Major-General of the army of their adoption; nor have they yet caused him to be furnished with the acts of the council, relative to the army. True it is they passed a resolution to that effect, but it never was complied with. Their object must have been to conceal, not promulgate their acts. "They have loved darkness rather than light because their deeds are evil."

I do not consider the Council as a constitutional body nor their acts lawful. They have no quorum agreeably to the Organic Law, and I am therefore compelled to regard all their acts as void. The body has been composed of seventeen members, and I perceive that the act of "suspension" passed against your Excellency was by only ten members present; the president pro tem, having no vote, only ten members remain when less than twelve could not form a quorum agreeably to the Organic Law, which required two thirds of the whole body. I am not prepared either to violate my duty or my oath, by yielding obedience to an act manifestly unlawful, as it is, in my opinion, prejudicial to the welfare of Texas.

The lieutenant-governor, and several members of the Council, I believe to be patriotic and just men; but, there have been, and when I left San Felipe there were, others in that body on whose honesty and integrity, the foregoing facts will be the best commentary. They must also abide the judgment of the people. I have the honor to be,

Your Excellency's obedient servant,

Sam Houston

Commander-In-Chief of the Army

The day after writing this letter Sam Houston departed on furlough to the Cherokee Nation in deep East Texas, not to return until the end of February in time to attend the Constitutional Convention, which convened on the first of March at Washington-on-the-Brazos.

CHAPTER SIXTEEN

As Bowie and his men left La Bahía for the Alamo, they were not fully aware of the degree to which the government and, as a consequence, the army was becoming fragmented. They knew that Grant and Johnson were embarked on a misguided campaign to the south and Matamoros, but did not realize how much Sam Houston's authority had been undermined. They headed for Bexar thinking of themselves as a vanguard of a force that would be steadily mustering to defend the frontier and eventually expel the enemy, making Texas free once and for all. Although their ranks had been thinned and their materiel depleted, they were confident and resolute as they set out. They remained in good humor as league after league took them further away from the squabbling and the posturing.

Jim had liked Bowie when he first met him and was pleased to have an opportunity to get to know him better. Riding side by side, their conversation began with little reference to the work at hand; both men understood the situation and knew what had to be done. They spoke of women and horses and their lives.

As the conversation meandered and finally began to wane, Bowie observed, "That's a fine looking animal you have there, Jim!"

Breaking into a broad smile that seemed to sum up his pride and his own admiration for Sal, Jim leaned forward and patted her on the neck. "She's the best!" And as if prompted by her snorted reply, he continued, "She was a gift from my brother when I left for Texas."

"You rode her all the way from Carolina?"

"I did, indeed, and what a ride it was!"

"You're from Edgefield District, you said?"

"Yes." Jim smiled, almost laughed, as just hearing the words Edgefield District stirred a hundred memories within him. "Do you know it?"

"Not exactly, but I've heard tell—they say everybody there is some rambunctious!"

"Oh, we're not so wild. We just always seem to be in the middle of things."

"Well, you're in the middle of something now, that's for sure!" And, changing the subject, he continued, "What did you think of Bexar?"

"I wasn't there long, but it seemed a place I might like." As he spoke these words, Jim realized that he was looking forward to returning to Bexar. From the first, he had been attracted to the place, and now in an odd way, it was becoming the center of his world. He remembered the saying, "All roads lead to Rome," but for him, all roads seemed to lead to Bexar.

Jim understood that Bowie's assignment involved taking a decision as to whether or not Bexar, and more particularly the Alamo, should be defended or abandoned. Although Jim admired Sam Houston and was prepared to follow his orders wherever they led, the possibility of abandoning the Alamo as part of an overall strategy did not sit well with him. Not only was it against his instincts to flinch, it didn't make military sense to him, particularly in light of the near anarchy now prevailing. He knew that the strategy for a successful campaign would rest on more than his own limited view of things, but he gave voice to his concern as he turned to Bowie.

"Do you think we should abandon Bexar?"

"Not if we want to win this war," Bowie said.

They rode on in silence for a while, each in his own way contemplating what had just been said. Then Bowie continued, "Sam Houston's a good man. But he's got lots of problems: what army exists, is spread all over the place, doing God knows what; politicians, if you can call them that, back in San Felipe—all at each other's throats. Here he is, faced with a Mexican army comin', like it or not, and he's depending on me to tell him whether to hold this line out here or pull back. Trouble is, we don't know when Santa Anna will get here, and with those kinds of uncertainties, we have to hold Bexar."

"And that means Goliad as well!"

"That's about the way I see it. There's not much choice, but I'm not so sure that old Sam appreciates the importance of Bexar to the Mexicans. They won't go anywhere else until they take it, and not just out of pride or sentiment either. They'll be strung out across that desert and in sore need of a waterin' hole where they feel comfortable."

"Then you've already made up your mind," Jim said.

"Mostly. If there's any chance at all, when you think about it, holdin' them here is about the only chance that Texas has. Besides, now that we had that showdown at Goliad, and with what Houston already knows of the situation out here, he'll be gettin' the army together pretty quickly. If only those quacksalver politicians back there'll stop squabblin'!"

Bowie's words made sense to Jim, and there was

little more to be said on the subject. "What's it like, living in Bexar?" Jim said.

"Well, it's not like the South. It's not even like San Felipe or Brazoria, or even Gonzales. And it's sure not like Louisiana!" Bowie thought for a few seconds, stifled a cough, and then continued. "But it's a mighty fair place—rocky, but with water and shade, and a distinct way of life—if you cotton to it, pretty enjoyable!"

"Then you never regretted coming out here?" Almost before these words left his mouth, Jim remembered the stories he had heard of Bowie's marriage to the daughter of a prominent Mexican family, and her untimely death while Bowie was off on some venture or other. He hoped he hadn't opened any old wounds.

If he had, Bowie showed no sign of it. But he thought hard before answering, and then in a tone that suggested much more than the few words he spoke.

"No, I never regretted it. This is a good place." Looking again at Jim, somewhat searchingly, he continued. "It'll be good for you."

Jim felt as if Bowie must have realized that more than just a thirst for adventure had brought him to Texas. Then Bowie, as if truly reading his thoughts, said, "What's it like back in Carolina?"

Paraphrasing Bowie, Jim laughed and said, "Well, it's not like around here, and everybody seems to be named Bonham or Butler or Smith."

Bowie interrupted. "Hell! We've got some Butlers back in Georgia. We really might be kin!"

Jim was about to respond when he noticed some movement on the crest of hill just to the west of them. He pointed past Bowie to the spot.

"Did you see that?" Jim said.

"No, but it's probably just some Comanche scout." In response to Jim's look of surprise, he said, "Don't worry, it's the Mexican army they don't like!"

Mention of the Indians induced Bowie to embark on a more detailed explanation of his vision for Texas, what they were facing, and what they would have to do to succeed. But the prolonged speaking brought on more coughing, which he finally squelched with a draw from a whiskey flask. Thereafter he grew silent again.

Jim would have liked to have drawn Bowie out further, but he had seen enough sickness and misery to understand that as his discomfort increased, Bowie's focus was becoming more inward and casual conversation a strain. And it was so; Bowie withdrew into the world of his memory and imagination, a sure escape from the realization that he really was not well. These feelings continued until finally they stopped for the night. It was cold and all he could think was to be warm. Finally that wish, aided by a few more generous drafts of whiskey, drowned out all other thoughts as he sank into a troubled sleep.

The next day the sun shone through and with it relief from the rain and cold of the past weeks. Spirits rose as they continued on to Bexar. As they had covered most of the distance the previous day, it wasn't long before Willis Moore, who had been acting as a scout, came riding back. "You can see a mission from just over that next rise!" he shouted as he neared the group.

"Good! That'll be Concepción," responded a now his-old-self-again, better-spirited, Bowie. In a pronouncement, which was to prove prophetic, he looked at Jim and said, "I reckon we're gonna find we've got our work cut out for us."

It had been less than three weeks since Jim had left Bexar and only a little longer since Bowie had been there. But both men were surprised at the changes that had taken place. These were immediately evident as they rode into the Alamo, which had indeed been stripped. Neill's letter to Sam Houston had been no exaggeration. Command had devolved to Neill, but as they were to discover, it was a hollow command indeed—little more than a hundred men, scattered around town in various living arrangements. Many of them were sick or recovering from wounds received in the earlier engagements, and critically short of supplies of all kinds. Their principal remaining assets were the artillery pieces left behind because they were too cumbersome for Grant and Johnson to manage.

The town itself had also undergone a change, albeit more subtle. There was an underlying tension probably undetectable to a stranger but immediately evident to Bowie. Even Jim sensed that it was not quite the same as when he had been there at Christmas. In spite of the perfunctory smiles, the faces of the people had changed. But this atmosphere did not prevent Bowie and Jim from soon being comfortably quartered in the home of Bowie's in-laws, the Veramendis.

In the eyes of his wife's family, Bowie remained one of them and was always welcome. To Jim's great delight, the family insisted on his being their guest as well. For Bowie, just being back in Bexar, no matter the conditions, served to lift his spirits. His mood was infectious, and so it was with a good deal of liveliness that both men approached the task of making ready for the Mexican assault.

Neill had done a fine job in maintaining morale and keeping the garrison together, but he was nearing the end of his tether. So Bowie and his contingent were a welcome addition to the force. Immediately, the newcomers set about helping to make things right within the Alamo itself. Green Jameson had for some time been directing the work of restoring the walls and improving the fortifications, and he had no difficulty in making effective use of the extra hands.

But there were other tasks as well. They needed to

replenish and reorganize their stores, and even improve the order and discipline among the men. It was the beginning of a period of renewed and intense activity and involved very hard work by everyone. Bowie was everywhere, shouting encouragement and leading by example, but he began to experience recurring episodes of illness. He did what he could to hide it from the others, but his energy level began to decline. He had good days and bad days, but more and more, they were bad. Jim, who had been at his side all along, did what he could to take up the slack. Through his cheerful optimism and hard work, he helped to keep up the spirits of the men.

Meanwhile, the news that trickled in from San Felipe was discouraging. The governor himself was under increasing assault from his political enemies, the extent of whose pettiness was now fully revealed, as was their role in enabling the actions of Johnson and Grant. The men of the Alamo, now desperately preparing for its defense, were appalled at this turn of events. Being anxious to reaffirm their loyalty to the duly formed government, they selected Jim as chairman of a committee to draft a resolution supporting the governor. While not a ringing document of the sort that would eventually flow from the Alamo, it nevertheless left little doubt as to the sentiments of those who stood in the breach. It was dated 26 January 1836, and read in part:

> "... *that we will support the authority of Governor Henry Smith in his unyielding and patriotic efforts to fulfill his duties and to preserve the dignity of his office, while promoting the best interest of the people against all ... designs of selfish and interested individuals.*
>
> "... *that the governor, Henry Smith will please accept the gratitude of the army at this station for his firmness in execution, as well as his patriotic exertions in our behalf.*"

In addition to Jim, it was signed by James Bowie, Green Jameson, Dr. Pollard, Jesse Badgett, Juan Seguin, and Gaspar Flores.

Texians who supported the cause of independence were looking forward to the constitutional convention scheduled to convene at Washington-on-the-Brazos on the first day of March. In everyone's mind, it was to be a watershed event and the citizens of Bexar, like those in other municipalities, were selecting delegates.

The dissension in San Felipe, however, had left the men in the Alamo fearful that their plight might be overshadowed by political posturing. They were not comfortable in entrusting advocacy of their interests to the delegates from Bexar. Determined to assure that the convention fully understood the urgency of the crisis at the frontier, they decided to send their own representatives, Jim Bonham and Sam Maverick.

On the day the vote was taken, Jim and two others had been on a scouting mission to the Frio River. They had been gone overnight and when Jim returned, he went directly to his quarters at the Veramendis. Evening was coming on, and he had not been there long before Bowie, too, returned. After a brief exchange of greetings, Bowie broke the news.

"Jim, we've decided that it may not be in our best interests to depend only on the delegates from Bexar. The men want you and Maverick to represent the garrison at the convention."

Jim looked searchingly at Bowie. Taking only a moment to decide the question, which would determine his destiny, he finally responded.

"I agree, we should be represented and Sam's a good choice, but not me."

"Why not? The men like you. They listen to you, actually more than they do Sam, and they think you'd represent us well!"

"That's just it! I do seem to have some influence with the men, but I'm not so sure I'd be very effective in that cauldron back in Washington. Sam knows those people, he's more suited to that sort of thing. I can do more good here."

"I told them that would be your reaction, and you're right! I know we're going to need all the help we can get in holding this place together!"

"This is where I belong!" Jim said.

"Very well, then it's settled. We'll find somebody else."

Another ballot was cast, and Jesse Badgett was named in Jim's stead. Within days, he would depart for the convention. Sam, much caught up in the affairs around Bexar and himself reluctant to leave the Alamo, announced that he would remain there as long as possible before going to Washington.

The election correlated with a turning point in the makeup of the force in the Alamo. In the face of ever increasing warnings of Santa Anna being on the march and the turmoil in San Felipe, Bowie was more than ever convinced that the Alamo must be defended, and Neill agreed with him. They drafted a letter to Governor Smith dramatically affirming their position and repeating what was to become the mantra of the Alamo— *please send men and supplies.* And their request was granted sooner than they could have imagined. Almost as the express rider left with the letter, help began to arrive.

The next afternoon, Travis and thirty men came in, to be followed within days by Davy Crockett and his jaunty Tennesseans, their hubris, and their imposing long rifles taken as sure signs that things were changing for the better. It seemed a serious buildup of the garrison had begun. The fifty men who had arrived within the short space of those few days provided a boost in morale far exceeding that which could be justified by their numbers. With the new blood came new energy, although dissension as well, found its way inside the walls of the Alamo.

Crockett had not been there a week when Neill was called away, leaving command to be shared jointly between Travis and Bowie, and also leaving the loyalties of the men split between them. A tense enough situation was made worse when Jim Bowie, his illness now beginning to prey on his mind, succumbed to a binge, which led to a full rupture between him and Travis. Fortunately, he soon sobered up and the discord was resolved as the two men agreed to joint command. The incident served to remind them of the fragility of their position.

Although he had cast his lot with the garrison, Jim was not to remain long in Bexar. Travis and Bowie had in mind other tasks for him. Having learned that Fannin and his men had recently withdrawn back into La Bahía, they saw an opportunity to consolidate the Texian forces. Knowing that Bexar would be Santa Anna's primary target, they reasoned that it would strengthen the defense of the frontier to move most of Fannin's command to the Alamo, leaving only a small contingent at the more defensible *presidio* of La Bahía.

Although such a combining of forces portended yet another struggle for command, both Travis and Bowie were prepared to deal with it. For his part, Travis foresaw no difficulty in relinquishing his position as ranking regular officer in the Alamo. After all, he reasoned, Fannin was an artillerist and more suited to conducting warfare from the parapets of a fortress.

Indeed, the idea carried an additional attraction to Travis in that such an arrangement would enable him to take up his role as commander of the legion of cavalry, to roam the plains as he had in the past, and harass the advancing Mexican army. In his mind it was the only plan that had a chance. But it would take Fannin's cooperation. And who better to make the case than Jim Bonham.

So it was, on the sixteenth of February, Jim had mounted Sal and rode out of the Alamo to plead the most important case of his career to a man with whom his relationship had been in steady decline since the day they met.

CHAPTER SEVENTEEN

Jim awakened to the sound of a distant cannon. Although it was not yet full light, it brought him back to the here and now. The fruitless meeting with Fannin, the hard ride to Brazoria and back to Gonzales, all that was behind him. Only the Alamo lay ahead.

It had been barely two weeks since he left to seek Fannin's aid, and six weeks since he had ridden into the Alamo with Bowie. Yet now, things were entirely different. The Mexican army, to the dismay of everyone, had arrived much sooner than expected. Even as the convention assembled, their countrymen on the frontier were struggling for their lives. Now, for Jim, nothing could have underscored the situation more than the rumble of yet another cannon, which spurred him to full wakefulness and the need to be on his way.

He carried Williamson's letter of false hope, as he searched his memory of the last few days to see if there was any opportunity he had missed, anything at all that would make that letter more valid and enable him not to have to brand it, at best, mere sophistry. He had gone over the possibilities until his mind was spinning and no matter how optimistic a view he took, it would be at the very minimum, six or seven days before any sizable unit other than Fannin's could relieve the Alamo. Any way he reckoned it, particularly in light of what Maverick had told him, and his own knowledge of the provisions, there just did not seem to be enough time.

With each passing day, Santa Anna would have less reason to hold back an assault, nor was he likely to take the time to starve them out. Clearly, he was a man in a hurry, and it was obvious that he intended to crush the revolution before it could gather momentum. The only chance that Jim could see was the Ranging Force. If they could get into position and attack the Mexican lines of supply, that might buy enough time. But Jim had to admit to himself, it would be a near miracle if even that could be brought about in time.

The news he brought could not be good, and he would have the unhappy duty of having to refute Willie's letter. *My God,* he thought, *Fannin! What a poor excuse for a leader! If only he had . . .* But there was no use in wasting time with such thoughts. There was nothing to do now but return with the truth. There would be no miracles. The men of the Alamo were, if not forgotten, then certainly victims of confusion and of the selfish ambitions of others. Almost certainly they would have to face whatever came, with only their own resources.

He wondered how his friends were faring; with courage he was sure, but a real test nonetheless. Thank God for Davy Crockett! His tireless good humor and his men, reputed to be peerless marksmen, must be much appreciated about now. Jim smiled to himself. Ole Davy certainly seemed like one who would never flinch. Daddy would approve.

As he rode along, his attention eventually turned to Sal as she carried him effortlessly towards his fate. It seemed that she had become almost part of him, so complete was the bond between them. "How many miles have you taken me?" he whispered as he felt her purposeful stride. *What a good friend, magnificent creature!* He reached down and stroked her neck. But she needed no reassurance, and he drew strength from her as he realized that a race across a battlefield lay at the end of this road.

A grim smile crossed Jim's face as he remembered the visions his appointment as a cavalry officer had evoked. Now he knew that he and Sal were the only cavalry there would ever be, not bad after all. Since the day he had arrived in San Felipe, his path had led to a series of unpredictable forks in the road. But at last he could see it as part of an inexorable process, which now yielded no more options. Transcending everything that had gone before, only grim determination and dedication to duty were all that was left to him.

His only goal now was to get back with his report and join his comrades in making a good account of themselves. He hoped that what now seemed inevitable would be worth it, and that Sam Houston could regroup the army in time to save Texas.

As he moved ever closer to the Alamo, each salvo was louder than before as the cannons continued their relentless pounding. From the sound, it seemed as if one of the batteries must be directly ahead. Jim began to worry about suddenly riding into the midst of a Mexican detachment.

Thus concerned, he was startled as a lone rider materialized from around a bend, galloping in his direction. He was coming fast and Jim soon recognized the man as Ben Highsmith, who himself was caught entirely by surprise and was clearly frightened. By the time he reined in, a look of relief crossed his face as he recognized Jim.

"Colonel Bonham, it's you!"

Ben, having been sent with yet another message to Fannin, had returned earlier in the morning. But the sight that had greeted him as he overlooked the Alamo had persuaded him that he would be throwing his life away to return. The Mexicans had established batteries on this side of the Alamo, one of them as Jim had suspected, close to this very road, and Ben had narrowly missed blundering into it. So he had turned back and headed for Gonzales. Now he undertook to persuade Jim to do the same.

"Colonel . . . Jim, there ain't no sense in it! Fannin ain't comin' and them Messicans has got a ring around that place as tight as my ass in a blue norther." He wondered if Jim had heard him. "One man in there more or less ain't gonna make a bit a difference!"

Jim neither acknowledged this latest news of Fannin, nor showed any sign of turning back.

"It's alright, Ben. Get on back to Gonzales. There's plenty you can do there!"

"But what about you? They wouldn't want you to come back."

"They know I'm coming back."

"It's suicide—and it won't help!"

"Maybe."

"What d'ya mean, *maybe*? I'm tellin' ya, that unless you got a mighty big bunch of men comin' down that road behind ya—and I know ya don't—then there ain't no chance in hell." He stopped as he realized that his words meant little to Jim. Then he continued, "See fer yourself. You ain't got much further to go. Just stay to the north of the road."

Jim looked at Ben with honest friendship and concern. For a brief moment that seemed an eternity, an awkward silence ensued. Jim had no desire to debate or to explain himself. He simply wanted to be on his way. Even Sal beneath him seemed restless and anxious to get on with it. He calmed her with a few reassuring strokes and again turned to look at Ben.

"I know you're only trying to talk sense." He hesitated for a moment, and then said simply, "But they deserve to know the situation. It'll take only one of us to tell them."

The youngster looked at him with astonishment.

"But it's . . . it's your life! None of your friends in there expect you to throw it away!"

Jim turned Sal in the direction of Bexar.

"Good luck, Ben!"

He didn't look back. He had heard these arguments all along the way, but the idea of not returning was counter to everything he believed, who he was. Just as a child from the moment of birth begins to learn his native tongue, so, too, are the values inculcated which will forever, and virtually inescapably, define his world.

So it was that Jim's heritage as well as his nature were home to his ideals. Together, they defined a place, a wonderful place where he was comfortable and could always live in the freedom he cherished so much. No matter the cost or the grimness of the prospects, the bondage of cowardice was not for him. His times had molded his character and foreordained his responses.

In his boyhood, the American revolution, with all its risks and sacrifices, was a recent and real thing. The battle of New Orleans, even the Napoleonic wars, were part of his world. Extravagant deeds and sacrifice in the winning of liberty and the preservation of honor were extolled as cherished ideals.

These things, however, carried a high price; *courage*, something he was fortunate to possess in full measure. Jim had often pondered the bravery that ordinary soldiers in unnamed armies throughout history had managed to summon in the face of almost certain death. While it was a threshold he had yet to cross, and though he might regret the circumstances that now put him in this situation, he was determined to do the duty that a fickle destiny had imposed upon him. So he continued down the road to the Alamo that had begun so many years ago at Flat Grove.

Long before it came into sight, he was able to distinguish the sound of rifle fire interspersed with the occasional roar of cannon. He knew the firing must be coming mostly from the Mexican side, because his friends would be conserving precious ammunition. Steering clear of the road as Ben had warned him, he finally came to a rise, and through an opening in the cottonwood trees, the *alamosas* as they were called, he could see it all—the Alamo besieged. Clearly, it was as bad as Maverick and Highsmith had described. His alarm at the sight was surpassed only by the sadness he felt at the news he was bound to deliver.

Few people at Jim's age know when their destiny has been fulfilled, but as he sat briefly looking at the old mission in the morning sun, preparing to face the gauntlet, he knew. Although he would never know if what he was about to do would matter much in the overall scheme of things, he took no more time thinking about it. Action overcame contemplation as he rode slowly forth, emerging from the trees.

Almost immediately, he saw the waving arms on the ramparts. It seemed his comrades had spotted him and would be ready to open the gates. If they had not, he would be dead sooner rather than later.

He moved Sal on past the powder house into the open, a slow deliberate walk at first. Then as he approached the place where he was sure to soon be noticed, he urged her into a gallop. Finally, a split second before he heard the first crack of rifle fire, they made a mad dash for the fortress, aware of each moment, as if looking at pictures in a book—as if it were happening to someone else—hearing the whine of bullets, hanging on to Sal who was now running like the wind. Conscious of her every breath and movement, Jim wondered for a brief moment if indeed his friends had spotted him—if the gates would open, expecting at any moment to feel bullets tearing through his flesh. *What would it feel like? My God, am I going to die now?* The walls were being peppered with rifle fire. Would the gates open? Just when it seemed that they may not, they did open. Suddenly, he was safely within the Alamo.

Willing hands tended Sal, as eager and expectant faces crowded around to hear Jim's news. The exhilaration of the ride momentarily masked the truth from his face. It was not difficult to smile, having just survived the dash through the Mexican lines. All around him stood men who would die with him: the hard-working and conscientious Jameson, the always cheerful and willing Holland, Dickenson, Ward, and others waving from the ramparts. Then he saw Will, calmly standing in the background, arms crossed, already beginning to read the message in Jim's face. In spite of his foibles, never a more exemplary leader, who was determined to deal with anything.

"Well, our emissary has returned! It's good to see you, Jim!"

Jim knew that the men would likely take his return as a sign that reinforcements were not far behind and be hungry to hear about it. While he would have preferred to end their euphoria quickly by shouting out the truth, he was obliged to report to Will first and allow him to decide how best to interpret the news he brought, and how to present it to the men.

Climbing down from the saddle, he hastily removed from his saddle bag the package of letters from the families in Gonzales and handed it to a man he did not know, but who identified himself as being from there.

The man seemed strangely familiar, and it soon came to Jim that this must be the father of the young man who had handed him the packet outside the Luna Bar two nights before.

"Are you Andrew Kent?" Jim asked as their eyes met.

"Yes, how did you know?"

"The resemblance is strong. It was your son who collected these letters."

Kent smiled at the thought of his son, but said only, "Well, we're all much obliged to get these."

Thinking too of Davy, Jim stifled the impulse to ask which man might be Jacob Darst. Though the welcome from those surrounding him was heartfelt, he felt compelled to cut it short and follow Will who was already walking towards the headquarters. As they entered the room, Jim suddenly became aware of Bowie's absence.

"Where's Bowie?" he asked with some trepidation.

"He's taken very ill, Jim. Not long after you left it was plain that he couldn't carry on. He asked me to take over sole command." Will had gallantly omitted recounting a further altercation he had had with Bowie. Anxious to hear Jim's news, he concluded, "You'll be able to see him later. But now, tell me, what news do you bring?"

Although he was not surprised, Jim was disturbed to hear the news about Bowie. But he put it out of his mind for the moment and quickly related the highlights of his trip. He handed Will the letter from Three-Legged Willie and explained how his own unhappy conclusions were so much at odds with what Will was about to read.

After reading Willie's letter, Travis looked up at Jim.

"Why would he write this? Ignore Fannin's express, and tell me that he's on his way?"

"I don't know, Will! To keep hope alive, I suppose.

Willie's a good man and your good friend. Nobody's working harder to help. But I fear he's indulging in some mighty wishful thinking. Fannin's not coming! He's torn with indecision. He even still seems to be looking to Robinson for instructions." Jim remained silent as his friend absorbed the truth, and then added, "There'll be no help from Fannin, Will."

The acceptance in Will's face made it easier for Jim to tell all that happened and to relate his own unhappy estimate of the situation as he had seen it unfold since leaving for La Bahía. Will listened stoically and did not disagree; nor did he seem surprised. The endgame of the whole mess had been clear to him for sometime now, but still he was not ready to completely abandon hope.

"I'm afraid you're right, but what about the others—Tumlinson, and Wharton's company?"

"Tumlinson, I'm not sure, but you can be certain that Willie will move heaven and earth to find him, as well as Wharton's men. They'll come, but when? There are probably others, too. It's for sure your messages have been effective. Everyone out there knows Santa Anna is here and that we need help. But they're all absorbed in the convention now. It comes down to whether there's enough time, and you know better than anybody how long we can hold out here!"

"Maybe a week, but honestly Jim, I don't think Santa Anna will wait that long. His whole strategy has been to act quickly and keep us off balance, and I must say, he's done a good job of it. He's got a full army out there now. Unless we have help from a real cavalry unit, it's doubtful a few companies of volunteers would make the difference. We need supplies, ammunition." His voice trailed off.

"Well, they are stockpiling provisions at Gonzales. Willie's got them grinding corn and drying beef."

Will half smiled as if he could picture the industry of Willie and the good people in Gonzales, but the more he assimilated what Jim had told him, the more it became clear, that it may well be too late already. He shook his head, then rose, walked to the door and sent for his officers.

It did not take long for the group to assemble. Save Bowie, who was too ill to attend, the others, in anticipation of hearing Jim's news, quickly crowded into the room. They stood around informally in sort of a semicircle, and looking at their expectant faces, Travis wasted no time in getting down to business.

"As you know, Jim has just gotten back from his mission to find help. We had no idea we would need it quite so soon when he left." His words were underscored by the sound of a nearby cannon, inevitably followed by that of a ball crashing into the courtyard nearby. Some of the group chuckled nervously, but their attention continued to be riveted on Will.

"He's been to La Bahía, then to Victoria and Brazoria, and finally Gonzales. I'm sorry to have to tell you that the news he brings us is not what we would like to hear." Responding to the grim silence, he continued. "Major Williamson—most of you know him as Three-Legged-Willie—has sent me a letter in which he states that Colonel Fannin is on his way here now with a relief force and that other units are either mobilizing, or are on their way here as well. He encourages us to do everything possible to hold out until aid arrives."

The men all looked at each other questioningly. *This doesn't sound so bad* was the unspoken message that passed between them.

"But Jim tells me that although Fannin made an attempt to come to our aid, he didn't get out of sight of Goliad before his wagons broke down and he turned back. He is now back in La Bahía . . ." *bewildered*, Will thought sarcastically, "and the latest word from him is that he is not going to make another attempt."

All faces turned towards Jim, and a voice from the group asked, "What's wrong with him, Jim? For God's sake, it's his duty to come!"

Jim felt the same way but answered the question by attempting to explain it as Fannin might. This drew no sympathy from men facing imminent destruction. Nor could they put from their minds their own privation, shortages which contributed mightily to the desperation of their situation and which were brought about by the two scoundrels with whom Fannin had allied himself, Johnson and Grant.

They knew Jim was no apologist for Fannin nor was he going to play devil's advocate. So no more questions were raised. None were needed, although the grumbling continued for a while. But they grew silent as Travis again spoke.

"As to the other sources of help, it's clear that our appeals have reached receptive ears and help could come from many quarters. But you know as well as I, what it really comes down to is *time*."

They all knew, only too well—dwindling ammunition and supplies, an enemy growing stronger each day—a simple calculus.

It seemed as if there should be more to be said, but really, there was not. A momentary silence pregnant with grim determination was all there was. There was nothing more to say about Fannin, nor was there any ranting or railing against Johnson or Grant; no bitterness expressed towards the ineptitude of politicians . . . just quiet resolution.

Travis ended the meeting with a simple statement of muted hope, "Let us see what tomorrow brings, but please be sure that all the men understand the situation."

Will need not have added that last admonition because before the officers had filed out, word had already
begun to spread—transmitted by pickets on the walls
above and by other soldiers within easy earshot of the
briefing. Much of the hope that had come through the
gates with Jim vanished as the word spread, yet there
remained a chance. Slim to be sure, but enough that in
the farthest recesses of each man's soul there resided a
faint glimmer that any moment help might arrive.

After the others left, Travis took a moment to address Jim's immediate needs. He explained that the
Veramendis had been able to bring some of his belongings into the compound, and he pointed to a cabinet at
the end of the room.

"I knew you'd be back to collect them." Nodding
towards his servant who stood just outside the door, he
added, "I'll have Joe find some quarters for you."

"Thanks, Will."

At that, Will left to begin making his rounds at the
ramparts. It had been only a month since he had come
into the Alamo and less than two weeks since he had
been in sole command. But it seemed he had commanded here forever, and Jim watched in admiration as
his friend set about dealing with the bad news.

Before going to his own quarters, Jim hastened to
find Bowie who was now bedridden. He went to the
little room along the south wall where Bowie lay and
was shocked to see just how sick he was. Bowie was
clearly fighting a losing battle with death. It stirred
memories of the battles lost by John and Simeon, and
once again the rage and frustration at the insidious
process of wasting away welled up within him.

At first he thought that Bowie didn't recognize him,
but as they made eye contact the spark of recognition
told him that he was mistaken. He was recognized,
indeed welcomed.

"Is there anything I can do for you?"

"Kick Sam Houston's ass!" Bowie gasped.

Bowie's remark, expressing as it did his frustration with the whole establishment, struck a chord with Jim. Bowie had always understood better even than had Sam Houston, the strategic need to hold Bexar. And he was prepared to do it. But to have been left in ignorance of what was going on and abandoned—uninformed and seemingly forgotten—while the one man who could have helped succumbed to political intrigue, brought bitterness, which in his feverish brooding he did not bother to conceal.

Although Jim understood Bowie's feelings, he realized his friend's comment was more rhetorical than a reasoned analysis of the general's actions. He merely replied with a smile, "That would be kinda hard. He's back at the convention, and I'm just not up to doing any more riding just now."

As he spoke, it occurred to Jim that Bowie may not even have realized that the general had returned from his furlough. He was about to make this point when Bowie, ignoring Jim's comment and struggling to retain his concentration, concluded his thought.

"Those stupid bastards in the Council," he muttered, "can't they understand? They've made a mess of everything."

They have for sure, Jim thought, but seeing no point in encouraging Bowie's agitation, he replied, "But we've got plenty to keep us busy here now."

Although he was in a state of near total collapse, Bowie remained alert for the moment and turned his attention to Jim. He took a hard look as if seeing him for the first time, and said, "You're a good man, Jim."

The only words that came to Jim were, "You, too, my friend." Then he reached down to shake his hand. "I'll visit you again later."

As Jim turned to leave, Bowie, in a voice barely perceptible, managed to say, "Wait," and as Jim turned to face him, he continued, "Jim, I know this is not what you planned or expected ..." and half whispered "whatever is?" Then stifling a cough and choking down some air, he added, "but it's worth it. Sam Houston is a good man. He'll make the most of it."

Jim didn't respond, but looked Bowie in the eyes as a moment of unspoken understanding passed between them. Bowie was further down the road they must both soon travel. Dying of disease, he could afford the luxury of resignation. But Jim was not ready for that. He had things to do. So he did his best to return the encouragement with a nod and smile, then turned and left.

CHAPTER EIGHTEEN

The room that had been assigned to Jim was small and sparsely furnished but afforded some privacy. It would have been a welcome haven in any case, but he was pleasantly surprised to find it had been recently cleaned and the cot covered with a blanket. More surprising, however, was the single rose emerging from the clay bottle, which had been carefully positioned on the small table. A woman's touch surely, but which woman? And where would she have ever found such a treasure? Simple as the gesture was, it had the same effect as those grander furnishings in the cell he had occupied in Pendleton.

The attraction of the cot led him to take a rest which, in spite of the incessant hammering of the Mexican artillery, became several hours. When he finally awoke, it was between salvos, and there was a frozen instant of serene quiet. At first he thought he was waking from a bad dream, and just as he was almost convinced it was so, the stillness was once again shattered and reality returned.

He was quickly on his feet, feeling vaguely guilty about some undetermined duty he must be neglecting. But having no post as yet, he went to the stable. There was Sal, rested and uninjured, ready to go again if he wanted. Now accustomed to the constant barrage, she was, nevertheless, nervous. At the sight of Jim, she whinnied and came over, moving her head up and down as if to acknowledge that everything was alright.

She had been well curried—by whom Jim could not even guess—and she stood before him hardly the worse for wear in spite of the gauntlet she had run, and all the hard riding of the past weeks. Sal was visibly more settled within minutes after Jim reappeared, and the reunion provided an inexplicable kind of reassurance to him as well. He stroked her for a long while before finally leaving the stable area.

After seeking out Jacob Darst to thank him and reassure him of his family's well-being, Jim went in search of Will to find out where he might be most useful. He assumed it would be at one of the artillery batteries, but was ready to follow whatever orders Will might issue. As he stepped out into the open near the corner of the old chapel, he noticed what had been a crumbled place in the wall adjacent to the opposite corner had now been replaced with an earth and timber palisade, the revetment consisting of a fearsome looking row of logs. The tops had been fashioned into spikes that looked as if they would deter a charge of elephants. Jameson had done his work well, and seeing Crockett's sharp-shooters manning these defenses made him happy—for the moment—to be on this side of the barricade.

The place where Bowie now struggled was further to the right near the main gate in one of several rooms alongside the base of the stone wall, which still stood enclosing the original mission compound. The roof of this string of rooms formed a platform for the defenders manning the parapets above. Likewise, within the chapel itself, similar rooms, such as the former baptistery near the front, provided a base for the defenses above.

Jim walked through the front door into the chapel to have a look. The nave itself was in ruins with no roof. What covering there was came from the breastworks, which had been erected around the perimeter. These were little more than walkways that connected the improvised gun platforms at either end, and were accessible by means of an earthen ramp leading up to two gun emplacements above the end of the church where the altar had once been.

As Jim reached the base of the ramp, he turned and looked back towards the front of the building. There, at the ramparts over the baptistery, was another artillery piece. Though he squinted as he looked into the western sky, he could also make out the flag fluttering high above. He returned the waves of the men above and retraced his steps to the front door. Stepping back out into the open, he stood contemplating the scene for a moment, then continued on his way to find Will.

Travis was in his headquarters and turned as Jim approached.

"Did you have a rest?"

"Yes, thanks. All I need. I saw Bowie earlier; it doesn't look good."

"No. I don't think he's going to make it." Will's words hung a pronouncement for all of them, which led him to add, "Jim, I fear your assessment of the situation is right. Santa Anna will probably arrive at these walls before any of our friends."

"When?"

"I don't know. There can't be much more time; maybe a couple of days. He's going to be anxious to get it over with!" After a pause, he said, "You know, some of the men still think Fannin might yet be on his way, or that other help is coming, and maybe they're right. But I'm only going to give it one more day; then I will have to make clear to them what seems evident now—we're on our own!" He took a deep breath. "I also intend to allow each man to decide whether he will stay to the end." As he spoke, he had been looking out across the courtyard, but now turned back to look at Jim. "Thanks to your splendid example, I don't expect many of them will be leaving!"

"I regret that I wasn't more persuasive with Fannin."

"I know. But Jim, you've done much to hold us together. Without your efforts, there might have been even more people running off after Grant and Johnson or on some other equally destructive course. God knows what the situation would be now!"

"Well it's for certain, Will, our work's cut out for us. We know the hand that's been dealt us!"

Travis shook his head, and speaking in a low voice, almost to himself, said, "I still can't understand—why the hell did Sam Houston disappear when we needed him the most?"

"We know what happened. He suddenly found himself without an army, victim of a few misguided individuals."

"*Misguided?* More like greedy and foolish, I should say!"

"That's all past, Will. Everybody back there understands the situation now. With Houston back, they'll come to their senses."

"Too late for us, Jim."

Jim didn't answer, and Will, his manner changing to one of determination, said, "Well, there's much to do. When they come at us, I want those Mexicans to think— to know—they've crossed the threshold of hell!"

A sardonic laugh came to Jim. "Hell we will make of it, I do believe everyone is ready!"

"Well then, I've just given some orders that will no doubt cheer you!"

Jim could not imagine what this might be, but he soon found out as Travis continued. "I've just finished touring the battlements, the entire fortress actually. I found the men steadfast and ready, as you say, but apprehensive. I've concluded that although we've been conserving ammunition by firing only three artillery rounds as signals each day, this evening we will fire six extra rounds and allow the sharpshooters to do their stuff. At the very least, we will ruin their evening *comida* as well as their sleep!"

As it happened, they did more than cause a few cases of indigestion. Getting the range with the first salvo, the artillery demolished a cantonment area, which purposely had been ignored by the Texians over recent days to encourage the enemy to grow complacent in that area. The disruption was further heightened as the Texians with their long rifles were able to pick off a number of the enemy as they scattered.

Travis was elated to see the salutary effect this small bit of offensive action had on the men and hoped that it caused some confusion among the enemy, who up until that time had been systematically improving their positions as the investment tightened.

Afterwards, and gratified by the men's reaction, Travis met briefly with the officers to review the practical details of their defensive plan. Most of the defenders had long since been assigned to their posts, so it suited Jim very well when he was assigned to join Dickenson in command of the artillery batteries on the parapets above the old chapel. From this vantage point, Jim could also make use of his knowledge of the approaches in watching for any sign of reinforcements. But he expected none.

The next morning the three signal shot limit was

reinstated and the never ending task of watching and waiting continued.

All the men, of course, were intent on keeping a sharp lookout for the help they hoped would emerge at any moment. But hoping and keeping watch as they might, no cheering force of Texian soldiers materialized. No reinforcements nor news of any kind arrived. Only Mexican soldiers. More and more of their units poured into the town as the defenders watched in glum realization that the enemy's numbers were not likely to be matched now, even if help were to come.

Finally, about an hour before sunset, the day reached a dramatic climax. Will, true to his resolve, stood in front of the chapel facing his men, all of whom—save those few who kept watch on the ramparts—had answered his call to assemble. With Mexican shells continuing to fall in the open space beyond, Will, with the sun in his face and gravity in his voice, began.

"Men, I have only a few words to say. You all know the news that Colonel Bonham brought us yesterday. Fannin is *not* coming." He let that simple statement sink in. "Nor is it likely that we will receive help from any other quarter. In the settlements, our countrymen, like us, have been caught by surprise. While it seems our position here is finally being understood, and we hear that preparations to help us continue apace, it now seems certain that we will be attacked in force before any reinforcements arrive.

"With your own eyes, you see the enemy's numbers, and you know what the outcome must be." The men all knew this but listened intently as Will continued. "It has befallen us to face the brunt of the enemy's fury, and there can be no question of surrender or retreat. Each day that we hold out is important, but I mean this to be more than just an action to buy time. We will fight to the last man, and we will fight with skill and dedication. We will make those who face us regret the day they ever crossed the Rio Grande!" A cheer went up, and Will continued.

"Each of them who may survive will not leave this place with the confidence he brought across the river. They will leave with doubt in their minds and fear in their hearts, and dread of the day that they should ever be called upon to face another Texian!" Another cheer as Will continued. "In that way they will carry our fury in their hearts wherever they go, and we will be present in every battle that follows." Then Will lowered his voice and spoke with calm deliberation.

"For whatever reason fate has laid upon our shoulders this task. We will do our duty! But I know there may be some of you who are not ready to face this. You may have reasons, which no man can fairly question. So I am offering anyone who wishes, the opportunity to leave, no questions asked." He drew his sword and traced a line in the sand.

"But those who will stay and fight, cross this line and stand with me!"

A momentary silence ensued. Then all the men, save one, crossed the line.

During the night, that lone man abandoned the fort. As Saturday morning dawned, clear and a little milder, his absence seemed to bind the rest together and finalize the compact between them. No one spoke of it, and they went about their business, playing out their roles as if in the final act of a tragic opera.

In the afternoon, fire from the Mexican cannons became sporadic. The Texians wondered—not with dismay, but with professional regard—if the Mexican army might soon be maneuvering into position for what only could be the inevitable assault. The defenders intended to be ready with the most effective response. To Dickenson and Jim this meant deliberation over where best to train their batteries so that the first salvos might do the most damage to the enemy.

But the anticipation of changes in the enemy's formations were as nothing compared with the changes in the hearts of the defenders. Although each prepared in his own way, as a group they had become as one. In contrast to the anxiety of the eleven previous days since the siege had begun, they were now not merely resigned, but strangely animated, even positive. It was as if a great weight had been lifted from each of them.

Petty differences had been forgotten, and they brought new energy to the task of preparing the defenses. They even joked, but they had changed—so much so that if stranger from another land had suddenly been thrust within the fortress and had not climbed the walls to see the assembled army outside, he would never have imagined that these men were facing certain death.

Such was the mood that had overtaken them. The disquiet, which only a day before had consumed them, had given way to resolution and to the freedom that comes with recognition and acceptance of reality.

Towards evening as Jim stepped out from the old chapel, Will called to him from just outside the corner of the long barracks.

"Jim, how goes it?"

"Good evening, Will. I reckon we've got our guns zeroed in and about as ready as ever they will be!"

"I'm sure of it! Would you join me for a minute?" Jim followed Will across the plaza into his headquarters, which they both entered in silence, and sat down. Will turned immediately to something he had been writing. Within a few moments he said, "I'll be sending this express as soon as it's dark. Is there anything you'd like to send?"

Although Will asked the question in a matter-of-fact

way, his asking it at all told the whole story. This would likely be the last express from the Alamo.

There were many people that Jim had thought of writing over the last few days: Lila Sue, his mother, Luke, Malachia. He had not brought himself to do it. Now there was no more time. Just as well. They all knew him, knew how he felt.

"No, nothing; thanks, Will."

As Will finished the letter, he put it in a packet with some other things and turned back to Jim.

"I'm sending this with James Allen. He'll go to Gonzales and then on to Washington. I want him to give a verbal report as well." Just then Allen appeared at the door.

"I'm ready, sir."

Jim was pleased that Will had chosen Allen. He was a bright young lad, one of the group who had come in from Gonzales, and maybe his return would lighten some of the pain soon to be felt in that town. After Will had finished his instructions and handed the packet to Allen, the young man turned to Jim as if seeking some instruction from someone who had done this sort of thing before. Jim understood and with a confident and hearty pat on the back, he added to Will's words.

"Be sure you stay clear of the powder house but still well north of the Gonzales road. And good luck!"

The councils of war were over. All had been said that could be said, and all had been done that could be done. Will himself, now carefully avoiding any profundities, could not but remark on the spirit of the garrison.

"The men have never been better. They're ready." Looking more directly at his friend, ". . . and you, Jim?"

"I am indeed . . . and you?"

Will nodded, and then added, "Thanks, Jim."

They shook hands in silence, and Jim left. He climbed up to his post on the chapel parapet and, relieving the others who had been on watch, suddenly found himself alone, kept company only by the Mexican campfires and noises in the distance. Their presence, ominous as it was, provided a curious kind of relief from the loneliness of the night.

But such thoughts were fleeting, and soon he found that he could not but reflect on his life. He thought mostly of what had been, not what *might* have been—the usual things, he supposed. He couldn't get John and Simeon out of his mind, but he forced himself, with a difficulty that surprised him, to picture the living: Mama, Luke, Lila Sue. What were they doing this evening, he wondered. He didn't know how much time had passed, but soon the big Texas moon had risen, and Dickenson had returned to take over the watch, leaving Jim to his own devices.

He went down to the stable where Saluda stood, stroked her silently for a while, and walked her slowly to the postern. Then, nodding to the sentry, he released her into the night with the fervent hope that she would survive and live. At first she loitered about, nibbling at nonexistent growth in the rocky soil, and then wandered off, somehow getting the idea. Jim climbed again to the rear wall of the chapel and watched her heading off in the direction she knew so well as the moon slipped behind a welcome cloud.

Jim looked up where the moon had been and offered an unspoken prayer. *God forgive me any wrong I have done, any hurt I may have caused. Bless my family and my friends. Give me—give us—courage. Bless us all.*

His was but one of many prayers in several languages being offered in and around the Alamo that night. He stood and gazed into the darkness for a while. When the sky cleared, he became aware that the Mexican cannons had grown silent. He returned to his bunk and fell into a fitful sleep.

He awoke at the first shouts and sounds of gunfire. It was dark, but he knew it was morning, and he knew immediately what it meant. He woke fighting mad, as if these sounds were a signal to unleash all the frustration and disappointment welled up within him. There was no reason to restrain it. His heart pounded as he raced up the earthen ramp to the parapet. In moments he and Dickinson, Esparza, and the others were at their posts. They laid their rifles along the wall and quickly manned the two cannons, as Jim looked over at the shadows now approaching. *You want my life . . . come and get it!*

"Fire!" The round from the first twelve-pounder spewed forth, almost immediately followed by the second as it roared in his ear. Jim took grim satisfaction in seeing both rounds fall in the midst of the advancing Mexicans, many of them now screaming in agony as they fell back from the blasts of the salvo. As they reloaded, the sounds of the other batteries joined in, and the fury of the battle seized him. He loved life, and these people were about to take it away from him, and he wanted to kill them for it.

They fired round after round, many of them canister and grape. Together with Ward's single cannon at the front of the chapel and Crockett and his riflemen below, they were inflicting devastating losses on all the enemy who came within their field of fire. But the plaza beyond the front of the chapel was their blind spot, obscured by the long barracks. It was from that direction that the shouting told them that the Mexicans had gained the plaza, necessarily having breached the north wall, and the west as well. They knew that soon they would feel fire from their own batteries being turned against them from the west wall.

As Jim looked in that direction, he saw the flag still fluttering defiantly. At its base Ward and another man, apparently the only ones still standing at the forward battery, struggling to load the gun. In that frozen moment, Jim watched as Ward's comrade slumped to the floor. He motioned to Esparza, and together they raced along behind the parapet to help Ward with the gun.

As they got there, Jim could see that the long barracks seemed still to be holding, but it and the chapel were all that remained to the defenders.

From the top of the ramp behind him there came a shout for more powder, and at the same time he saw that Crockett was being outflanked by the enemy in the plaza. Ward's eight-pounder had but a single charge left. It took no council of war for the three men to know where to place the shot for it to do the most good—to help Crockett, and perhaps gain time to get more powder from the armory below.

They trained the gun point-blank on the Mexicans now crowding the plaza beyond Crockett's position. As they had fought to turn it, Jim caught a quick glimpse of Dickinson and the others at the far end of the chapel, having taken up rifles and firing down the earthen ramp into the void below his position. The shouting was now intense, and as they fired the cannon Jim turned again, this time to see several Mexican soldiers running towards them along the breastworks. They had apparently come up the ramp at the other end, meaning that the rear batteries had been overrun and the powder room now definitely cut off. Jim no longer saw Ward, but he and Esparza both picked up rifles they had placed against the parapet and fired point-blank at the oncoming enemy, dropping two of them. Esparza handed Jim another rifle, and as Jim fired he saw, out of the corner of his eye, Esparza toppling into the void below.

Now more Mexicans came. Jim was reaching for the pistol in his belt when he was hit. There was no pain, but he was aware of a powerful blow to the stomach as an irresistible force drove him back. He was lying on something. Was it Ward?

As if in a dream, he watched each distinct movement of the Mexican officer as he came forward and hauled down the flag, and ever so slowly—*Why was it so slow?*—he saw him attach his own flag, the flag of Mexico, to the halyard. Then, as he began to raise it, Jim felt the pistol still in his hand. He raised it and fired into the chest of the Mexican. The flag, like a great leaf, began to flutter down, its bright colors turning black as they shut out the first light of the morning sky.

CHAPTER NINETEEN

A little more than twelve years had passed since the fall of the Alamo. Texas had flourished as an independent republic for ten of those years, finally joining the Union as the thirty-sixth state. It had been an era of growth and consolidation, but there had also been much adversity. In the past year Corpus Christi and Galveston had suffered terrible epidemics of yellow fever. In fact no towns on the Gulf had escaped. New Orleans and Mobile had been hard hit, as had the seaports of Mexico. Veracruz was a place of sickness and distress.

But up in the mountains, in the valley of Mexico, Mexico City was a haven. Flowers bloomed, the sky was bright blue, and the air was cool and fresh. In contrast to the fetid climate on the coast where life seemed a daily struggle and fear of disease an overriding concern, there was time to enjoy life.

In the spring of '48, Bentley's Circus was in town. The populace were enjoying performances of dance companies from Spain and Italy, the theater flourished, and in the bullring the corridas had seldom been better.

The *fondas* and cantinas were always busy. There was a sense of vitality that more nearly resembled a flourishing European capital than a city under occupation by a foreign army for more than six months.

The United States and Mexico had been at war since the summer of 1846, and Santa Anna had once again been a key figure. After early victories in the North by Zachary Taylor at Buena Vista and Monterrey, the Army of the United States, under the command of General Winfield Scott, had come ashore at Veracruz in April of 1847. In a succession of quick and sometimes costly victories, they had fought their way up to the valley of Mexico, finally occupying the capital in September. Engagement with guerrillas continued into the winter, but essentially the war had been won by the United States.

By late November a cease-fire generally ensued, and by early February a peace treaty had been signed by the Mexican government. It only remained for the United States Congress to ratify it and that ratification to be verified by the Mexicans before the war could be declared officially ended.

Meanwhile, key parts of the country beyond the capital had been occupied by the Americans, and there was a sense of the future being on hold, as both sides awaited finalization of the treaty. The stakes were high. By its victory the United States was about to annex New Mexico and California and fix the southern border not only of Texas but of itself as a newly defined continental power.

Yet as the Mexican people struggled to embrace peace, months had slipped by waiting for the politicians to finish their games of cat and mouse. A large portion of the population had never much enthusiasm for the war in the first place, so it had been only a matter of days after the fall of Mexico City before an easy fraternization with the occupying army had begun. It was more pronounced in the cosmopolitan environs of the capital, to be sure, but general throughout much of the country nevertheless. Now, a sort of ennui had set in. As pleasant as life had almost become, both the citizens and the army of occupation were becoming restless and wanted it finally to be over.

Less exciting than the capital, and certainly less frenetic, Cuernavaca was a place where life was even more pleasant. The new military governor of the region, Colonel Milledge Luke Bonham, had arrived with his regiment, the Twelfth United States Infantry, on the tenth of March after a two-day march from the capital. The regiment became the principal unit in the brigade-size force that occupied the region as Luke succeeded the original holder of the post, General Smith. The command had settled down for an indefinite period in this most charming of places.

Luke, like all of his men, had been happy to quit the unhealthy environs of their previous billet at the convent of Ensansia in Mexico City where they had been billeted most of the time since the cease-fire. Though final ratification of the treaty was not a foregone conclusion, their hopes were high that within a matter of months they would be on their way home. It could not come soon enough for Luke, but he was thankful to be spending the waning days of the conflict in such serene and beautiful surroundings.

Everything about it suited him. Encircled by majestic mountains, it seemed a place of perpetual spring. The air, while crisp, was not so rarefied as in the capital. Riots of colorful flowers abounded, while humming-birds darted among blossoms he could not name. The delight was not just to his eyes; the fragrance of the orange blossoms everywhere seemed made sweeter by the gentle trickle of the ubiquitous fountains, each seeming to echo the sounds of others throughout the city and

bringing a kind of measured music, which complemented all other aspects of the environment. Such also
was the courtyard of the villa in which he made his
headquarters. Overlooking it all, the shaded verandah
outside his office on the second floor was indeed a place
of serenity, a kind of Arcadian retreat that until arriving
in Cuernavaca, he could have only imagined.

But now in mid-April, the waiting was wearing on
him. He had been dealing with various annoyances, but
none had disturbed him more that a recent dispatch he
had received. It described how, inexplicably, Santa Anna
had been cordially received, even *protected* from the
relentless pursuit of the Texas Rangers by an American
colonel somewhere near Santa Anna's hacienda at
Encero.

Luke continued to be amazed at Santa Anna's resil-
ience. In the years following his acts of butchery at the
Alamo and Goliad and his ignominious defeat at San
Jacinto, Santa Anna had eventually been deposed. At
the time this new war began, he was in exile in Cuba. But
he had been recalled by a nation desperate for leadership. Once again with his peculiar combination of brilliance, daring, and somehow ultimate ineptitude, he
had returned to lead Mexico to yet another disaster.

His return was marked by his landing at Veracruz
on September 14th, 1846; yet it had taken but one year to
the day until the stars and stripes were raised over the
National Palace in Mexico City. After the fall of the
capital, as a last gasp, he had undertaken the investment
of Puebla, since early in the war occupied by American
troops. It was a key point astride their lifeline—the
National Highway between Veracruz and Mexico City.

The siege had lasted for a month, and had it not been
broken by the brilliance and initiative of General Lane
and the untiring efforts of the Texas Rangers, the entire
American army could have soon been in dire straits

with even the outcome of the war in doubt. In collateral actions at nearby Huamantla and finally at Atlixco, the organized resistance had ended. Santa Anna once again had tasted failure at a key moment. Having already resigned the presidency, he was reduced to orchestrating guerrilla attacks on the occupation force.

Soon it became evident even to the citizenry that the *guerrilleros* were closer to being bandits than patriots. The Generalissimo's credibility waned even further, and his status became that of fugitive rather than national leader.

Winfield Scott's successor, General Butler, had authorized the issuance of a passport to him. While waiting for passage, Santa Anna had found the safe haven, which now so disturbed Luke. How ironic that the man who more than any other had set in motion the forces that had precipitated this war would once again escape—free to do *what* in the future? Nevertheless, Luke was pleased that elements of his regiment had participated in the actions at both Huamantla and Atlixco, his only regret being that they had not finally run Santa Anna to ground.

As he stood on the verandah gazing at the smoking peak of Popocatépetl in the distance and rehashing these events in his mind, Luke suddenly became aware that the sound of the fountain had competition from approaching footsteps on the hard tile behind him. He turned to see Tom Seymour, who had taken over active command of the regiment since Luke had assumed his present role. He was met with the greeting, "Hi there, Colonel B., enjoying the view?"

"It's the most relaxing place I know, Tom!"

"Can you believe that Hancock and his friends actually climbed it?"

Luke nodded in admiration of his young adjutant, while both men stood in silence for a moment gazing at the volcano. Tom was about to speak when Hancock himself appeared in the doorway.

"Ah, Lieutenant. Good day."

"Good morning, sir" and acknowledging Tom, "Colonel Seymour." He turned again towards Luke. "We have just received this dispatch." He handed him a large sealed envelope and stepped back to wait with Tom in silence as Luke opened it and read it without expression.

After several minutes, which seemed longer by far to the others, Luke looked up and broke into a smile.

"This should make you both very happy!"

"The treaty?" Tom guessed.

"Yes! Ratified by the Senate at the end of March and received in Mexico City two days ago. The Mexicans, of course, have not yet had time to verify it, but we are to make preparations to leave here and can expect to receive orders before the end of next month. The entire occupation is expected to be ended before summer is over!"

Hancock, with a broad grin on his face finally said, "Then it's official, sir? The war is over?"

"Not quite yet, officially. But apparently verification is so much a certainty that General Butler has ordered us to go forward with 'all haste' in making preparations, and be ready to leave here on short notice not later than the end of May. We will rendezvous with other units in the city, and then it will become a matter of an orderly withdrawal of the entire army down to Veracruz."

"You believe the Mexicans will sign off on it then?" Tom asked as the last vestige of skepticism left him.

"Yes, I do, and it's about time. We'll be leaving all right, but not tomorrow; there is much to do. We're going to be very busy." He thought for a moment.

"First, we must notify the *Alcalde*. I want him to hear

it from us. He must understand that our withdrawal will be orderly, that we will brook no nonsense in the process, and leave this place in good condition." Then, turning to Hancock, he asked, "Do you reckon he will be in his office by now?"

"He's usually there at this hour, sir."

"Good! Then please go directly to him, present my compliments, and determine the earliest time I might see him. Tell him that it's important!"

"Yes *Sir!*" Hancock smiled, saluted, and did a smart about-face and was gone.

Luke had always understood that success with the occupation depended in large part on the cooperation of the local hierarchy. Not only was civil order at stake, but the ultimate well-being of his troops in an environment, which no matter how friendly it seemed, always held the potential of becoming hostile. Not all Mexicans were delighted to host a Yankee army, but Luke had worked hard to minimize potential problems and to develop the positive aspects of this grandest of all shotgun weddings. Fairness in his actions and assurance of respect for local customs by his troops had become his stock in trade.

Because he had been careful to maintain a certain formality and correctness with the local gentry, he had earned the good will of most of them. Luke had come to see beyond their feudal trappings and appreciate their struggle to establish institutions, which would enable an enduring modern form of government consistent with their own culture. But since winning their own independence, they had yet to find a way of bringing it about, and remained vulnerable to the likes of Santa Anna who would always be prepared to subordinate the country's interests to their own.

Luke's impression was that most of the people with whom he dealt cared little about the sparsely populated lands to the north, nor could they be expected long to hold them, if not from the United States, then from Britain or some other continental power. The injury to their pride however, from losing this vast territory, would be a bitter pill indeed. Nevertheless, he privately believed that in the long run Mexico would be better off, still a huge country, consolidated within what seemed more natural borders. In any case, he had no reason to expect anything but their good will and fullest cooperation as he readied his forces for withdrawal.

Luke's mind raced over what seemed like hundreds of details as he digested the reality of the occupation being almost over. Finally, he turned back to Seymour.

"Well Tom, it looks as if you'll be in Connecticut before the snow flies again!"

"I can hardly wait!"

"I know." Then, remembering that Tom had not yet announced the reason for his visit, he added, "Tom, was there something on your mind before we received this grand news?"

"Nothing so important as what we have just learned, just some details. Really, I suppose, just to chat." He laughed.

The men had become close friends. Tom, knowing Luke well enough, could tell that he had given up on whatever had preoccupied him earlier and would now be focusing on preparations for the withdrawal. He was suddenly struck with another aspect of the news, something that until now had been left unsaid.

"There are a lot of fine people we'll be leaving behind."

"There are indeed. I'm thankful that the remains of my dear cousins were returned home."

He was alluding to Pierce Butler who had commanded the volunteers from South Carolina, the Palmetto regiment, and to young Andrew who had been a lieutenant in the same outfit. Both had died heroically at the bloody battle of Churubusco. Only by the greatest effort, both in Columbia and in the field with the army, had it been made possible to return their remains.

Remembering that battle from when he had been serving with the Ninth Infantry regiment, Tom observed, "The Palmetto's losses were truly staggering."

Replying, almost to himself, Luke said, "For *all* the regiments, yours as well, Tom."

"Yes." Tom paused, remembering those days of the past summer. Almost as if to erase the faces of fallen comrades from his mind, he turned the subject back to Luke. "How was it that you were not with the Palmettos?"

"I could have been, but I chose the regular army."

Sensing that his friend would explain no further without prompting, and yet realizing that he seemed to want to talk about it, Tom continued.

"And what led you to that?"

"*Manifest Destiny*," he laughed. "Like you, Tom, I really believe we are riding the wave of history, and young career officers such as Hancock are going to make it become a reality. Our country will be greater than we could have ever imagined!"

"But couldn't you have served that idea just as well with the Palmettos?"

"Of course, but it was Pierce's place to lead that regiment, and I would have been in the way. But there's more to it than that. By accepting a commission in the regular army, I sought to make clear that my concern was with the broader interests of the United States. We all know the political issues that divide the country over this war, and they're not entirely baseless. But the causes and the goals, which have been enunciated by the president, are valid. I'm not here fighting for the extension of our *peculiar institution*. Even if I were, it's inconceivable in the setting of the vast western lands. For instance: where would they find the slaves?" He thought for a few moments, then continued, "I can tell you, neither Pierce nor Andrew sought that either. That makes it even sadder, good men giving their lives even as their motives were being questioned."

"But doesn't serving at all, no matter which unit, leave you, as a Southerner, open to those questions?"

"Of course, but it makes it a longer stretch for those who want to make an issue of it, and perhaps may give them pause to remember what it says in the Bible about casting the first stone."

Luke stopped there. He had strong feelings about the losses suffered by the Palmetto regiment, to his mind an unnecessary sacrifice in a battle that had already been won. He felt himself about to express sentiments better left unsaid. He had been distressed at reading the news accounts of the triumphal return of General Shields to the United States; in particular, his visit to South Carolina. It had been his brigade in which the Palmetto regiment had served.

Although the general's war record had been highly acclaimed, it was to Luke, unseemly that Shields should be traveling around Carolina in a railroad car named *Pierce Butler*, all the while taking bows and receiving honors from people whose sons he had led to slaughter. Particularly galling to Luke was the quote from a speech given at South Carolina College, in which Shields addressed the cadets.

"I wish I had you at Churubusco . . . what I could have done with you there!" *Yes — get them all killed,* Luke had thought as he read the account. Certainly there was no question of Shields' personal courage. But to Luke, it was a bitter metaphor that Pierce should continue to support Shields, even if only by means of his name on a railroad car. It stuck in Luke's craw and went against everything he held dear, beginning with his family motto—*esse quam videri*—to be rather than to seem. Stopping himself before he vented, Luke changed the subject.

"Forgive me, Tom, I know you, too, lost a lot of wonderful friends—Ransom and others—and there'll be much sadness in New England for a long time to come!"

"Yes, but I'm looking to the future now, as I am sure you are."

"Indeed!"

Tom left, but Luke's reflective mood did not. *Well, it seems that it really is over.* Luke stood thinking about the campaign and the long road that had brought him here to this unlikely paradise. He had assumed command of the regiment when his predecessor, Lewis Wilson, had died of yellow fever shortly after they arrived in Veracruz. Then there had been all the bloody battles up to the valley of Mexico; Paso de Ovejas, Cerro Gordo, Contreras, Churubusco—until finally, Chapultepec was stormed. Tom Seymour had participated in raising the stars and stripes over the castle.

Finally, the occupation of Mexico City: at first, a flush from the heady wine of victory, but eventually something akin to the doldrums, illness among the troops, dissension and political maneuvering at the highest levels of the army, growing concern with the well-being of his family, and now—Cuernavaca. It had been a long and painful journey, but it was nearly over. Luke was proud to have taken part in it, but now at age thirty-five, he was anxious to go home and to get on with his life.

Finally his thoughts did indeed turn to the future and to what he would do when he got back. Returning to Ann was foremost, and he could not help but wonder how it would be with her. Would they be as strangers after so long a separation? After all, by the time he could get home, it would have been more than a year since he had seen her. And what of little Sallie? Would she remember her father? And his mother; she had taken a bad fall during his absence, and was really getting too far along in years to deal with the demands of the plantations.

Then there were the terrible voids left by the deaths of Pierce, Andrew, and the others. How hollow now seemed the brave words he had invoked in Edgefield to send them off on that day that now seemed so long ago. *By God! Even though they had been poorly used, they showed what they were made of!* But it pained him to think of it.

His ruminations were interrupted by the return of Lieutenant Hancock. Within little more than an hour of having left, he had returned to tell Luke that the *Alcalde* was available now, if it suited the esteemed colonel. It did suit him! He was comfortable in going himself to visit the *Alcalde* at his office. He could have summoned him, of course—he had little doubt that had their roles been reversed that would have been the case. But that was not his way. Yankee officers . . . Luke smiled to himself . . . *me, a Yankee* . . . did not stand on such ceremony. Winning the war spoke for itself.

Before leaving on the short ride, he left word for his staff and the unit commanders to be assembled for a meeting, to commence immediately upon his return. There was much to do.

By the next morning, the pending withdrawal was common knowledge. Ratification of the treaty by the American Congress had by no means been a sure thing. Nevertheless, it had been anticipated. The news, while cause for some quiet celebration, was received calmly by the army and the citizenry alike, exactly the way Luke wanted it to be. It was now simply a matter of time before the provisional Mexican government, assembled at Querétaro, ended it all with their final approval.

Even though he had been expecting it, the actual fact of an imminent departure energized Luke. He had not realized how enervated he had become. Along with personal concerns, months of worry that foes of the treaty in Washington might at the last minute cause it to be rejected, had taken their toll. But now, the threat of limbo lifted, he felt like a new man.

Late in the morning of the second day after his visit with the *Alcalde*, Luke's orderly appeared, an envelope in hand.

"Beg your pardon, sir, this message for you has just arrived. The man who brought it is standing by, should you wish to reply now."

Luke took the envelope. He noticed the fine paper with only his name inscribed in a beautiful hand on the cover; clearly not an official document. He and opened it. The message read:

Esteemed Colonel Bonham —
Understanding that the opportunity may soon pass, it will do me great honor if you are able to dine with me at the hacienda, Saturday afternoon next.

Luke recognized immediately the signature, no less than the patriarch of the local gentry, known to all about simply as Don Alfredo, and one of the few among that group whom he had not met or even seen. While his orderly waited, Luke sat down and penned his acceptance.

Chapter Twenty

As he set out for Don Alfredo's hacienda, Luke was accompanied by Joseph Malone, his sergeant-major. Not only did Malone's presence satisfy the minimum demands of protocol, but Luke enjoyed his company and regularly chose him for such assignments. These occasions also afforded Luke opportunities to stay in touch more directly with the concerns and morale of the command. They had an easy going relationship, and despite the difference in rank, they felt comfortable in each other's company. Both were excellent horsemen who looked forward to a stimulating ride as they broke into a canter upon reaching the outskirts of town.

Luke was a tall and graceful figure who sat on a horse with noble bearing, as did Malone. Together, clad in their dress uniforms, sabers alongside their saddles, they presented an impressive sight as they made their way to the *finca* of Don Alfredo.

In less than an hour they arrived at the main gate. Luke had passed it several times since coming to Cuernavaca but could only guess what lay beyond. It was an impressive stone and timber structure, adorned with bits of wrought iron filigree and opening into a road that led up a long slope, irregularly flanked with clumps of trees and disappearing over a ridge. Beyond, purple sierras loomed in the distance, icons of this still exotic land.

They were met at the gate by a delegation of three men: a young, well-dressed *caballero* whose English precluded little more than rudimentary introductions, and two older *vaqueros* whose wizened faces suggested that they belonged to a culture about which Luke really knew very little. Correct and smiling, the young man affected a demeanor that made the visitors feel welcome but offered no suggestion of familiarity. With the gate closed behind them, the escort led them up the road at a walk with only the clatter of hoofs and calls of birds punctuating an otherwise palpable silence.

As they reached the top of the rise, a jewel-like valley opened to their view. Just low enough to be hidden by the ridge over which they were passing, it spread out before them—a kind of paradise, hidden from the view of all, save those fortunate enough to live there.

What Luke took to be the main house was the center-piece of a collection of buildings: barns, stables, and others, the entire ensemble under venerable tile roofs, rambling over a verdant landscape. The architecture was simple, a happy combination of stone, stucco, and timber that seemed almost to have sprung from the earth itself, and was adroitly punctuated with touches of blue, black, and ochre color at doors and windows.

Bits of ironwork and a vine trailing flamboyant flowers from the loggia above the front entrance com-pleted the tableau. The land itself seemed dominated by green pastures, liberally sprinkled with trees, and con-taining several ponds, which evidently were fed by a small stream that trickled across the valley. Malone and

Luke looked at each other in silent appreciation at the beauty of the scene.

As they descended, they saw two men waiting near the front of the main house. One of them, a distinguished looking older man, was obviously Don Alfredo, and the other, seemingly a servant. No other family, or household retainers were to be seen, although Luke caught a brief glimpse of two other men entering a distant building.

"Bienvenidos!" called Don Alfredo, his warmth and expansiveness immediately apparent and belying the formality of the invitation and their reception at the gate.

"Don Alfredo?" Luke responded as he dismounted.

"*Sí*, of course! I am so pleased that you were able to come!" He responded in English, much to Luke's relief.

It being an unofficial affair, Luke had decided not to bring a translator, leaving it to his host to deal with any possible language problem. But with that obstacle cleared, a slightly more relaxed Luke returned the greeting. In the course of the next several minutes, he introduced Sergeant Malone and learned that the head of the delegation, which met them at the gate, was the *patron's* grandson. It soon became clear and mildly surprising to Luke that this *comida* was to be a private affair attended only by himself and his host. Others would be taking the midday meal, of course, but not with them. Malone took their horses, and following the escort, disappeared around the end of the building.

Broadly smiling, yet patrician in his demeanor, Don Alfredo conducted Luke to a shaded terrace nearby. Together with cascades of flowers, it was enhanced by a nearby brook, which seemed to spring from a rock formation only a few yards from where they sat.

"The beauty of your hacienda is much to be admired, Don Alfredo," Luke said.

"Thank you, Colonel, in many ways it is, I hope, the truest expression of my life. Obligations and duty have often taken me far from this place, but it's always in my thoughts—a sort of *ancla*—anchor of my existence. I suppose some would consider it foolish to become so attached to a place, but it's my way." He finished with a sort of shrug and a smile.

"A worthy effort, sir. I understand completely!"

Then ensued one of the most pleasant repasts Luke had ever experienced. The food was fine and most appropriate for the occasion; the wine was excellent and did its work in stimulating a conversation, which touched on a wide range of subjects, but without mention of any specific business that might have been the cause for the invitation.

In the course of their talk however, Luke learned that his host was very well informed of the mind-set of his countrymen assembled at Querétaro, and if there was any purpose to this meeting, it was to inform Luke that the treaty would indeed be affirmed. It happened that among the delegates was Don Alfredo's son, and as they lingered over coffee, Don Alfredo explained himself a bit further.

"Although I have been aware of your sensitive handling of your responsibilities here, my son's role in the negotiations obliged me to wait until it was assured that the treaty would become reality before I felt it proper that we should meet. Now that the time is come, I must say it has been a pleasure, and I wish to express most sincerely my thanks at the manner in which you have discharged your duties."

"You are kind, indeed, Don Alfredo. Thank you!"

Then, rising to mark an end of the meal, Don Alfredo continued. "Since you admire the hacienda so, perhaps you would enjoy a brief tour before you depart?"

"Most certainly! It would be a great pleasure!"

Don Alfredo then showed him some of the treasures within the house, as well as a few of the more important rooms, and then outside several of the adjacent buildings. As the tour ended and they emerged from inspecting the inner workings of a handsome stone mill, Don Alfredo sent for Sergeant Malone and the horses. As they waited, Luke continuing to regard the mill with admiration, his host facing out towards the nearby pasture. Luke then noticed that Don Alfredo had become distracted and was looking past him over his shoulder.

Luke turned to see what had caught Don Alfredo's attention. Never in his life had he been more shocked. Chills ran over his body as he caught his breath and grasped the trunk of a nearby tree for support. He could feel the color drain from his face, and he heard his host's voice as if coming from the bottom of a well.

"Colonel! Are you ill?"

Luke could not answer immediately. He could only stare in disbelief, because there, before him, stood . . . could it be? *"Saluda!"*

The name involuntarily slipped from his lips. Another chill passed over him as the great bay mare, until then intent on the sugar she was expecting to receive from Don Alfredo, stopped in her tracks and faced Luke squarely. For a moment man and horse stood there, frozen in time, and Luke was overcome with emotion. He was barely able to repeat the word, "Saluda". . . and then, as if they were back in the pasture at Red Bank and the last twelve years had never happened, she turned and walked slowly over to him.

Don Alfredo, too, was stunned. He knew he had witnessed something extraordinary but was not sure what to make of it.

"You know this horse, Colonel?"

Without immediately answering him, Luke reached across the fence and rubbed the mare's chin in the same way he had when she was a colt. Finally, as emotion receded and he became more composed, he turned to his host.

"Yes, Don Alfredo, I do know this horse. But tell me—how do you come to have her?"

"My son brought the horse back from Texas—from Bexar—after the battle of the Alamo."

"My brother died at the Alamo. She was his horse."

Both men stared at each other in near disbelief. Then, Don Alfredo, fighting hard not to seem to be offering an apology, continued.

"Miguel, my son, was on the staff of General Santa Anna. It was Miguel who was selected to bring back the dispatches with reports of the battle, and he did so, riding this horse." He paused as he sought to determine how Luke was taking this news. Then he added, "Of course he was not there when the actions took place at Goliad or San Jacinto."

Don Alfredo would like to have told Luke how disgusted Miguel had been at Santa Anna's butchery at the Alamo, and how he and all of his family had been sickened when they heard the further news of Santa Anna's shameful slaughter of Fannin and his men at Goliad, and the dishonor of his personal conduct at San Jacinto. But to say this to Luke at this time would have sounded disingenuous in the extreme, and beneath his dignity. He could say no more and simply let the facts as he had explained them rest.

Luke stood looking at Don Alfredo for what seemed an eternity but was actually less than a minute. His expression conveyed no feeling. He was, in a way, numb. He could muster no hatred for this man or for his family. He believed that they were honorable people and quite possibly had even lower regard for Santa Anna than did he. Directly addressing the concerns that must be coursing directly beneath the surface within his host, he said, "*Señor*, if you are concerned that somehow I may hold your son or your family responsible for what happened at the Alamo those many years ago, please rest easy, and be assured that I do not."

Although he tried to conceal it, Don Alfredo was visibly relieved.

"You are most gracious. Were I in your position, I am not sure how I would react."

In a voice full of emotion Luke replied, "The same, I am sure." The words expressed an unspoken bond between honorable men which transcended nationalities. "You can imagine my surprise. It's hard to believe that after all these years . . ." his voice trailed off. "But can you tell me more? Some details?"

Don Alfredo told him all he knew about how Miguel had found Saluda and then finished his narrative.

"And she has been a special animal, a favorite, for all these years. We have, of course, ridden her less and less as she has grown older, but she has remained—how would you say it—*vivaracha, alegre.*"

"Sprightly?"

"*Sí,* sprightly, all these years. We call her *Guapa.*" He stopped and looked at the horse who was indeed a handsome one. "And you, Colonel . . . called her Saluda. Was that—*is* that—her name?"

"Yes, she was named after the river that is near our home."

"Is there a Rio Saluda in Texas?"

"Not that I am aware. We come from South Carolina." Then Luke recounted for Don Alfredo how Jim had come into possession of Saluda and how she had come to be at the Alamo.

"Truly a soul-stirring story, Colonel! And there is yet one more piece of it which I can supply you." Seeing the quizzical expression on Luke's face, Don Alfredo hastily continued, "Come, follow me."

He led Luke to another beautiful stone building some distance away. If anything, it was more handsome that the mill which Luke had admired so much. The limestone bore a patina that only time can bestow, and at every hand the craftsmanship and the fittings were of the highest quality. Yet it was a stable.

They entered at one end under the sculpted head of a horse and proceeded down a long corridor formed by stalls on either side. At the end they passed through another door, and Luke found himself in one of the most beautiful tack rooms he had ever seen. Almost immediately, he spotted it—hanging on the wall, the bridle that was part of the tack with which Jim had been outfitted as he left Edgefield. But he waited for Don Alfredo to speak.

"Here—here is the bridle which *Guapa* wore when Miguel found her."

As his host handed it to him, Luke could suddenly remember that day when he had placed this very same bridle in Jim's hand, a bridle that would take him on the final adventure of his life. He could not restrain tears from welling up in his eyes. Finally, in a not-too-steady voice he said, "And here is the Palmetto imprint with which old Jonathan always marked his work."

"Yes, *Señor,* we have always wondered about that mark and, I must say, admired the sentiment which is inscribed upon it—*esse quam videri.*"

"Even now, you will see it on my own tack," Luke said almost to himself. Then he finally turned and looked across the room. "A beautiful room, Don Alfredo. I hope you will soon be able to enjoy it in peace."

"It has always been peaceful here." He smiled.

At that, both men, as if obeying some unspoken command, stepped out through a side door into the sunlight. Once again Luke drank in the beauty of the place, his gaze settling on Saluda who stood as she had been left waiting. In silence they walked over to her. Luke once again stroked her chin, patted her shoulder, and then turned. Don Alfredo had stopped a short distance away, near where Sergeant Malone had brought the horses. As Luke faced him, he stepped forward, and assumed an air of some formality.

"Colonel Bonham, it has been both a pleasure and a privilege to look after the horse *Saluda*. As I understand, you will in the near future be departing our country for your home. If you will allow me, it would be my pleasure to return this special animal to her true owner. I will have her groomed and brought to you whenever it suits your convenience."

"Thank you, sir, you have been the most gracious of hosts. And your care of Saluda—*Guapa*—befits more than anything I can imagine the memory of my brother. You will always have my gratitude. I will make the arrangements soon."

The formality seemed fitting as an end, not only to the wanderings of Saluda, but to an uneasiness that had haunted Luke for many years.

The battle of the Alamo was finally over.

~ FINDING JIM BONHAM ~

SOME HISTORICAL NOTES

Jim Bonham's significance as an historical figure may be measured by the historical importance of the Alamo epic itself. His actions gave life to the ringing words of Travis and embodied the spirit of the defenders who stood in the face of an overwhelming enemy.

One of my earliest recollections is as a schoolboy studying Texas history. I remember the textbook: it was gray, something less than an inch thick, and the inscription in the front consisted of a single quotation: "Thermopylae had its messenger of defeat, the Alamo had none." This puzzled me, because I knew that James Butler Bonham had returned to the Alamo with a message that defeat was imminent. Of course, I didn't know what or where Thermopylae was, and I had never heard of Leonidas, so it seemed logical that the recipients of such a message be those who were about to be defeated.

Telling the story necessarily involved what I believe to be a logical development and reconciliation of known facts. Although dialogues were invented, attitudes and even some situations projected, they are a faithful reflection of Jim Bonham and his life as I believe I have come to know it. No known historical facts or dates were altered for the sake of the story, and wherever possible, the names of the people are real. A summary of most of my principal sources of information, follows.

THE EARLY YEARS (1807 - 1827)

The details of James Butler Bonham's family life and his antecedents are well documented by official records, deeds and wills, headstones, and notations in the family Bible. And over the generations various family members have studied and recorded family history. Most notable among these were three men, all of whom were named Milledge:

Milledge Luke Bonham, Luke as he is called in the book, was Jim Bonham's younger brother. After serving under

General Bull in the Seminole War, he visited Texas about two years after the fall of the Alamo and did what he could to settle his brother's affairs. While there he met with Sam Houston, as well as with Mrs. Dickenson, and "the two men who sought to dissuade Jim from returning to the Alamo."

Descriptions in the book of Luke's military service in the Mexican War are faithful to the record, and he was mustered out of the army in the summer of 1848. He eventually went on to serve in Congress, then as a General in the Confederacy, and as Governor of South Carolina. He died in 1890, a father of fourteen children (including one who died in infancy) and leaving an extensive collection of papers, which may be found in the Caroliniana Library at the University of South Carolina.

Milledge Lipscomb Bonham was the fifth of fourteen children born to Luke and Ann Patience Griffin Bonham. He became a distinguished jurist, serving as chief justice of the South Carolina Supreme Court, and wrote several papers and letters in which recollections of his father were recounted. These papers also may be found at the Caroliniana Library, as well as at the University of Texas and in The Alamo library. He was fortunate to have known his father well, and as their lifetimes overlapped by thirty five years, he had ample opportunity to hear firsthand accounts of his uncle Jim, particularly about the events leading up to Jim's departure for Texas.

Milledge Louis Bonham, son of Milledge Lipscomb, earned prominence as an historian and became head of the department of history at Hamilton College in Clinton, New York. He wrote, but did not publish a manuscript entitled *The Life and Times of Milledge Luke Bonham*, in which he sets forth much of the information passed along to him by his father and his grandfather. A copy of the manuscript may also be found in the Caroliniana. Among his other writings was an article entitled, "James Butler Bonham: A Consistent Rebel," which was published in the *Southwestern Historical Quarterly* for October, 1931. He named a son Luke, and of his grand uncle, he wrote:

"...*In Texas he defied Santa Anna; in death he defies oblivion.*"

The most comprehensive compilation of the genealogy of the Bonhams in American was prepared by Elmer P. Hazie. It is available at the New York City Public Library and at other institutions.

Life in Edgefield District of South Carolina during the first half of the nineteenth century is well-documented in countless books. In addition to this kind of general reading, a good bit of information was obtained by perusing the collections of the Saluda Historical Society and the Edgefield Historical Society.

Sources of information on South Carolina College (including the visit of Lafayette) were Edwin Green's history of the University, and books by Daniel Hollis, LaBorde, and Hungerpiller [see bibliography]. The archives of the College (now the University of South Carolina), in particular those of the Clariosophic Society, yielded insights into college life at the time, as well as the names of Jim's classmates, many of whom went on to distinguished careers.

NULLIFICATION AND EARLY LAW PRACTICE (1828 - 1834)

James Bonham's participation as an aide to Governor Hamilton and commander of an artillery battery at Charleston harbor during the nullification crisis in South Carolina (1830-32) are documented in official records. It is likely that he regarded Hamilton as a mentor as well as a friend, and noteworthy that Hamilton, in addition to serving in Congress with Sam Houston, eventually played a key role in financing the new Republic of Texas. And like Jim Bonham, he died a hero's death...giving up his life preserver to a mother and daughter following a shipwreck in the Gulf of Mexico. Hamilton's son served briefly under Luke in the Mexican War.

It is possible that during the nullification crisis, Bonham may have met James Fannin who had stopped briefly in Charleston while on his way to Havana. Clarence Wharton mentions the visit in his book, *Remember Goliad* [see bibliography]. If they did meet, this might account for Fannin's reference to Bonham as *"...my friend..."* followed by the comment *"...the artillery is also his favorite corps"* in his letter of referral to Governor Smith dated 30 November 1835.

Records of subsequent events during the time he lived in the Pendleton area are less well documented. However, from

Paula Mitchell Marks [see bibliography] we learn of his acquaintance with the young Sam Maverick and discover that the Maverick Plantation, *Montpelier,* was next door to that of the family of the young woman with whom Bonham has been romantically linked, Caroline Taliaferro.

Other bits of information about this period were obtained from references contained in the papers of Milledge Luke Bonham. These are best exemplified by the recounting of an anecdote by Chancellor James Parsons Carroll, who was James Bonham's roommate at college. It was the story of Bonham's having been jailed for contempt of court. This event was confirmed by Benjamin F. Perry in his sketch of the judge in the case, John F. Richardson [see bibliography]. This sketch however fails to correlate a date with the incident, and many people have assumed that it took place before the nullification crisis. However, in my reconstruction of events I have placed it in early 1834, shortly before Bonham moved to Alabama. This determination was made because it is the only time period during those years for which court records and newspapers are not available. And believing that such an event would have, at the very least, been in the court records, it seems reasonable to assume that as the correct time period.

Unrelated to this incident, but interesting nonetheless, is the appearance of the Leonid meteor storm the preceding fall. By all accounts it was particularly spectacular that year, and although usually less flamboyant, it remains an annual event that we today can share with the people of those times.

ALABAMA (1834 -1835)

Principal sources for the account of Bonham's time in Alabama include: James Bonham's letter to his mother, October 3, 1834, a copy of which can be found in the Alamo Library; *The Wardlaw Chronicles* by Diane Wardlaw, Simeon Bonham's will; a biographical sketch of A. C. Horton by Matthew Ellenberger; the account of the relationship between Dellet and Travis by William C. Davis in his book, *Three Roads to the Alamo;* various accounts of the Mobile Greys [see bibliography]; and Milledge Luke Bonham's account of his last visit with his brother.

TEXAS (1835 -1836)

James Bonham's arrival in Texas can be fixed by Fannin's letter of November 30th, 1835 recommending Bonham to Governor Smith; by the Governor's message of the previous day to the Council, in which he announced *"Some of the Mobile volunteers have arrived ...and called on me..."* and also by Bonham's note of December 1st, to Sam Houston, in which he volunteered his services.

An interesting aspect of the history of this period, particularly insofar as James Bonham is concerned, is the participation of the Mobile Greys. As all accounts acknowledge, Bonham helped to recruit the group during October, 1835 in Mobile. But in making the trip to Texas, the group apparently split up, most traveling by sea, but a few overland with Jim Bonham. The Greys were reunited shortly after arriving in Texas and soon proceeded to Bexar, reaching there about mid-December, shortly after the battle in which General Cos was expelled. Jim eventually saw them again when he was sent to Bexar just before Christmas. By then, a newly commissioned officer in the regular army of Texas, he was most likely responding to orders to escort the reunited Greys and other units to the fortress at Goliad to participate in what Sam Houston expected to be a general mobilization. That he made the trip was also confirmed by the recollections of R. R. Brown, which were published in the *Texas Almanac* in 1859.

The fact of an almost contemporaneous announcement appearing in the Brazoria newspaper (January 2nd and 3rd) announcing his intent to open a law office there should not be taken as proof of Jim's presence in Brazoria. It merely confirms that his plans, no doubt made earlier in the month of December, had been overtaken by events. These movements of Bonham, considered in light of his direct correspondence with Houston, and Houston's remark later in January that Bonham ought to be a Major, suggest that Bonham's recruiting duties may well have expanded into his being Houston's agent in trying to hold together a deteriorating situation among the volunteers at the frontier.

Upon returning from La Bahía to the Alamo with Bowie, Bonham seems to have taken an active role in the restoration of the fortress and leadership of the garrison. This is evidenced by his chairmanship of the committee which drafted the resolution of February 21st supporting Governor Smith. And Paula Mitchell Marks writes that he declined the opportunity to join Sam Maverick as one of the representatives from the Alamo to the Constitutional Convention.

I am persuaded by none other than William Barret Travis that Bonham made but one trip to Fannin. The wording of his messages of March 3rd, and the specific ways in which he alluded to Bonham, strongly suggest that had Bonham been the bearer of an express which was sent after the arrival of the enemy, Travis would have mentioned it. His not having done so suggests that Bonham was probably not at the Alamo when the siege began. It seems more likely that Bonham, after his unsuccessful meeting with Fannin, went to other places in search of help and finally, on his way back to the Alamo, wound up in Gonzales at the end of February. He departed for the Alamo on March 2nd, the same day that Sam Maverick left the Alamo for the convention! The likelihood of their having met on the road is obvious and strongly suggests that Maverick was indeed one of the two men (later mentioned by Jim's brother Luke) who sought to dissuade him from returning to the Alamo.

With reference to Travis, some historians are skeptical as to whether he ever actually challenged his men to remain with him in the Alamo by tracing a line in the sand with his sword. If he did not, then Zuber and Moses Rose probably deserve some sort of literary prize for concocting one of the most enduring myths in history. So much so, that *a-line-in-the-sand* has virtually become part of the language! It seems likely to me that Travis did indeed draw the line and accompanied the act with a dramatic speech. After all, Rose had nothing to gain from the telling of a story that did him no credit. If he had reason to lie about his presence at the Alamo, he could have come up with almost any kind of self-serving tale. Although neither Mrs. Dickenson, nor Travis' servant, Joe, related the incident, there could have been many explanations for their not having done so. But the fact of their having been present and survived the massacre could have seemed a compelling reason for Rose to tell a story which was essentially true.

Some believe that Travis remained hopeful almost to the end, and they cite as evidence, a letter, dated March 1st, from

Williamson (in Gonzales) to Travis, delivered by Bonham upon his return on March 3rd. The original of this letter, presumably having been brought back to Mexico, has never been found. But a translation of it, taken from a Mexican publication of the time was discovered. In this letter, Williamson is purported to have written:

You cannot conceive my anxiety: today it has been four whole days that we have not the slightest news relative to your dangerous situation and we are therefore given over to a thousand conjectures regarding you. Sixty men have left this municipality, who in all probability are with you by this date. Colonel Fannin with 300 men and four pieces of artillery has been on the march towards Bexar three days now. Tonight we await some 300 reinforcements from Washington, Bastrop, Brazoria, and S. Felipe and no time will be lost in providing you assistance. As to the other letter of the same date, let it pass, you will know what it meant: If the multitude gets hold of it, let them figure it out....

Your true friend
R. M. Williamson

P.S. ...For God's sake hold out until we can assist you...I remit to you with major Bonham a communication from the interim governor. Best wishes to all your people and tell them to hold on firmly by their "wills" until I go there.

Williamson...Write us very soon

On the basis of this letter, it is claimed by some that Bonham returned to the Alamo believing help was on the way. However, this argument is fundamentally flawed. It is only necessary to read Fannin's letter of February 27th to J. W. Robinson to see why this is so. Relevant portions of Fannin's letter (emphasis mine) read as follows:

I have to report, that yesterday, after making all the preparations possible, we took up our line of march, (about three hundred strong, and four pieces of Artillery,) towards Bexar, to the relief of those brave men now shut up in the Alamo.... Within two hundred *yards of town, one of the wagons broke down.... It was expedient to return to this post and complete the fortifications, &c [sic].... **I sent an express to Gonzales to apprise the committee of Safety there of our return....***

Remembering that 1836 was a leap year, the copy of the express to which Fannin alludes reached the Committee of Safety in Gonzales by the time Williamson wrote his letter on March 1st, and before Bonham's departure on March 2nd. This is confirmed by Dr. Pollard in his account of the events at the time. Thus, Jim Bonham did know that Fannin would not be coming. Moreover, he also heard the same news again when, on the road to Bexar, he encountered Ben Highsmith who had just left Fannin.

Travis, in his famous letter of March 3rd to the President of the Convention, seemed to confirm that he had received something other than good news, when he wrote:

*...Col. Fannin is said to be on the march to this place with reinforcements; **but I fear it is not true,** as I have repeatedly sent to him for aid without receiving any. Col Bonham, my special messenger, arrived at Labahia fourteen days ago, with a request for aid; and on the arrival of the enemy in Bexar ten days ago, I sent an express to Col F. which arrived at Goliad the next day, urging him to send us reinforcements (none have arrived. **I look to the colonies alone for aid;** unless it arrives soon, I shall have to fight the enemy on his own terms. I will however, do the best I can under the circumstances, and I feel confident that the determined valour and desperate courage, heretofore evinced by my men, will not fail them in the last struggle, and although they may be sacrificed to the vengeance of a Gothic enemy, the victory will cost the enemy so dear, that it will be worse for him than a defeat....*

Not exactly the words of a man who has just received a message that help is imminent!

Looking again at the Williamson letter, the question also arises, how would Williamson have known the strength of Fannin's relief force (300 men and four artillery pieces) if he had not seen Fannin's express? Assuming the Williamson letter is authentic, why then did he write what he almost certainly knew to be untrue? One can only speculate, but a plausible explanation may be that Williamson, understandably, was engaging in some wishful thinking, doing his best to keep hope alive among the defenders. Perhaps he believed that he or someone else could yet prevail on Fannin to change his mind, and that by the time Bonham delivered the letter, Fannin would indeed be on his way. And if not Fannin, then perhaps others.

Whatever the case, it seems a certainty that when Bonham returned to the Alamo on March 3rd, he knew well the state of things, and particularly that Fannin was not coming. From that time forward Travis also knew that they could expect no help from Fannin *"...I look to the colonies alone for aid..."* and it was James Bonham who told him.

THE MEXICAN WAR (1846 - 1848)

Milledge Luke Bonham's role in the Mexican War is well chronicled by his grandson, Milledge Louis Bonham. Also in Milledge Luke's papers may be found many of his letters from Mexico. General background information on life in the army and in Mexico during the occupation was obtained from Bruce Winder's book *Mr. Polk's Army,* and from perusal of *The Star* and *North American* newspapers, which were published with the army during the war.

When he was military governor of Cuernavaca, Milledge Luke's adjutant for a short time was Winfield Scott Hancock, who one day would be the candidate of the Democratic Party for president. His second-in-command was Thomas Seymour, a future governor of Connecticut, who would also be a lifelong friend. Milledge Luke named his fourth son Thomas Seymour Bonham. These interesting coincidences in mind, I found, in one of Milledge Luke's last letters to his wife before departing Mexico, his announcement that he was bringing home a surprise...a horse...and sure enough, also among the papers, is the shipping receipt! The possibility of another coincidence of the kind which were profusely spawned by that war was immediately evident. Could he have found his brother's horse? Both Luke and Thomas Seymour write of being entertained by the local gentry during their time in Cuernavaca, and it is not inconceivable that the mare could have been brought back to one of the *fincas* in the vicinity. However, there is no known record of the fate of Jim Bonham's horse. One account has her dropping dead of exhaustion and bullet wounds the instant Jim returns through the gates into the Alamo; another claims that the animal was unscathed. And more than one historian, apparently confusing Seguin with Bonham, states that the horse Bonham rode was borrowed from Bowie. Taken together, these conflicting accounts are an invitation to speculation, and left me less constrained in reaching my own fanciful conclusion.

Was it Jim's horse that Luke brought home? Probably not...but it *could* have been!

William N. Bonham
San Antonio, June 1, 2003

BIBLIOGRAPHY

Barefield, Marilyn Davis. *Records of Wilcox County Alabama*. 1988.

Bauer, K. Jack. *The Mexican War 1846-1848*. University of Nebraska Press, 1992.

Brooks, U. R. *South Carolina Bench and Bar Volume I*. Columbia, SC: The State Company, 1908.

Brown, John Henry. *Life and Times of Henry Smith*. Austin: Steck, 1935.

Brown, R. R.. *Expedition under Johnson and Grant*. Texas Almanac, 1859.

Burton, Orville. *In My Father's House Are Many Mansions: Family And Community In Edgefield, South Carolina*. Chapel Hill: University of North Carolina Press, 1985.

Chabot, Frederick C. *The Alamo Mission Fortress and Shrine*. San Antonio: Chabot, 1936.

Chariton, Wallace O. *100 Days in Texas—The Alamo Letters*. Dallas: Woodware, 1990.

Clarke, Carol Lea. *Imagining Texas: Pre-Revolutionary Texas Newspapers, 1829-1836*. El Paso: The University of Texas at El Paso, 2002.

Davis, William C. *Three Roads to The Alamo*. New York: HarperCollins, 1998.

Ellenberger, Matthew. Biographical sketch of Albert Clinton Horton. *The Handbook of Texas Online*. The Texas State Historical Association, 1999.

Elliott, Claude. "Alabama and The Texas Revolution," *Southwestern Historical Quarterly*, (January, 1947).

Fehrenbach, T.R. *Lone Star, A History of Texas and the Texans*. New York: Macmillan Publishing Co., Inc., 1968.

Freehling, William W. *Prelude To Civil War, The Nullification Controversy in South Carolina 1816-1836*. New York: Harper & Row, 1965.

Glenn, Virginia Louise. "James Hamilton, Jr. of South Carolina." Ph.D. Dissertation, University of North Carolina at Chapel Hill, 1964.

Gray, Col. Wm. F. *From Virginia to Texas, 1835*. Diary.

Green, Edwin L. *A History of The University of South Carolina*. Columbia, SC: The State Company, 1916.

Grimes, Ann Graham. *The Immortal Thirty-Two*. 1995.

Gulick, Charles Adams, Jr. The Papers of Mirabeau B. Lamar. Austin: A. C. Baldwin & Sons, 1924.

Hollis, Daniel Walker. *University of South Carolina, Volume I, South Carolina College.* Columbia, SC: University of South Carolina Press, 1951.

Hungerpiller, J. C. "A Sketch of the Life and Character of Jonathan Maxcy, D. D." *Bulletin of The University of South Carolina,* No. 58 (July 1917).

Jenkins, John H. (editor). *The Papers of The Texas Revolution 1835-1836.* Austin: Presidial Press, 1973.

LaBadie, N. D. *San Jacinto Campaign.* Texas Almanac 1859.

LaBorde, M. *History of The South Carolina College.* Columbia SC: Peter B. Glass, 1859.

Marks, Paula Mitchell. *Turn Your Eyes Towards Texas.* College Station: Texas A&M University Press, 1989.

Maurois, André. *Adrienne: The Life of The Marquise de La Fayette.* New York: McGraw-Hill, 1961.

McAlister, George A. *Alamo The Price of Freedom, A History of Texas.* Big Spring, Tx: Docutex Inc. 1990.

McDonald, Archie P. *William Barret Travis A Biography.* Austin: Eakin Press, 1995.

O'Conner, Kathryn Stoner. *The Presidio La Bahía del Espiritu Santo de Zuniga 1721 to 1846.* Austin: Von Boeckmann-Jones, 1966.

Perry, Benjamin F. *Reminiscences of Public Men (first series).* Philadelphia: John D. Avil & Co., 1883.

Roell, Craig H. "Remember Goliad! A History of La Bahia," Texas State Historical Association, 1968.

Sanderson, Richard. *Leonids 1833: The Night of Raining Fire.*

Sutherland, John. *The Fall of the Alamo.* San Antonio: The Naylor Company, 1936. (First draft)

Wardlaw, Diane. *The Wardlaw Chronicles.*

Wharton, Clarence. *Remember Goliad.* Glorieta, NM: Rio Grande Press, 1994.

Winders, Richard Bruce. *Mr. Polk's Army.* College Station: Texas A&M University Press, 1997.

Tim J. and Terry S. Todish. *The Alamo Source Book—1836. Austin:* Eakin Press, 1998.

Bexar Archives: *Cuartel del Alamo. Election of Deputies.*

Archives at The Alamo Library

Mobile Archives

Mobile Historic Preservations Society

State of Texas Archives

Texas Historical Association monographs

University of South Carolina Archives